Copyright 2013, HMS Pegasus, by Bria

MW00444859

HMS PEGASUS.

a Giles Courtenay story by Brian Withecombe

Brian Withecombe
Badger's Holt,
16 Weybridge Walk,
North Shoebury
Essex SS3 8YJ
01702 216435

Other Giles Courtenay adventures in Kindle

The Seagull and LeCorsair
Aphrodite's Quest
Amazon at the Nile
The Winged Avenger

ONE

His Britannic Majesty's 74-gun ship of the line *Pegasus* rode the uneasy swell coming from the west south-west, barely noticing it. There was a fair lop on the sea, the crests tinged slightly white as the wind pushed the sea before it. The water sluiced down the fat side of the ship as its press of sail pushed it onwards, towards the nor'east.

The ship's captain walked out from beneath the poop, sniffed the air and walked deliberately to the compass. The quartermasters at the double wheel straightened as their Lord and Master approached and the officer of the watch looked more alert than he had been for the majority of the morning watch, which ran from 4am to 8am. Six bells rang out from the foc's'le belfry, denoting it was 7am.

The officer of the watch touched his hat and tried to smile.

"Good morning sir. Course nor by nor'east. Wind pushing up from the west sou' west."

"Thank you Mr Stevens. We should sight land today."

"Aye sir. Home."

"Just so. Dorset, is it not?"

"Aye sir. Charmouth."

"Well, I am sure you will have the chance to get there for a while, even if it is short! Unfortunately whilst we are in the midst of this war there is a shortage of ships and good officers to man them. Do you yearn for a frigate? Something smaller than a ship of the line perhaps?" He saw the hesitation on the officer's face. He took him by the arm and led him away to the lee nettings on the broad quarterdeck. "You may speak freely Mr Stevens. I'll not jump down your throat!"

"It's not that sir. At the end of each cruise, well, there is always the chance that officers will be offered other appointments but I am happy here. With Mr McAteer promoted and in Antigua, and Mr Fenwick now our Senior, well…"

"Are you trying to tell me that you wish to keep your present appointment, Mr Stevens?"

The young officer reddened "Aye sir. I am. If that is alright with you, sir?"

"Oh. I think I can manage Mr Stevens! Now I feel the wind has changed slightly. You may like to give attention to the trim of the sails, yes?"

Stevens hurried away. There was the sound of footsteps on the planking. The Captain turned.

"Good morning Sir Giles. Are you well this morning?"

"You mean James, am I looking forward to getting home and seeing Jessica? The answer has to be of course I damn well am!" But he was smiling and his words had no offence. James Fenwick, First-Lieutenant of the *Pegasus,* smiled broadly and nodded.

"Trafford is arranging your breakfast sir."

"Excellent. I shall go and enjoy it then. The ship is yours James."

Fenwick smiled again, touched his hat and stepped aside as his Captain walked below the poop to his cabin.

It was September 1799. *Pegasus* had been away in the Caribbean since early in the year. She had been sent as part of a small Squadron under the flag of Vice-Admiral Spencer-White first of all to Antigua, and then on to St Kitts, where the Squadron had been sent with orders to help crush a slave rebellion. The orders had been executed, by the Captain of this stately two-decker, Captain Sir Giles Courtenay, Bart. The Admiral had shown little interest, or indeed stomach for the task, and in the end on the pretext of being needed elsewhere, had left Courtenay to sort out the rebellion. But Courtenay's real interest in the Caribbean had been to recover a former command, the frigate *Aphrodite*. She had been part of the Squadron, but had been taken by her crew, who had mutinied against their Captain, a vicious aristocrat called Lord Tolman. They had sailed their ship into enemy hands no doubt under the impression they would be treated as heroes. She had been located in a heavily defended port on the Spanish Main, but undeterred Courtenay had made a plan, sailed into the port, cut out the frigate, sunk a Spanish ship of the line, and made good his escape. He had also rid himself of an enemy.

There was a deep family feud between the Spencer-White family and Courtenay. A few years ago, as plain Lieutenant Courtenay he had been the Senior Lieutenant of a handy 22 gun sloop of war called the *Seagull*. On patrol off the French coast they had been set upon by a French National frigate, and the Captain, a petulant man called Prankash, had been killed. He was part of the Spencer-White family and they blamed Courtenay, even though it could have just as easily been him who was killed on that day as he was standing next to his Captain when the man was struck down.

Since then Spencer-White had done his best to have him killed, captured, or discredited. So far every plan had failed. Spencer-White had been most ably assisted in his nefarious plans by his Flag-Lieutenant, Matthias Harding, who in reality was little more than a hired killer.

On board a captured lugger, sailing into the Spanish port with the ship ablaze as it headed for the Spanish 74, Harding had died on the end of Courtenay's cutlass.

Fenwick came out of his thoughts as there was a yell from the mainmast look-out high above the deck.

"Deck there! Sail-ho, dead ahead! Looks like a brig sir!"

"Mr Owen. My compliments to the Captain. Tell him we have sighted a brig, dead-ahead."

The Midshipman hurried away.

A few moments later the look-out reported the brig was flying a signal. It was the challenge, followed by the flag for despatches on board.

The Midshipman in charge of signals turned to Fenwick with a puzzled expression on his face.

"Sir, she is the courier brig *Rapid* and she says she has despatches for us."

"Very well Mr McBride, I shall see the Captain." He looked around as the Sailing Master, Owen Davies, appeared on the quarterdeck. "Morning, Owen," he said very quietly. Davies' eyes followed him as the Lieutenant walked under the poop.

The sentry outside the Cabin saw him coming. He slammed his musket butt to the deck and yelled.

"First-Lieutenant, *sir!*"

The doors opened and Kingston, the cabin servant, smiled a brief welcome. Fenwick walked in and saw his Captain sitting on the bench seat under the salt sprayed windows enjoying a mug of coffee.

"Hello James." said Courtenay. "Some coffee? What is this about that sail? What is she?"

"Courier brig, and she says she has despatches for us sir."

"What? That's a little strange, I would have thought? That brig, which was in Antigua when we left, passed us in mid-Atlantic I seem to recall. She would have had more than enough time to get home and get her despatches to their Lordships in Whitehall, who would know we are well on our way home."

"Perhaps they are sending us off somewhere before we get home, sir. Diverting us to blockade or something similar."

Courtenay smiled at Fenwick's face.

"I doubt it James. We need some work being done to the ship. She needs a spell in dockyard and her bottom scraped."

"Aye, I think she could sail better that's for sure. Our trip to, and all around the Caribbean and down to the Main has added plenty of weed and other growth to the copper. What the hell is going on then.?" He paused as Trafford came into the cabin.

"Morning sir. That brig is gettin' close, Sir Giles."

"Thanks Alex. James, send her a signal to close on us and lie under our lee. Heave-to when she is up to us and we will see what is going on."

Later, as the brig came up to the 74, Davies stopped the ship, and the small brig tacked neatly and hove-to on her lee side. A boat was lowered and an officer, who Fenwick identified as the Captain of the small command, climbed down into it. Five minutes later he was climbing *Pegasus'* tumblehome.

Courtenay, never one to stand on ceremony, ran lightly down the gangway ladder and greeted the man at the entry port.

"Captain Sir Giles Courtenay sir? I am Commander Crompton, at your service sir."

"Crompton eh? Welcome aboard Commander. What was so important, not far from home, that you should trouble yourself......."

"May we go to the cabin sir? What I have to tell you is, er, *confidential.*"

Courtenay smiled and led the way to his cabin.

"Please sit Commander. Now what the devil is going on?"

"I believe you know my Uncle sir?"

Courtenay smiled. "His Lordship? You are a lucky man sir, to have such an Uncle."

Crompton smiled. "Yes sir, he is a very kind and gracious Uncle, but I earned the right to wear the King's Coat and to command the yonder ship sir!"

Courtenay's smile broadened. "Of course you did. I believe it would not be your Uncle's way to show favour where it was not deserved. Now young man, out with it, what the deuce is going on?"

Crompton pulled a thick envelope from his pocket. "These are orders for you sir and Lieutenant Fenwick and Mr Owen Davies. They are in respect of a Court-martial." He looked at Fenwick, who was standing stoney-faced beside his Captain. He glanced for a moment at Alex Trafford standing on the other side, closer to the windows. He sensed the bond between these three men. Even as he looked at them he saw Trafford and Fenwick exchange glances.

"Whose Court-martial Commander?" asked Courtenay, knowing the answer.

"Yours sir." He paused. "Sir, I am not supposed to know the content of those orders but the Admiral, who holds you in great regard sir, told me privately, then made sure my ship was the one to deliver them to you. I was charged with ensuring you received them and that I told you what is happening, sir."

Kingston appeared next to him with a tray and glasses. Crompton looked at him, took a glass and swallowed all the contents.

"Sir, you are charged with hazarding your ship by disobeying orders and attacking the Spanish port of La Manta which was outside your patrol area, but" he hurried as he saw Fenwick about to interject, "most importantly, with murder of a King's officer, sir."

"Matthias Harding." said Courtenay flatly.

"How did you guess sir?" asked Crompton

"It was not difficult Commander. Not difficult at all!" He looked at the young officer for a moment, one eyebrow raised quizzically.

"I know of the feud sir." The other replied, sensing Fenwick and Trafford taking a step forward. "My Uncle tells me many things, all of which I keep entirely between us. He knows he can trust me sir. Thus, I know of the problem with Lord Cairns."

"Who?" interjected Fenwick before Courtenay could say anything.

"Sorry, you would not know. Sir Wilberforce Spencer-White is now Lord Cairns. It is he who has brought the charges." He looked acutely unhappy.

Courtenay smiled. "Do not look so gloomy Commander. It is not your fault nor that of your Uncle. What are your Orders?"

"I have to return to Plymouth sir, and take with me Mr Fenwick and Mr Davies. They are to be witnesses and therefore will be offered accommodation suitable to their rank and station until the Court-martial can be assembled." He lowered his head. "I am very sorry sir, to have to bring such news to such an officer as yourself."

"As I said Commander, it is not your fault." replied Giles calmly. He turned to Fenwick. "It is alright James. Pack your things and arrange to transfer to *Rapid.* Alex, pass the word for the Master to do likewise please."

"It ain't fair sir!" the coxswain said.

"The truth will out Alex," he murmured quietly, "the truth will out. Now go and speak with the Master."

Fifteen minutes later the First-Lieutenant and the Sailing Master were standing with long faces at the entry port whilst their baggage was lowered into the small boat which was hooked onto the main chains. They turned as Courtenay appeared next to them. They both lifted their hands to their hats and Giles nodded to them as they turned towards the side of the ship. Fenwick turned back and made to open his mouth and say something but Giles shook his head and the Senior said nothing. He followed the Sailing Master down into the boat and several minutes later, Courtenay watched as they climbed up the small side of the brig. Thirty minutes later the brig was out of sight, heading for Plymouth. *Pegasus* followed at a more leisurely and sedate pace.

Several hours later as dusk was closing in, *Pegasus* dropped her anchor in Plymouth Sound. Trafford was standing on the quarterdeck as Courtenay rapped out his orders and the ship came to rest. Then he looked towards the shore which was now fast disappearing into the darkness.

"Mr Beare. There is a guard-boat approaching. I suspect that the Port-admiral's Flag-Lieutenant will be aboard. Send him to the cabin." With that, he turned and walked beneath the poop. Trafford saw the expression on the Second Lieutenant's face. Beare simply touched his hat and turned away to supervise the men who were bustling around on the deck below, coiling ropes, readying boats for lowering, the various jobs that had to be done when a ship reached port. High above the deck the topmen were making sure the sails were furled neatly, so that no criticism would attach to their ship whilst it rode at anchor for being untidy.

Trafford looked all around him for a moment, then strode after his Captain.

'Port-admiral's Flag-lieutenant, *Sir!*' barked the cabin sentry.

The dapper Flag-lieutenant stepped carefully over the coaming into the cabin and strode to the desk behind which Courtenay was seated.

"Captain Sir Giles Courtenay sir? I am Flag-lieutenant to Vice-admiral Sir Louis Montford, who is the new Port-admiral here at Plymouth. You met with the *Rapid* brig sir, I know. Your Senior and Sailing Master are in, er suitable accommodation ashore." He had a clipped, impersonal way of talking and Courtenay gained the impression he was enjoying all this. He had something approaching a sneer on his face. "You are to hand your journals to me sir, as they are required for the use of the Court. I am to inform you that the Court-martial is to take place in three days' time at the Port-admiral's residence."

He paused and looked down at Courtenay. "You may appoint the person who is to defend you sir, of course. I would suggest you do this without delay."

"Three days is precious small time, Mr er, what *is* your name since you have chosen to withhold it?"

"de Vere Preston sir."

"Well Mr Preston, three days is small time. What if I am unable to find a person who is prepared to defend me?"

"That is not my concern sir. I only deliver the messages. The journals, sir?"

Courtenay knew they would be required. He had them on the desk. He simply nodded to them. For a moment Preston made no effort to pick them up. Trafford stepped forward, Preston glanced at him and saw the angry glint in his eye and hurriedly took them from the desk.

"You may stay aboard sir, but obviously you must not leave Plymouth."

Courtenay smiled. "Of course not. Thank you Mr Preston, you are dismissed." Red-faced, the Flag-lieutenant left.

"This ain't bloody fair Cap'n!" burst out Trafford as the man left. "You done nothin' wrong! And who is going to defend you at such short notice? It's all been done so that you don't have any chance of defending yourself!"

"Thank you for your concern Alex, but this is entirely to be expected. Tell me, has Major Strathmore left the ship yet?"

"No sir. He wouldn't have left you knowing about this Court-martial, Sir Giles!"

"Good, then be a good fellow and ask him to come and have a word would you?"

Trafford left, a quizzical expression on his face.

The following morning, Courtenay was enjoying, as far as he was able, his breakfast when he heard the ages old call from his ship to an approaching boat. He listened for the reply but didn't hear it. Kingston had already managed to get some fresh provisions from shore and had proudly announced that he had some sausages, fresh from Mr Wall. Two sausages, nicely fried, with some fresh eggs were being consumed slowly by Courtenay when the Midshipman of the Watch made his appearance.

"Well Mr Harvey? Was that boat something to do with us? I did not hear any reply to the challenge?"

"Please sir, there is a lady on board the boat with one other gentleman and they are requesting permission to come aboard. The gentleman is not a Navy Officer sir, nor from the Military. He is a civilian sir!"

Courtenay smiled. "Civilians do exist Mr Harvey, believe it or not! But a lady…?"

Trafford burst into the cabin, a grim smile on his face.

"'Tis Miss Jess….Lady Courtenay Sir Giles, and your Father!"

Courtenay hurried out from under the poop and down to the entry port in time to see a fine hat with blue feathers appear at the top of the stairs, closely followed by his wife's beautiful face. She had eschewed the bosun's chair and climbed the side of the ship.

"Jessica!" he hugged her to him, oblivious of the grins and stares from his crew. She put her arms around him and kissed him. Even one or two of the hardened Warrant officers turned away. Courtenay looked as the man made his entrance. Over Jessica's shoulder he smiled at his Father.

"Father, how good to see you!"

"Giles my boy, how are you?" The two men hugged and then Courtenay led the way to the cabin. Kingston had already arranged some more chairs and was hovering with a tray.

"Kingston, how are you? Are you looking after my husband as I instructed you?" asked Jessica as soon as she saw the man.

He blushed, and nodded. She turned and held out her hand to Trafford. "Alex Trafford, I am glad to see you safe and well!"

"Ma'am."

"Now then Giles, what is all this about a Court-martial in less than three days' time?" Courtenay senior said angrily. "My god, that is no time at all to be preparing a defence! Who is going to represent you? I know it has to be a fellow officer, but if I can be of any assistance?"

"Nicholas will be defending me, and do not worry Father. Everything is in hand. You may speak with him shortly. How pray did you find out about all this?"

"Lord Crompton told Jessica and she came down post-haste to see us. Did you kill that man?"

There was only Kingston and Trafford in the cabin.

Courtenay looked his Father straight in the eye. "Yes Father, I killed Matthias Harding, but.." he added as his Father went to speak, "it was in a duel. He had been wanting to call me out for quite some time. On board that lugger, which was by then well alight and heading for the Spanish ship in La Manta, he suggested we finished our business. He was none too happy when I chose cutlasses, but he was in no position to really argue. I was defending myself Father. He wasn't quite the duellist he thought he was!"

Jessica was not the kind of woman who would put her hand to her mouth at the thought of the horror or a duel. She had seen too much for that.

"The man deserved to die Father, and surely if dear Giles here killed him whilst defending himself...."

"He should be found not guilty." Courtenay's Father finished for her. "I fear, my dear, that the Navy may have its own views on that!"

"Harding was a murderer." said Giles sharply ."He had a girl called Emma Harper killed in Antigua after he had tried to make it appear she was really Mercy LeFevre and that she was not dead at all! Of course we found out, and Nicholas put her somewhere he thought was safe, only it wasn't safe enough. Somehow he found out and killed her. I think that Spencer-White knew, which is why he sent Harding on that last patrol with us which resulted in us being at La Manta. He wanted him out of the way!"

"Can you prove all this, son?"

"Yes Father, I do believe we can!" He took Jessica's hand and squeezed it gently.

Courtenay senior smiled. "I will leave you two alone for a while. Where can I find Nicholas Strathmore?"

"Alex, be so kind as to show my Father to the Major's quarters, will you?"

Courtenay's Father got up, smiled at his son and followed the coxswain out of the cabin.

Three days later, and the Court-martial gun outside the Vice-admiral's residence boomed to signify that the proceedings were about to commence.

The Court-martial was held in a large room in the residence. There were five officers comprising the Board. In the centre sat Vice-admiral Montford, with a Rear-admiral Courtenay did not recognise on his right. The rest were captains from two other seventy-fours in the Sound, one of which had only arrived the night before, and one who was the Port- captain.

Courtenay was standing near a chair in front of the table behind which the Board sat. His sword was on the table. To his left was a table at which Strathmore was seated and to his right was another table with the prosecuting officer, a sour looking Captain.

Behind Strathmore was a short row of chairs. Courtenay senior and Jessica were seated there, anxiety showing clearly on their faces. Giles looked at them and smiled briefly before turning back as he heard the Court Clerk come to his feet.

The Clerk of the Court stood, with a piece of parchment open in his hand. He looked down at it through his half-glasses and started to read in an important voice.

"Captain Sir Giles Courtenay, Baronet, *presently* Captain of His Brittanic Majesty's ship *Pegasus,* of seventy-four guns. You are charged with two most serious offences. First of all, that in disobedience of orders given to you whilst on the Antigua station by Vice-admiral Sir Spencer-White, now Lord Cairns, you did quit your station and hazard your ship by entering the port of La Manta on the Spanish Main solely to attempt to effect the recovery of the frigate *Aphrodite.* Secondly, you are charged that whilst attacking the said port of La Manta you did commit murder on a fellow officer, namely Matthias Harding, then holding the appointment of Flag-Lieutenant to Sir Wilberforce Spencer-White. How do you plead, sir?"

Courtenay was standing. "Not Guilty sir"

Montford spoke. "You may sit Sir Giles. I was a mite surprised to see Major Strathmore defending you. Are you not supposed to be elsewhere Major? I am reliably informed you have an appointment in London?"

"I was indeed supposed to have taken up my new appointment sir, but I have been given dispensation by the Commandant-General to undertake this service."

Montford smiled gently. "I see. Very well, Major." He turned to the prosecuting Captain.

"Very well Captain Bridge. Let us get this most disagreeable business out of the way as fast as we are able, what?"

TWO

As Bridge stood and started to shuffle his papers Strathmore rose to his feet and looked directly at Rear-admiral Montford.

"You will excuse me sir, but although the charges against Captain Courtenay have been outlined, what is far from clear is who has brought these scurrilous charges against him. I consider that Captain Courtenay has a right to know his accuser."

Vice-admiral Montford fixed him with a stern grey eye but Courtenay noticed the corners of his mouth were twitching a little, as if he was amused and trying not to smile.

Bridge stepped forward and interjected. "This is out of order Major! Really, whatever next? It is enough that these grievous charges have been laid." He turned to the Court and Montford nodded, apparently in agreement.

"Quite so Captain Bridge, quite so. I am sure it is of no consequence at all that these charges have been laid by Vice- Admiral Lord Cairns. Please be seated Major Strathmore, you will have your chance shortly."

Giles hid a grin and Strathmore pulled apart the coat-tails of his tight-fitting red uniform coat and sat, but as he did so he turned and looked at Courtenay senior who simply gave a small smile and a nod. That had been neatly done. It would serve no good to the prosecution that the charges had been brought by a man who had a grudge against a Captain with the fine record Giles Courtenay had.

"I intend to show to this Court-martial," Bridge was stating, trying to look important, "that Captain Sir Giles Courtenay, the accused, murdered Lieutenant Matthias Harding, who at the time was serving an appointment as Flag-Lieutenant to Sir Willoughby Spencer-White, who is of course….,"

"Yes, yes Captain Bridge," interrupted Montford, "we all know he is now Lord Cairns. Please proceed."

"Er, yes sir. On the night of 10th July 1799, according to the journals and orders of Captain Courtenay I have examined, and from the statements which have been taken from the First-Lieutenant and Sailing Master of His Britannic Majesty's ship *Pegasus,*" He darted a look at Montford who was patting a yawn to extinction. One of the other officers was staring at the ceiling. "well, the accused planned to cut-out the frigate *Aphrodite* from the Port of La Manta on the Spanish Main. He was well off-station and therefore hazarding his ship."

"Did he?" asked Montford.

"Well, er."

"Did he or didn't he? Major Strathmore, you I understand were there. Did Sir Giles succeed or not?"

Strathmore stood. "He most certainly did sir. The journals should show you sir, that not only did the Captain cut out the *Aphrodite* he also sank a Spanish 74!"

"Thank you. Let us deal with this matter of disobeying Orders first." Montford looked at Giles Courtenay. "Sir Giles, do you agree you were off-station?"

"No sir. My orders were simply to patrol to the south'rd. That is supported by the entry in the Order journal, sir."

"H'mm. What took you to La Manta then? How the deuce did you find out *Aphrodite* was there? Captain, we all know you used to command her and you did so with distinction. Wanted to get her back badly did you?"

Courtenay looked at the floor for a moment. He lifted his head and looked at each member of the Court in turn. "Yes sir, I did want to get her back. Her crew had been sorely treated and even though there is no defence to mutiny there was the good name of my old command. As for knowing she was in LaManta, well sir, with my orders was a letter stating that I could find *Aphrodite* there. I have no idea from where it came sir."

"Where is this letter?"

"It was with the Orders journal sir."

"Captain Bridge?" asked Montford, "where is this letter?"

"I have no idea sir."

Montford glared at him. "If the members of the Court will permit me?" He looked around. No-one said anything. "Very well. It seems to be that Captain Courtenay's orders were very loosely worded. I believe him when he said he received intelligence that his old ship was at LaManta, and there was nothing in his Orders which prevented him going perhaps a little further to the South than his Admiral intended. Damme, Captains have to be able to use some initiative! This charge is a slur against Captain Courtenay's name. I dismiss it."

Bridge could hardly contain his anger but he stood and spoke very calmly.

"Very well sir, but there is still the grievous charge of Murder, and for which I will be demanding the death penalty."

"Well, get on with it, man!"

"During the raid on LaManta, for some reason Lieutenant Harding accompanied the accused on the lugger which was used as a fire-ship. No doubt Captain Courtenay will tell us why in due course."

Montford was waving a hand. "Yes, what the devil was he doing there Captain? He was Spencer-White's Flag-Lieutenant after all, and the Admiral wasn't there!"

Courtenay stood. "I have no idea as to why he was sent in the *Thrush* frigate sir. However, in being sent he became one of the officers I had available for the raid. I invited him to join it and he agreed."

He sat down and Bridge waved his papers in the air. "There you are sir, the accused has said he invited the deceased to join in! What for? I have uncovered the fact there is something of a feud between the Spencer-White family and the accused. Harding was the Admiral's Flag-Lieutenant, and naturally would support his Admiral. It is my submission that the accused saw this as an opportunity to gain some revenge on the Admiral!"

Courtenay sat stoney-faced. He knew the eyes of the members of the Court were on him.

Bridge was rampant. He smelt victory! "I think sir, that now is the time to call evidence as to what happened on that night. I call first of all Midshipman Smythe. He was the Midshipman who served on the lugger with the accused." He really was starting to get the wind into his sails.

Smythe walked stiffly into the room wearing his best uniform. It was an extremely smart Midshipman's uniform from one of the best Naval tailors in London. His Father owned a very good part of Gloucestershire. He gave his formal details. Bridge looked at him sternly and then spoke.

"Now then Mr Smythe. What appointment do you hold in *Pegasus?*"

"One of her Midshipman sir."

"How senior are you?"

"Not very sir." That brought forth some smiles and a little laughter around the room. Montford rapped lightly on the table with his knuckles.

"You were with the accused on the night in question at LaManta were you not?" Bridge continued.

"Yes sir. The Captain asked if I would go with him on the fireship, and there were a few of us in all. The Captain, Mr Harding, the Captain's cox……"

"Yes yes, Mr Smythe. Now then, presumably there came a time when you had to leave the lugger?"

"Yes sir. We fired her and the Captain let her run in as far as we could against the Spanish two-decker before we took to the boats."

"Did he go before you?"

Smythe smiled. "Oh no sir, the Captain would not have done that. He told me to go over the stern to the boat with the rest of the men. Then his cox'n came down the rope."

"So that left just the accused and Mr Harding on the ship?"

"That left Captain Courtenay and Mr Harding there, yes sir."

"What happened next?"

"Trafford, the Captain's cox'n, was worried that the Captain had not joined us so he climbed back up to see what was happening sir. After a few moments they both climbed down and joined us in the boat. We pushed off and went to join the rest of the boat crews who were going to cut-out the frigate sir."

"And nothing was said about Mr Harding not being there?"

"The Captain said he was dead, sir."

"Thank you Mr Smythe."

"No questions sir" from Strathmore.

Smythe got up and walked out, but not before he smiled at his Captain.

Bridge shuffled his papers again. He was always shuffling them. "Call Lieutenant James Fenwick."

James Fenwick marched in and sat down in the witness' chair.

Bridge hovered over him. "Mr Fenwick, what is your appointment?"

"I have the honour to be First-Lieutenant of the *Pegasus* sir, under Captain Sir Giles Courtenay."

That took Bridge aback. He had been expecting something else.

"Is it not true sir, that you are the step-son of Lord Cairns?"

"It is sir, to my everlasting shame!"

Bridge tried a strategic withdrawal. "With the Court's permission, I would like to put this officer's evidence back for the present."

Montford fixed him with his steely gaze. "Why? Perhaps Major Strathmore has something he would like to ask of the Lieutenant first? Major?"

Strathmore rose languidly. "Thank you sir. Good morning Mr Fenwick. What do you know of Matthias Harding?"

"He was little more than a paid assassin. He was my step-father's means of settling many a little problem, usually with someone else on the wrong end of a duelling pistol or a sword! He was a bully, and scum!"

"Thank you Mr Fenwick." Strathmore sat down, smiling. Montford had a slow smile starting to play on his lips which he hid by coughing and bringing a handkerchief to his mouth.

"Thank you Mr Fenwick." said Montford. "Do you value your appointment?"

"I do indeed sir. I hope to continue in the same when this is over and the Captain is returned to his command."

"You were only involved in the cutting out, were you not?"

"Aye sir. Nothing else, although I would have relished being on the fire-ship with the Captain!'

"Thank you Mr Fenwick."

Fenwick rose, smiled at Courtenay and marched out.

Bridge was on his feet again. "It is clear sir, from just what the Midshipman said, that Matthias Harding was murdered. He and the accused were the only two on the ship and only the accused came off. It is perfectly clear sir. The comments by Mr Fenwick were completely unjustified. Matthias Harding was an Admiral's Flag-Lieutenant and entitled to the respect which accompanies the appointment."

There was some murmuring from the members of the Court.

"That, Captain Bridge, is doubtful!" barked Montford. "Any further evidence?"

"No sir, the facts speak for themselves."

"Really? Major Strathmore, have you any evidence?"

Strathmore rose, unrolling a sheet of paper. "I have two pieces of evidence sir. One is the Captain's coxswain, Alexander Trafford, and the other is this statement. You should sir, have the original as I placed it aboard a brig which was due to leave Antigua shortly after the Squadron, but which would of course, arrive a lot earlier. The brig did indeed get here first sir. I checked."

"We do not have the statement Major."

"Perhaps sir it would be as well to listen to the evidence from Trafford first and I will then read you the statement, which I took the precaution of having notarised in Antigua by the Governor."

Bridge was getting redder and redder. "Sir, I really must protest! Major Strathmore has now said he intends to call a common seaman to give evidence which no doubt is designed to further blacken the name of an officer! Surely you will nor permit this? After all sir, a common seaman giving evidence in an Officer's Court-martial!"

"All I am interested in, all this Board is interested in, Captain Bridge, is finding the *truth* and I care not a fig if the truth comes from a *common seaman* as you put it, though I do not share your views in that regard." He turned to Strathmore. "Call your witness Major Strathmore."

Trafford, wearing his best blue jacket and white trousers, with a new pair of black buckled shoes, and carrying his tarred hat, walked into the room and to the chair.

"You may sit, Trafford." said the Clerk of the Court. Trafford sat.

Strathmore rose slowly to his feet.

"Would you confirm your appointment please for the Court?"

"Aye sir. I am coxswain to Captain Sir Giles Courtenay presently Captain of 'is Britannic Majesty's ship of the line *Pegasus*."

"How long have you been the Captain's coxswain, Trafford?"

"Since '96 sir. When we were after that damned woman pirate. You remember the one sir."

"Yes, I remember her Trafford." Strathmore looked inwards for a few seconds, reliving that last fight on board the sloop of war *Seagull.* "You were with the Captain on the fire-ship at LaManta, then?"

Trafford smiled broadly. "Aye sir. He never goes anywhere like that without me being there!" There was a small ripple of laughter from the few members of the public who were seating in the room. There are always some, who usually come to delight in the misfortunes of others.

"Who was on the lugger apart from the volunteer crew?"

"Mr Smythe sir. Good lad. Goin' to make a fine officer one day if 'e lives long enough. The Cap'n, and Mr Harding, sir." As he came out with the last name, Montford gained the distinct impression that if Trafford could have spat he would have done.

"What happened when the ship was fired?"

"The Captain orders the crew off. Mr Smythe followed the lads and then the Captain ordered me over the stern. I got down into the boat expecting to see Mr Harding right after me and then the Captain. But no-one came down and all the time the ship was burning more 'n more and gettin' closer to the Da...Spanish ship, sir."

"What did you do?"

"Well, sir. The Cap'n can look after himself but after a few moments I got a mite worried, so I shins back up the rope. The lugger had a low stern so it didn't take a few seconds."

"What did you see when you got back up to the deck, Trafford?"

"I saw Mr Harding attacking the Cap'n." There was a sharp intake of breath from one of the Captains behind the long table, and from some of the audience. "With a cutlass, sir!"

"You saw Sir Giles being attacked by Matthias Harding with a cutlass, is that right?"

"Aye sir, it sure is! The bast.......sorry sir, Mr Harding, had picked the wrong weapon to take on the Cap'n. His type are more used to fancy swords and pistols."

Montford rapped on the table. "What do you mean Trafford, 'his type'?"

"It was common knowledge on the lower deck sir, that he was a duellist. Sword or pistol it made no difference from what I 'eard. But you don't fight a duel with a cutlass sir, not in my experience." Before anyone could say anything, he added "I seen a few of them in my younger days sir, between officers. Usually over cards sir."

Montford smiled. "Please continue Trafford."

"Well sir, Mr Harding was nowhere near as good with a cutlass as he obviously thought he was. The Captain was better, simple as that sir."

"In other words Harding was killed by Sir Giles who was defending himself?"

"Yes sir. The Captain sliced 'is innards sir.' Gasps from the audience and when Trafford looked around he saw more than one lady having a fan waving air in front of her face. One of the men didn't look too happy either. He wondered what they would think if he told them how Courtenay had ended it. He could still remember Harding's severed head rolling across the decking.

"No more questions sir." from Strathmore. Bridge was on his feet, hurrying to stand over and try to intimidate the coxswain. Trafford fixed him eye to eye.

"So you admit, er Trafford, that you saw the accused kill Mr Harding?"

"The Captain was defending himself. Ain't no law against that, surely?"

"Are you certain of this? You have been with the accused for a number of years, after all. You are loyal to him. I can understand that, as will the Court, but are you totally certain of what you are saying. If you are telling lies you will be………"

"Captain Bridge." This was the Rear-admiral. "The witness has said he is certain. All your intimidation and threats are not going to get this man to say anything else! He is a professional seaman. He is not going to risk himself by telling lies. Please continue!"

"No more questions sir." Bridge skulked back to his seat.

Strathmore rose again. "Thank you Trafford."

Trafford got up, and as he turned to go just briefly touched Courtenay's sleeve. Montford saw it and so did Jessica Courtenay. She knew the bond which had grown between the two men and Montford now knew it as well.

"Now sir," the Marine Officer was saying. "This statement which I took and which I had notarised before it was placed on the courier brig when it left Antigua. You say sir, that there is no sign of it?"

"No Major. Not a trace." Montford did not look happy.

"Then sir, it is as well that I had a number of copies made, all signed by the witness and all notarised." He handed a piece of parchment to the Clerk of the Court, and then another to hand to Bridge.

"I pray sir that you refer to this statement, which I took personally from one Eliza Flynn. As you will see sir, this is a deposition from this lady who says that on the night Emma Harper was murdered she saw a Navy officer outside the house she was occupying. She was certain as to the type of officer sir, because she saw his aguillete. There were only two officers on Antigua at that time who wore that insignia and the other was the Flag-Lieutenant to Rear-admiral LeGrange. The description given in the statement fits Mr Harding exactly. Emma Harper was murdered that night, sir."

"What has she to do with all this, Major?" asked Montford.

"Emma Harper was paid by Matthias Harding to impersonate a woman pirate by the name of Mercy LeFevre. She was fairly similar and Harding planned to try and convince Sir Giles that LeFevre was still alive even though both he and I knew for certain she was dead. It was all part of his campaign against Sir Giles. We, Sir Giles and myself, caught Miss Harper and forced a confession out of her which I have here. Again, this has been notarised." He handed it to the Clerk of the Court who passed it on to Montford. He read it and passed it around the others then sat back. At last, Bridge was able to see it.

"It is absolutely obvious sir, that Harding killed Emma Harper because of her confession. Being seen outside her lodgings on the night she was killed, being identified by her as the person who had paid her to impersonate LeFevre, well sir, as Captain Bridge said earlier the facts speak for themselves. I believe sir that the legal expression is *res ipsa loquiter.*" He turned to Courtenay's father who smiled and nodded.

Bridge was on his feet, approaching the table. "Sir, you cannot possibly admit this evidence. It was given in Antigua and we have no way of knowing whether or not any of this is true!"

"Captain Bridge. This witness statement was notarised before the Governor! Do you disbelieve him, sir?" Montford was getting angry.

"Well no, sir, it is just that we do not know if the witnesses were paid, or……"

Strathmore was on his feet, grim-faced but well in control.

"Sir, I took those statements. They were given freely without any threats, nor indeed promise of reward. I object sir, to the accusations of Captain Bridge!"

Montford was diplomatic. "Rest easy Major. I am satisfied they are authentic. So it seems clear gentlemen that Harding was a murderer as well as being a general ner'do well! I think we will retire. It is almost time for luncheon. If you gentlemen would care to join me, I think we can reach a decision."

Everyone stood as the members of the Court-martial rose and filed out.

The small group walked along the quayside close to the Admiral's residence until there was a clear view out across the Sound. Courtenay stood for a moment looking at his ship, anchored well out so that any would-be deserter would have a long swim to the shore even if he managed to get past the Marine sentries on the ship and the guard boats which pulled regularly around the anchorage. There were many other boats as well, coming and going. Any daytime deserter would have a hard time.

Trafford, who had walked along slowly behind Courtenay, his Father and Lady Jessica saw him straighten his back a little as he stared at the ship of the line.

"Never fear sir. You'll be back aboard and everything will be back to normal soon enough!"

Courtenay smiled suddenly, but just as suddenly it disappeared. He turned to his Father.

"I wonder how long it took Bridge to realise I had not given any evidence, Father?"

Courtenay senior chuckled. "A few moments, I am sure. No longer, but by then it was too late. The chance to say anything had gone." He looked at his son. "Tell me Giles, what would have said had you been asked if you had killed Harding?"

30

"The truth, Father. I *did* kill him but I did not *murder* him. It was a duel, which is of course forbidden, but more to prevent junior officers killing their seniors!" He looked at his wife and then placed an arm around her shoulders.

"It is becoming chilly Jess, are you all right?"

"I am perfectly alright thank you dearest. What I would have given to have been on that fireship with you! I would have shot the man in cold blood for what he had tried to do to you. And that man Spencer-White, or Cairns or whatever his name is now! Fancy bringing charges against you when he knew his man was a murderer! He ought to be shot!"

Courtenay and his Father chuckled. Trafford grinned broadly.

"How long will they take, dearest?" asked Jessica.

"It sounded as if they were going to make up their minds over luncheon, my dear." said Courtenay senior. "I have a feeling it may well be Vice-admiral Montford who makes up his mind and the rest will follow! How about something to eat? Giles?"

"No thank you Father." Jessica shook her head, some curls dancing against her face as she did so. There were footsteps behind them and they turned to see Fenwick approaching.

"Ah, James, hello."

"Sir. Lady Jessica? How do I find you? Well I hope, and not too distressed by this morning's happenings?"

"Thank you Mr Fenwick. I am very well although I wish this were over."

"I am sure it will be Lady Jessica. That is, once everyone has enjoyed a good luncheon!"

They all smiled. Giles looked at his senior.

"Your little speech in Court will shortly reach the ears of Lord Cairns James, you know that."

"Aye sir."

"Is your Mother settled in her new home?"

"She is indeed sir and," turning to Courtenay senior, "it was most gracious of your lady wife to suggest my mother took up the position of teacher in your local school sir. The accommodation which accompanies the position is very much to her liking and she is most grateful. I am sure sir, that she will find some way of passing to you and your wife her feelings in the matter."

"Mr Fenwick, we were most sensible of your Mother's situation after Giles had recounted her predicament to us. Cairns is a monster sir. There was a vacancy and your Mother is a teacher. The solution was simple. Please pass our very good wishes to your Mother when next you see her which I am sure will be very soon. She must come and visit one day."

"And James," added Courtenay, "you are always welcome. Not only at my parents' home, but wherever Jess and myself are living. I was most honoured by your comments this morning."

"I said the simple truth sir. That is all."

The time passed all too quickly. Courtenay was looking towards the Admiral's residence when he saw the officer approaching, the Commander who was the accused's 'friend'. He pulled his coat into position and walked towards him.

They filed into the room. The five members of the Court were seated as before behind the table. On it's polished surface was Courtenay's sword. The hilt was towards him. Not guilty. He stood in front of the Court as Montford spoke.

"Captain Sir Giles Courtenay. You are most honourably acquitted of all the charges against you sir. You may return to your command. Pray continue to serve his Britannic Majesty and our service in the most positive way you have done since you gained your commission. This Court wishes to express its gratitude for the services you have rendered. It is known that you were responsible for putting down the rebellion on the island of St Kitts. It is known that you served your Admiral whilst in the Caribbean in a loyal and noble fashion, fully consistent with the high tenets of our service. It is also known you received little credit for what you did, and instead have been made to attend here and be subjected to a Court-martial. Good-day to you sir."

The members of the Court filed out and Giles turned to hug Jessica and shake hands with a grinning Strathmore. Just then the doors at the end of the room burst open and Admiral Lord Crompton strode in. He stopped in front of Courtenay.

"H'mm. Looks like I have missed the end of the damned charade! I am most damnably sorry my dear Courtenay, that I did not get here earlier. I should have been here this morning, and I would have had something to say about this, believe you me! As it was I was waylaid by some damn committee which usefully wanted my opinions, and was I am sure arranged by some friend of a certain person." He took Courtenay by the arm and turned away from the others but Jessica would not be put off and turned also, raising one beautiful eyebrow. "Anyway, when I found out that Montford was sitting I didn't worry. I knew he would know what to do."

"I beg your pardon my Lord?" said Jessica, "You make it appear you were aware of what the outcome would be! Do you mean my dear Husband has been put through this needlessly?"

"My dear Lady Courtenay," smiled Crompton, taking one of her hands, "unfortunately this, ah, charade was totally necessary. Montford knew what sort of man Harding was. We all did. The general view would be, if the truth were known that your Husband here did everyone a favour by putting him down." He chuckled. "By god, I would have liked to have seen it Sir Giles. Cutlasses! I bet that man was not quite as clever with one of those, was he?"

Courtenay smiled. "No my Lord, he was not."

"You see Lady Jessica," Crompton continued, "I suppose it might have been possible to stop the Court-martial but that would have meant there would have been complaints in the corridors of Admiralty that one of my officers was being protected. No, that was not the way to do it. The best way was what happened today. Your Husband has been tried and honourably acquitted. That is the end of it. He leaves here today without a stain on his character. The other way there would always have been doubts expressed by certain people everytime the name of Captain Sir Giles Courtenay came up for promotion. Do you understand my dear?"

"Yes I suppose so. It is so unfair!"

"Life is unfair Jess," said Courtenay. He turned to Crompton. "I am free to return to my ship sir."

"Yes, but I am sure you would far rather spend some time with your wife, would you not? I can give you a few weeks. Mr Fenwick can have command in the meantime.

Do him good, not that he will have much to do since *Pegasus* is going to be warped into the dockyard the day after tomorrow and have a partial re-fit."

"She could certainly do with her bottom being scraped, sir."

"Giles, that sounds most rude!" interjected Jessica. They all laughed.

"The Port Admiral will ensure you retain as much of your crew as he can manage. You know how it is. Too few men for our ever demanding ships, but you will retain your officers and the professionals if you wish?"

"I think there may be one or two of the men who wish to try for some promotion sir, but I really would appreciate retaining as many as possible. I fear however that some of the younger members of the wardroom may have their heads turned by the chance of service aboard a frigate or a sloop sir. I would not stand in their way of course."

"Well we will have to see. Now then, I am staying in a most reasonable hotel not far from here. I would be most honoured if you would all join me for supper? Mr Courtenay, I do not see your wife sir. Is she well?"

"She is sir, but she could not bring herself to come and watch the proceedings. I intend to return home now and give her the glad tidings."

Giles took his Father's arm and steered him out of the room into the afternoon sunlight, which was fast disappearing behind some dark clouds.

Crompton turned to Strathmore, who had been hovering in the background.

"Well Marine, well done on defending Sir Giles! Will you join us?"

"Thank you sir but no. I promised that as soon as I had completed my mission here I would leave for London and my appointment there, which I am sure is going to be challenging in the extreme." He rolled his eyes towards the ceiling and Crompton smiled gently.

"Well, never fear Major. I am sure my friend the Commandant-General will be able to find an appointment more to your liking in a while. In the meantime, some time at Court will not come amiss, eh? Think of the ladies!" Strathmore turned away hiding a smile. Was there anyone Crompton did *not* know?

Courtenay returned, and once again hugged his wife.

"Very well, we will sup at eight." said Crompton. "Once you have had your leave Captain you will report to me at Admiralty, where we will discuss what I have in mind for you or I should say, what Nelson has in store for you!"

"Admiral Nelson, sir?"

"Yes. For some reason he has asked that your ship be appointed to his Mediterranean Fleet. Now, I am going to rest for a few hours. Eight sharp now. I have little time for bad time-keeping!"

THREE

The wheels of the smart coach crunched on the gravel of the courtyard in front of the imposing stone house. The House had a magnificent view over the Firth of Forth to the Royal navy base at Leith Roads. The coach swayed on its springs as the coachman brought it to a stop at the foot of the steps which led up to the imposing main doors, which at the moment were swung inwards to reveal an elegant lady with a huge smile on her face.

Before the carriage door had opened she was down the steps and as her nephew alighted and trod on the gravel, she flung her arms around him and hugged him to her.

Captain Sir Giles Courtenay, Bt, smiled at his Aunt.

"Hello Aunt Marcia! I trust I find you well?"

"Giles, Giles, I am all the better for seeing you! And look at you now. A Baronet, no less!" She turned as Giles put out a hand to help down a young lady.

"Jessica my dear, how wonderful you could come and see us at last! Are you well after your trip?"

Jessica smiled at Giles' Aunt and they kissed each other. "I am so sorry we have not been able to come and see you since the wedding Aunt, but......"

"Oh toosh my dear, I understand. I too was young once! Come, it's a wee bit drafty standing here. There's a good fire in the drawing room and cook will make some tea for us." She turned and looked around.

"And where is that man of yours Giles? I thought you went nowhere without him?"

"Alex Trafford had some family to see. I gather someone recently died. He has not had the chance to see any of his family for a long time. I told him to take whatever time he wants."

"Are ye sure he will return when you go back to your ship Giles?"

"Of course he is Aunt," interjected a smiling Jessica, "they have been through too much together." She smiled up at her husband. "The thought of either deserting the other….."

"Enough my dear. You have only just arrived here."

They were now in the drawing room and taking advantage of the roaring log fire in the grate.

"Mother and Father are most terribly sorry they could not come Aunt," Giles was saying, "but Father is rather busy at the moment and could not get away. I am sure they will be up to see you soon though."

"Och, that one works too hard. Just think Giles, if your Mother had had her way, you might have been looking after the practice for him by now?" She laughed, a most pleasant sound, and Giles and Jessica joined in. The door opened and a maid came in with a laden tray. Giles noted and so did Jessica that there was also a decanter of whisky and one glass on the tray. Marcia looked at Giles. "Thought you might appreciate something a wee bit stronger Giles!"

The following morning found Giles down at the quayside, watching a small number of sailing boats scudding about in the Roads. There were a small number of ships at anchor. A sloop was the largest, and two cutters which were probably in the Revenue service. Boats were being rowed back and forth between the ships and the quayside. He stood aside as a cart came along with a large load of supplies and watched with professional interest as a boat came alongside the quay from the sloop. There was a harassed Midshipman in charge. Giles smiled briefly. He was wearing a plain blue cloak over his uniform and had his hat inside the cloak. No authority. He could watch the comings and goings without anyone constantly making sure they were on their best behaviour.

The Midshipman was getting angry. "Watch what you are doing Sanders, you fool! You'll have the Captain's supplies in the water if you are not careful!" He looked away, his attention caught elsewhere and did not see the look the man called Sanders gave him. The man turned and saw Courtenay watching him.

"What are you looking at mate?"

"Nothing in particular I can assure you. Just enjoying the view. Ships always fascinate me!"

"If you ain't careful mate, you might get an even better view. Cap'n is always on the look-out for new hands and you look fit enough! Per'aps I ought to get the press over 'ere?"

"Oh God, not again!" Giles breathed. He stood his ground, looking out at the sloop. "What is she, 18 guns? Flush-decked?"

The man called Sanders paused unhappily. This one knew about ships. The Midshipman turned back, sensed the tension and stepped up Courtenay.

'I am most terribly sorry sir, is this man annoying you?" He turned to Sanders. "By God you scum, if I catch you harassing a gentleman again I'll see your backbones at the gangway!"

"Easy, Mr…..?" said Courtenay slowly. "He meant no harm. We were just passing the time of day. I was remarking on your ship. What is she called?"

"*Corncockle,* sir. Commander Golding sir."

"And you are?"

"Midshipman Spicer sir."

"Well Mr Spicer, may I make a suggestion? Treat your men with respect. They have little, and some have nothing, but they have their pride and they deserve respect for the job they do and the privations they have to suffer. One day Mr Spicer, your life may depend on one or more of your men. Treat them badly and they will not support you, believe me. Look after them and they will be there when you need them. And now Mr Spicer, I am going to take my leave and watch your exertions from the warmth of that Tavern yonder. Remember what I said."

"May I ask your name sir? You seem to know a lot about our life!"

"Courtenay, Mr Spicer. Goodday to you. My compliments to your Commanding Officer. Tell him he is a lucky man to have such a fine looking ship."

The man called Sanders stood stockstill, mouth agape.

Courtenay walked off, with Sanders staring after him.

"Sanders, what are you gaping at?" snapped Spicer.

"Don't you realise 'oo that is sir?"

"What do you mean?"

"He said 'is name is Courtenay. That's Captain Sir Giles Courtenay! 'e commands a 74, called the *Pegasus!*"

"Don't be a fool man, how do you know that?"

"My brother in law is 'er bo'sun, sir, that's how!"

Courtenay entered the Tavern, oblivious to the stares of the men on the quay. The Landlord gave him a smile, and filled a tankard for him.

"Care for some fine cheese Master Giles?"

"I can see my Aunt has been keeping everyone well informed Hamish!"

"Aye, that she has! Proud fit to bursting, so she was!"

Courtenay smiled. "Will you join me and have a wee dram Hamish?"

"That I will, aye, and thanks." As he poured the drink the Landlord took in the appearance of the slim tall man in front of him. He had known Courtenay for many years. Had watched him grow up, still remembered the day he had gone off to join his first ship. Now he was a Captain of a ship of the line and a Baronet, but what had it cost him? He knew Courtenay was in his twenties but he could see grey hair in his sideburns and lines on his face that were not there a few years ago. He realised Courtenay was looking at him, tankard raised.

"Here's to you Master Giles!" Courtenay smiled at the memory.

"Old friends." he said and they raised their drinks silently.

Two days later, Courtenay saw the sloop shortening its cable and preparing to up-anchor. Jessica was with him this time, standing near the quayside. She looked up at him and saw him watching the ship with professional interest.

"How does she compare with your old *Seagull,* dearest?"

"She doesn't! She is smaller and what we call flush decked. In other words she has no quarterdeck. She is smaller and carries less guns which I fancy are also smaller in size. My old sloop carried quite a punch Jess. No, *Corncockle* does not compare. And I will lay you odds she did not start life as a British ship. She has French lines about her." He rubbed his chin. "Probably the Brest yards."

He looked down at her. There was snow on the ground and although she was wearing a thick cloak he could sense her shivering.

"Come along. You are getting cold. Time we were getting back." He turned her and she tucked her arm inside his as they walked away from the quayside.

Three days later *Corncockle* was back with something of a sad tale to tell, as Giles Courtenay found out the following evening. Aunt Marcia had decided to have a small dinner party. Giles had looked on knowingly when his Aunt had announced the fact. He had seen Jessica looking at him and he had said wryly that he knew his Aunt's 'small' dinner parties of old. She looked on thirty or so as being 'small'. However this time she had meant it and there were no more than ten people, including the Admiral in charge of the Leith Roads Naval base and his wife.

Rear-admiral Jerard Porter seemed a pleasant enough person on the face of it. His wife was a fairly quiet lady but not after she had sampled some of Marcia's fine wines. Dinner was however a pleasant affair and Marcia suggested they all adjourn to the drawing room for coffee and port or brandy.

Giles Courtenay sat next to his wife on a well-stuffed sofa, and the Admiral, holding a brandy glass half-full, sat down in a nearby armchair and looked directly at him.

"Well, Sir Giles. I'll not say I have not heard of you because you have recently had accounts of your efforts in the Caribbean gazetted of course. I also saw the report of the Court-martial. That man Harding was a professional killer and I for one am very pleased he is no longer with us." He suddenly chuckled. "I am sure however that Spencer-White is none too pleased, though!" He became serious. "Serve him damn well right. Hear he is now a peer of the Realm, eh?"

"Yes sir, that is correct." said Courtenay carefully. Jessica was watching him, he knew.

"Have you heard about the damn French privateer who has been causing mayhem in these parts Sir Giles?"

"No sir, I cannot say that I have." He felt Jessica tense.

"Privateer! Pirate more like. Letter of Marque from the Revolutionary Council and the man thinks he can run up and down our coastline as he pleases!"

"What sort of ship Admiral?"

"Probably one of their bigger corvettes. Twenty two guns and fairly heavy calibre as well. Sent out *Corncockle* to find her and bring her to action. Did ye hear what happened to her?"

"No sir. I noticed she is back at her moorings though."

"Two days out there was a violent storm. Real bad one. Fishing fleet down the Forth here ran for shelter. During the storm some lines broke loose as they do, and a block came down. Golding was underneath it. Died straight away. Would not have known a damn thing. Good captain as well. His senior, and only Lieutenant was too inexperienced to know what to do although he should have done of course! Her Master got her back here. I'm short of vessels as you know, so what am I to do?"

"Find another Captain for the sloop sir, although I confess I do not know from where at the present time! It will take time for you to get a replacement. The weather has not been too good either for travelling on the roads."

Jessica was looking at her Husband and was smiling slightly. Marcia saw the look, saw the two Naval men in deep conversation and decided to break in.

"Coffee, gentlemen?"

Giles looked up and smiled but shook his head. Marcia put the pot down on a low table and sat down on the other side of Jessica.

"What's to do Jessica?"

"I have the distinct feeling that Admiral Porter here is trying to find a way of asking dear Giles to help him out of a bad situation Marcia." She put out a hand to stop Marcia saying anything. "And I also have the feeling that Giles' mind is at work. I can always tell from that look on his face. I have seen it so many times from the African coast to the Island where Papa and myself were held prisoner, and to that Court-martial farce!" Marcia patted her arm and smiled, but she was concerned.

Admiral Porter downed the rest of his brandy and scowled. "I know Sir Giles. Deuce take it, I cannot allow that damned pirate to sail up and down the coastline burning fishing boats whenever he feels like it!"

"What about the revenue cutters sir. They seem to be doing very little? I thought they were employees of the King as well?"

"Yes, but they would hardly get anywhere near that Frenchie without being blown out of the water!"

"Perhaps not sir if all three ships were to work together and Mr Frenchman could be let us say, *deceived?*"

Porter smiled. "Well yes, but I would have to press the cutters' crews into the service to do that!"

"You have the power sir. All you have to do is to find someone to captain the sloop until, of course, you find a permanent one."

Porter eyed Courtenay. "Why is it Sir Giles, that I get the distinct view you have an idea how to take this Frenchman?"

"Oh just an idea sir. All you need is someone who could execute it."

"Well Sir Giles, perhaps I could prevail…."

Courtenay shook his head. "No sir, I am most terribly sorry but I am afraid that is out of the question. I am here on leave with my wife and when I return I have orders to report to Admiral Lord Crompton. I value my leave sir."

He stopped as he felt Jessica's hand on his arm, squeezing it slightly. He turned and looked at her, smiled and covered her hand with his.

"I would of course sir, be most happy to share my thoughts on what you could so to stop the Frog. Perhaps I could attend on you in the forenoon watch sir?"

"Capital Sir Giles, capital. Shall we say two bells? If that is in order Lady Courtenay?' Jessica inclined her head and smiled. Marcia gave the Admiral a look which could have curdled fresh milk.

Later that night, Giles and Jessica Courtenay lay entwined in bed in the moments before sleep overtook them

"Giles, I am very surprised at you."

"Why on earth should you be? What have I done to merit such surprise?"

"That poor Admiral Porter! You could see he was at his wits' end to know what to do!"

"My dearest Jessica. He is an Admiral. I am a Captain. I receive my pay to command a ship, an Admiral receives his Flag and his lofty pay to manage men, ships and *problems.* That is what he is there for! I just do as I am bid."

"I am nonetheless very surprised at you. I thought at the very least you would have offered to take charge of that sloop, whatever its name is and go after that insufferable Frenchman. I could tell that was what you were dying to do!"

Giles laughed. "And how my darling, could you possibly know that!"

He could almost feel her smiling in the dark. "Because Giles, I know you too well. Far better than you think I know you in fact. You are a man of action, not a man to stand by and see someone with a problem, knowing you can help and not being willing. What would you do Giles?"

"Set a little trap. Now sleep Jess and no more questions!"

"So that is what you have in mind Sir Giles?" Admiral Porter got up and walked slowly to the massive log fire in the grate. There was snow underfoot outside and the chill was permeating into this room. "Set a trap for the damn Frog. Will he fall for it?"

"I think so sir. It is a question of the French Captain seeing what he wants to see. If I have it right by the time he realises he has seen wrongly it will be far too late!"

"And what does Lady Courtenay think of the idea of you going in temporary command of the *Corncockle*?"

"It was her idea sir."

Porter turned and looked at him, one eyebrow raised. "Really? Most young Navy wives would have wanted to keep their husbands close to them for as long as their leave lasted! A most charming young lady if I may say so?"

Courtenay inclined his head. "Thank you sir. You are most kind. I am most fortunate but my wife is not the kind of person to weep and wail when I have to leave her. She has seen and gone through a lot at my side. She understands. I think if I offered to take her with me she would accept with alacrity!"

"H'mm. Look after her my boy, she will be worth her weight in gold to you. When do you intend to go aboard and put your plan into action?"

"Before the turn of the tide sir. I wish to be away down the Forth on the ebb. You will do as I ask, sir?"

"Aye, of course I will. I will issue an immediate order to the Revenue Cutters to place themselves under your command."

"Perhaps sir, you could send the orders straight away? I would like them to be away well before I raise *Corncockle's* hook." He got up and crossed the room to a table where the local chart was spread out. Porter looked over his shoulder. "Ask that they meet me tomorrow night sir, six miles off St. Andrews?"

"Very well. That damned privateer is supposed to be further to the north, but I understand." Porter looked carefully at Courtenay. "I am most grateful to you Sir Giles. You do not have to do this for me."

Courtenay smiled. "I am pleased to be of assistance sir. If you will forgive me?"

"Very well Sir Giles. Your orders will be ready for you within the hour."

Courtenay stood up straight from the chart, picked up his hat and cloak and strode to the door.

Outside was the carriage, with an anxious Jessica inside. She was huddled inside a thick travelling rug as the cold air came in with the opening of the door.

"Did it go well darling?" she said.

"Too well. He accepted!" Jessica laughed. "Right Jess, home so that I can collect a few items. I have no intention of being out in the North Sea in this kind of weather for too long so I will not take much.." He looked at her anxiously. "Jess, are you sure...."

She smiled up at him. "You just promise you will take no chances and that you will come back safe and sound!"

He smiled. "I will do my best with both!" He rapped on the roof of the carriage and it moved away, snow pellets ratting against the window.

The shrill of Boatswain's pipes died away as Courtenay removed his hat to the small quarterdeck of the sloop *Corncockle.* He looked at the line of officers, all three of them, and two were Midshipmen, and then the warrant officers. The only Lieutenant stepped forward.

"Good morning Sir Giles. Welcome to the *Corncockle* My name is Pardew. I am the Senior aboard." He turned to a tall, thin and stern-faced man. "This is Mr Bradshaw, the Master. We are at your command sir."

"Thank you Mr Pardew. Have the hands lay aft if you please." Courtenay turned and watched as the men were herded towards the aft end of the ship. He found it strange there was no proper quarterdeck because he had always served on ships which had one. Here, the deck was flush and there was no real division between main and quarterdecks. He cleared his throat and thrust his cloak over his shoulders so the men could see his twin epaulettes, reaching into his coat at the same time for his orders. Just as he was about to do so he heard some voices at the entry port, and turned an impatient eye to the starboard side of the deck where the sound of a small boat alongside could clearly be heard. Pardew stepped forward.

"Be quiet there! What the devil is......." As he spoke a familiar figure appeared at the top of the ladder. Pardew looked at Courtenay and saw him smiling broadly.

"Be easy Mr Pardew. It is my cox'n, Alex Trafford, come to join!" Trafford stood next to the burly form of the Boatswain's Mate as Courtenay spoke to the crew.

"Lads, I do not come among you as your proper Captain. I was saddened by the manner of your last Captain's passing. It is one thing to die in battle or suffer the misfortune of disease, but quite another to die in the way he did. I have been asked to act as your temporary Master and Commander for one very special mission. By the time we return here to Leith Roads a new and permanent Captain will have been appointed. There is a French privateer threatening the coast and our local shipping, including our fishing fleets. Our job is to catch him. And by the grace of God I tend to lay him by the heels! We sail before the tide ebbs. Mr Bradshaw, prepare to up-anchor if you please!"

Bradshaw touched his battered hat. "Aye sir."

"I will show you the cabin sir." said Pardew. Courtenay smiled at the very young officer and let him lead the way. Trafford followed at a respectful distance, being eyed by some of the crew.

"What the deuce are you doing here Alex? I gave you leave to go and see your family, for God's sake!" Courtenay was shaking the man's hand. Pardew had left after showing Courtenay his quarters.

"Oh, long story Sir Giles. When I got home I found my mother had died two years since. My sister had taken up with a local man, even got two kids I knew nothing about! He didn't want to know about me and she was taken up with running a house and looking after the kids so I went back to Tor Bay, to your Parents' house, and they gave me directions as to find you. I would have stayed in Tor Quay, but your Father, he said if he didn't send me onto find you, you would never forgive him!"

Courtenay smiled. "Absolutely right. Did you see Jessica?" There was none of this standing on ceremony with Giles Courtenay.

Trafford smiled broadly. "Aye sir, that I did right enough! Got some stuff packed away she sent over. She said you went before she had a chance to pack anything for you! Got a nice cheese, and some fresh bread. Few bottles of your favourite Claret as well.'

"Good. Was she, well you know……."

"Was she alright sir? Aye, worried sick about you already o' course, but, well, Lady Jessica is a strong lass."

There was a knock at the screen door and Pardew stepped over the coaming.

"Ready to proceed sir. Anchor is hove short."

"Very well. Have you ever taken the ship to sea Mr Pardew?" He watched the young man's face.

"Well I er, no sir, I am afraid I have not as yet. Commander Golding always insisted on doing it himself."

"I see. Well now is a good time to see if your training has paid off. There is never going to be an easier time to get a ship under way than in a nice calm anchorage! I shall be up presently Mr Pardew."

The man left. Courtenay looked at Trafford and they smiled, then turned to the door together.

On deck the snow had stopped and a quick glance told Courtenay that all was ready. Men were strung out along the yards ready to let drop the sails. The men at the capstan were waiting for the order to raise the anchor clear and the anchor watch were ready to cat it home. Pardew turned, touching his hat.

"Carry on Mr Pardew if you please. Take the ship to sea!"

The man hesitated for a moment, saw a small smile playing on Courtenay's face, and turned, bringing up his speaking trumpet.

"Up-anchor! Hands aloft, let go the topsl's! Hands to the braces there!"

The anchor came up, the men aloft let go the sails, and the ship started to slide sideways.

"Heave on those braces!" Pardew was yelling. The yards came round and the sails bellied out with the slight wind. The ship gained steerage way and the helmsmen stared aloft, gauging the set of the sails.

The master stepped up to the wheel and looked at Pardew. "Course, sir?"

"Weather the Forth Mr Bradshaw. Then…."

"And then Mr Bradshaw, you will lay off a course for St. Andrews. We have a rendezvous tomorrow evening with the Revenue Cutters who slipped out of Leith earlier. Six miles off-shore." interjected Courtenay.

"Aye aye sir."

Courtenay turned to Pardew. " Satisfied?"

"I will be in a moment sir. The braces need some attention."

"Good. I am but a temporary Commander Mr Pardew. You are here permanently. It will do your position in the ship a power of good if your men can see you have the confidence and *the ability* to handle the ship. Now, she is yours whilst I look at the charts and then I shall tell you what we are about." Courtenay turned and went down to companion, with Trafford following.

After a slightly round-a-bout course *Corncockle* was nearing the rendezvous with the Revenue cutters. There was a yell from the mainmast look-out.

"*Deck there!* Two ships dead ahead. They be the cutters from Leith!"

Courtenay turned to Bradshaw. "Excellent, Mr Bradshaw. Very well done indeed. And that look-out has good eyes because it will very soon be dark." He wrapped his cloak around him. Trafford saw it and smiled. Courtenay hated the cold. He preferred the Caribbean or the Med. "Have the men lay aft Mr Bradshaw. It is time we told the lads what we are doing."

The men once again came aft and many had curious stares on their faces. This youthful post-Captain, who commanded a powerful 74-gun ship of the line and who was a Baronet, had come among them like a whirlwind. He had been through the ship, speaking to seamen and warrant officers alike. He had shown genuine interest when the man called Sanders, plucking up courage, had actually had the nerve to speak to Courtenay before he was spoken to. Courtenay had simply smiled when the man had blurted out that he was the brother in law of *Pegasus's* boatswain.

"Henry Oates? Good man, Sanders. I am lucky to have him. Your brother-in-law?"

"Aye sir. Married my elder sister some years back."

"Well I hope he has made the most of his leave Sanders, because I shall expect him to be back aboard *Pegasus* when I return to Plymouth!" Sanders had knuckled his forehead as Courtenay had nodded to him and passed on.

The men were gathered.

"Lads, I told you we had a special mission. You will have heard the yell from the look-out. Those cutters are the Revenue cutters which you last saw at anchor at Leith. They have, er, been pressed into *our* service for what we have to do. I have never been one for fancy talk. That Frenchmen we are seeking is bigger, more heavily armed and has more crew than we have. We need help to take him which we are going to do by subterfuge. We are going to make him think we are a French corvette and that we have two cutters as prizes. When we sight the Frog you will load the guns with double shot and grape. I intend to get two broadsides into him before he can reply, run alongside and board him. I shall be speaking with the Captains of the Revenue ships in a little while. We will be reinforced by those men not required to man the ships. We *will* prevail lads, make no mistake."

He turned to Pardew. "Dismiss the hands Mr Pardew and when we are close enough signal the Cutters' Commanding Officers to come aboard."

Courtenay stood slightly stooped under the low deck beams of the sloop's cabin. He had his hands clasped behind him as the screen door opened and Pardew announced the Revenue Captains. Trafford stood in his usual position near the door.

One of the Revenue men made no bones about his complaint.

"What the devil do you think you are doing Captain, er, *whatever* your name is! We are Revenue men not Navy. Our complaint isn't with some Frenchman *you* should be taking care of!" The man was quite elderly and had a full bread, very grey. He was broad in the beam and stood as tall as Courtenay.

Courtenay turned. Trafford started forward, mouth opening no doubt to teach this Revenue man a lesson in manners but Courtenay held up his hand. The other revenue officer looked on with interest. He had a firm, alert face, and clearly was interested in the proceedings.

"I am Captain Sir Giles Courtenay. I presently command a 74 gun ship of the line, but I have been asked by Admiral Porter to assist him with this problem of the French privateer. Gentlemen, I am surprised to hear you say it is not your problem." He turned on them angrily. "Dammit to hell, a fight with a Frenchman is the duty of anyone who wears the King's coat! You may be Revenue men but you serve our King, or is it that you do not?" He turned an angry aye on the Revenue man who had spoken.

"How dare you....!"

"I dare sir, I dare, because I cannot believe I have heard a King's officer telling me that he has no fight with a Frenchie because he is not in the Navy! Admiral Porter. Did he or did he not place you under my orders in accordance with the authority he has as Senior Naval Officer at Leith Roads? Was it or was it not done with the permission of your superiors in Leith?" There was silence. "I asked you a question gentlemen, I believe I am entitled to an answer!"

The younger man stepped forward. "My name is Harris, Sir Giles. Edward Harris. You will have to forgive Ferguson here. He has been far too long wrapped up in his own wee problems with the smugglers to recognise a real threat! What d'ye want us to do?"

"Thank you Mr Harris. I want you to transfer to the *Corncockle* all and any men who are not really needed to sail your ship. A handy cutter like yours can, I am sure, make do with a small number of men, but in any event you will not be required to do anything else than act as bait."

"Bait?" asked Ferguson.

"Aye, bait. We are going to fool the Frog into thinking your ships are my prizes. I am going to make it appear I am a French Corvette. I intend to close with the Frog and that is why I need the extra men."

"Foolishness Sir Giles." exploded Ferguson. "Madness! My men are used to fighting smugglers not French seamen."

"They will be very similar to smugglers Mr Ferguson. She is a privateer not a French national ship and I would imagine her crew are the scum of the earth. Surely not a match for Revenue men, or are they?"

Out of the corner of his eye he saw Trafford smiling.

"Of course they are not Captain. Just because my men are Scots doesn't mean to say they can't fight! If ye remember….."

"Mr Ferguson. There is no need to lecture me on the fighting qualities of the Scotsman. My Mother, my Aunt, are Scots. The McPherson clan. I am half Scot. Does that help?"

Ferguson grumbled away under his breath for a moment. "MacPherson you say? And what d'ye want us to do if this here Frenchie comes a'calling?"

"Nothing. You will be spectators at what I hope will be a short sharp fight. When we have secured the Frenchie we will return to Leith where no doubt your men will be able to regale their friends for some time of their deeds!"

"Aye, weell, I suppose we have some lads who can fight you can borrow. I'd best get going." He paused. "MacPherson you say?"

'Yes. Marcia MacPherson is my Aunt." He saw the Revenue man's eyebrows arch. He obviously knew the name. "Mr Ferguson. Use the night to get a French flag bent on so that when dawn comes, it will appear you are a French prize. And you Mr Harris."

"And you Sir Giles?" asked Harris.

"Oh, I think with the dawn you will suddenly find yourself being escorted by a French corvette!"

Four bells rung out from the belfry. It was the forenoon watch. The decks had been holystoned, the men had eaten, and the look-out was scanning the horizon.

Below decks the men sent over from the cutters were trying to make themselves comfortable. It wasn't very easy in an already crowded mess-deck.

Courtenay was pacing the deck near the wheel. Pardew was watching the clouds scurrying above with the fresh wind over the larboard quarter.

."Mr Pardew. I am sure you will tell me that it is of the finest calibre, but what of the gunnery in this ship?"

Pardew turned and smiled. "No need to worry about gunnery sir. The gun crews will not let you down. Commander Golding insisted on a high state of efficiency."

"I am sure he did. Let us see some drill. Call all hands and we will have gunnery practice." He saw the look on the young Lieutenant's face. "I have no doubt whatsoever that you do believe the gunnery on this ship to be first-rate Mr Pardew, but I will be taking this ship into action if we are fortunate to attract the Frog and I need to know just how efficient the gunnery is! Now, please attend to my orders!"

"Aye aye air!" Pardew turned away, and in a few moments the men were tumbling onto deck and running to their guns.

The guns crews untied lashings, ran in the guns, opened ports, loaded guns, ran out, pretended to fire, ran in again, sponged out, and did it all over again. Eventually Courtenay ordered a halt.

"That was smartly done Mr Pardew. Congratulate your crews from me. I hope that they will perform under fire in the same way! Has this ship seen much action?"

"Mostly small fights sir with luggers, small privateers, brigs."

"Nothing as large is this Frenchie though?"

"No sir."

"Well never fear Mr Pardew, there is a first time for everything!"

Bradshaw was climbing onto the deck from the companion and Courtenay saw him look doubtfully first of all at the large French Tricolour streaming from the mizzen gaff and then at the two cutters both of whom were flying the same flag over their own colours. Then he looked up at the low grey scudding clouds and sniffed the air. Courtenay smiled to himself. Sailing Masters were all the same!

"Something bothers you Mr Bradshaw?" he asked mildly.

"In for a blow sir, I'm sure. I think it might be a good idea to find some shelter. I'm sure those lads in the cutters will find it hard if it gets bad, coping without all their crews!"

"I agree. Alter course two points to larboard and signal the cutters to follow. According to the chart there is a useful bay ahead?"

"Aye sir. Good enough for us!"

The three ships lay at anchor in the small bay. The two cutters were side by side, a few cables apart and only moving slightly at their anchors. *Corncockle* was to seaward of them. Grey day finally gave way to a dark night. Snow showers passed across the ships but the wind gradually eased. Morning founds the decks with a thin white layer and there was snow on the halliards and rigging.

Courtenay appeared on deck as light began to grow, clutching his cloak around him. Pardew was stamping his feet but stopped as soon as he saw Courtenay appear, and just behind him, Trafford.

"Good morning Mr Pardew." said Courtenay. "Prepare to up-anchor and signal the cutters."

"Aye aye, sir. Pardew turned and starting yelling his orders and Courtenay turned to look out to starboard in the growing light.

"Alex, hand me that glass, would you?"

Trafford, guessing something was not quite right, passed him a brass telescope from the rack and watched as Courtenay levelled it. Then he turned and looked himself, but the light was still quite bad.

Courtenay closed the glass and turned to Pardew.

"Mr Pardew. I have the feeling we have found our quarry. There is a ship out to sea. We are still hidden, I am sure, against the backdrop of the land and it is still quite dark. The ship looks like one of their corvettes. Get the anchor up quickly and make sail."

"Aye aye, sir!"

The anchor was soon hove short and Bradshaw was on deck issuing his orders to the men aloft. Within moments the sloop was under command, and with the cutters following but well astern, she moved out of the bay. Courtenay was in the starboard ratlines, leg twined around them holding him steady as he raised the glass once again. He jumped down onto the deck.

"Mr Pardew. Clear for action if you please. That is the French ship we have been looking for. Remember what we planned. Load but do not run out. Keep the men out of sight. She is over to our starboard bow, so we will run out and join her to larboard. Double-shot the larboard battery and add grape for good measure."

The crew of the sloop went to quarters, and as Courtenay watched, they rushed hither and thither in apparent confusion but each man knew exactly what he was doing and where he was going. Courtenay looked over the sloop and was impressed.

"Very good Mr Pardew. Now let us see what Mr Frenchman is up to shall we?"

He climbed into the ratlines again and looked through the glass. Trafford was now able to see the other ship and although no colours were being shown he could tell just by looking that it was a French ship.

"No mistaking her cut Sir Giles!"

"None whatsoever, Trafford." muttered Courtenay absently. 'Ah, she has seen us. There go her colours!"

A large Tricolour was being hauled up to her gaff to stream out in the wind. That had eased considerably but there was still more than sufficient to enable the ships to manoeuvre at will.

"Mr Bradshaw. Lay off a course which will take us up to her on her starboard side if you please." He looked astern and saw the two cutters following obediently. *Corncockle* had 9-pounders on her maindeck, and the cutters only had pop-guns of 6-pounders, but nonetheless if she could get in two broadsides and get alongside to board in the smoke and the confusion even the cutters with their smaller armament could cause damage if they crossed the French ship's stern and gave her a raking.

The gap between the ships lessened. The crew of the British sloop were clearly nervy. Several of them paused in their work to look at the Tricolour on their own ship, to the French ship which grew larger with every passing minute and there was a certain amount of muttering amongst them which a Petty Officer quelled with an angry roar.

Pardew turned to Courtenay. "Men are getting a little edgy sir."

"I know. It is one thing to be sailing towards the enemy with guns run out and the proper colours showing, and another to be sneaking up on him not knowing whether he has seen through our little ruse and is waiting for us to get within range! My information is that he has 12-pounders, which can out-range us as well."

Courtenay looked back at the French ship. Not far now. The ship was edging round to run down on the Frenchman's starboard side. He turned and looked at the signal halliards and at the Midshipman who was there. It was the Midshipman from the quayside, Spicer.

"Are you ready with our colours Mr Spicer? It is important that you get them aloft before we open fire."

"Aye aye sir. They are bent on ready."

Courtenay smiled, and the Midshipman called Spicer smiled back but Courtenay could see it was forced. The lad was scared stiff and why not? Courtenay looked at Trafford and he grinned.

"I'll try and keep an eye on him sir!"

Courtenay looked again at the French ship, which was now on *Corncockle's* larboard side on a converging course. He looked back at the deck. The crew were for the most part hiding behind the bulwarks near their guns. There were men near the side with orders to wave at the French ship as they came closer.

Courtenay looked at them and then yelled. "Come on then lads, wave at the bastards!" They looked at him for a moment, then turned and started waving energetically. The sloop was closer. The French ship was still on the same course and Courtenay noted that the Captain had shorted sail. He smiled. The gun ports on the French ship were closed. There were men looking at them from the privateer, which he had seen from her counter was called *Corsair*. He had noted that with a start. Memories of another, deadlier *Corsair,* had flooded his mind, and the lovely Mercy LeFevre. Beautiful and deadly. A vicious, murdering woman pirate. He and his sloop of war *Seagull* had destroyed her and her ships. He still carried the scar from the ball he had taken as she had tried to kill him before she had been killed by his First-Lieutenant and friend, Tim Spellman. The corvette was now close and *Corncockle* was ranging up on her starboard quarter. Any moment now.

Trafford, looking at the preparations on the gundeck happened to see one of the crew pointing astern, and when he looked he could not believe what he was seeing.

"Cap'n, look! One of those Revenue cutters has hauled down the Frog flag an' run up her own colours!"

"What the *bloody* hell!" snarled Courtenay, following Trafford's pointing arm. It was true enough. The Tricolour had disappeared from the leading cutter which was now flying only her own colours. "What the devil is that idiot Ferguson playing at?"

"They've seen it sir!" Trafford was now pointing at the French privateer where there were a number of Frenchmen gesticulating wildly.

"Mr Pardew! Run out the guns. Fire as you bear and I'll want a broadside into the Frogs after that! Clear the starboard battery and arm the men. Mr Bradshaw! Put your helm over and get us alongside. I'll trouble you Mr Spicer to strike that flag and run up our colours!"

Courtenay undid the clip holding his cloak in place and slipped it off, showing his twin epaulettes. He dragged out his sword, took the scabbard and threw it into a corner. Some of the men on the deck near the wheel looked on as Trafford calmly passed him two pistols which he clipped onto his belt. They were seeing their temporary Captain in a different light.

The *Corncockle* suddenly exploded in flame and smoke as the first guns opened fire. They might be small 9-pounders but double shotted, with grape, and aimed slightly high, their contents scythed across the French side like a hailstorm and a number of men were hurled to the decking. One or two French gunports were opening and here and there a gun muzzle showed but it was too late. Even as the first gun fired the British sloop reloaded and replied with a full broadside. The ship heeled over to starboard under the force of the guns then came back and was alongside the French privateer. Yardarm grated against yardarm and a number of British sailors threw grapnels to hold the ships together. A number of privateersmen appeared at the side of the French ship waving their swords, knives, muskets, pikes, anything with which to fight, and starting yelling but on the sloop, two swivels went off and packed charges of canister cut the Frenchmen down.

Courtenay ran down the deck to where the ships were closest, Trafford right behind him as always. He paused for a moment and looked at Pardew.

"Clear the larboard battery as well Mr Pardew, arm all the men. Get those Revenue men up here in a moment. I wish to keep them as a reserve for now!" He turned to the other men, now all armed to the teeth with a homely collection of weapons including boarding axes and long pikes. "Come on lads, follow me and let's take this Pirate!" He jumped for the other ship's side and even as he was clambering over the top, a swivel nearby exploded and cut down more men as they were going to start firing on them. With a roar the crew of the *Corncockle* stormed after Courtenay.

Courtenay dropped onto the gangway and immediately had to fend away a slashing sword from a person who appeared to be dressed as an officer. The man stumbled away then shrieked as an axe came out of nowhere and embedded itself in his back. A burly seaman from *Corncockle* picked him up and threw him over the side where he was mashed between the two hulls.

A seamen attacked Courtenay with a cutlass but Courtenay was able to parry away the untidy slash and run the man through the chest before he was able to recover. He pulled one of the pistols from his belt and shot another man who was about to stab a

British seaman. Trafford was despatching another Frenchman but there were a lot of them, and after hacking, stabbing and slashing for what seemed ages Courtenay realised they did not seem to be making a lot of headway.

He turned and leaned over the side and waved to the Midshipman, Spicer. The lad waved back and ran to a companion. Moments later there was loud yelling and the Revenue men swarmed onto deck and started to climb over onto the Privateer.

The extra men now helped to begin to push the French back. Courtenay ran a man through the stomach and as he fell away, hands clutching himself, pushed him out of the way, jumped over another inert form and sprinted along the gangway for the quarterdeck ladder. An officer stopped him at the foot, extending his sword and lunging skilfully. Courtenay traded blows with him, parrying his thrusts and lunges, then pushed him back against the ladder. Trafford looked on, feeling pity for the Frenchman for just a moment before turning and seizing another by the scruff of his shirt and pulling him away from a wounded man. He spun him round, slashed him across the stomach with his razor-sharp cutlass and watched as the man saw his entrails spill onto the bloody planking. He fell forwards onto the bloody mess.

In the meantime Courtenay had the French officer pinned against the ladder. He brought his fist round and caught the man on the chin, then as he staggered his right arm brought his sword round again and the man screamed as he felt the point enter his stomach. Further and further in, until the man went limp then Courtenay brutally pushed him over the side. The man was still alive as he hit the water but his eyes had a brief glimpse only of the sky above him before he died, crushed between the hulls as they surged against each other.

Courtenay was on the quarterdeck the other pistol in his hand, Trafford and half-a dozen others with him. There was a fancily dressed man on the deck by the wheel. He had been terribly mangled, one leg gone, blood everywhere. There was a youngster kneeling over him and two other seamen. One made a threatening gesture and before Courtenay could lift his pistol someone else shot him dead. The other dropped his cutlass and raised his arms. Courtenay looked down at the deck. His men were winning. More and more of the privateers were throwing down their weapons.

He strode over to the youngster and Trafford hauled him to his feet. There were tears running down his smoke-blackened face.

"*Mon Pere, mon pere!*"

"Jesus Cap'n. Must be the Captain's son!" The youngster, who was about 16, broke free and knelt again by his dead Father. Trafford again lifted him to his feet but this time gently.

Courtenay turned to the maindeck and felt snowflakes striking his face. The snow grew thicker. Pardew appeared.

"The ship is ours sir!"

"Well done Mr Pardew, well done indeed! I should have known that no privateer was match for our fearsome Jacks!"

Pardew allowed himself a small smile. He was hatless, as was Courtenay, his sword was bloody to the hilt and he had blood splashed over his breeches and uniform coat. He had fought hard.

"Well Mr Pardew, you and your men are to be congratulated. I will make sure the Admiral hears of this. First of all however we must check the butcher's bill. Then, you will take command here as Prizemaster and we will select a scratch crew to enable you to get the ship back to Leith!"

Pardew's smile was a little broader. Courtenay knew precisely what he was thinking. Perhaps this was another, important, step up the ladder of promotion.

FOUR

Giles Courtenay stretched his legs out in front of the roaring log fire, and curled his right hand around a large cut-glass goblet of fine Brandy. Jessica sat next to him, staring into the dancing flames as Marcia MacPherson poured some coffee for them all.

"Do you really have to go back tomorrow Giles? It seems hardly any time at all since you came here, and then some of the time was spent with you chasing that wretched French Privateer!" she said.

"I am afraid I have no choice Aunt. I have to report to Admiral Crompton at the Admiralty. Then it will be back to sea."

"You don't have to sound so happy about it Giles!" scolded Jessica, taking her husband's hand.

Giles smiled. "Sorry Jess. You knew what you were letting yourself in for when you married me!"

Jessica held up her hand. "I know, I know Giles. You are married to the Navy first and me second!"

"I would not put it *quite* that way Jess. We will still have some time together when we get back to London. I do not suppose for one moment I will be sent off straight away." He turned to his Aunt and took a cup of coffee. "In any case Aunt, you will have

Mother and Father and the girls here soon. They will keep you busy over Christmas and Hogmenay!"

"Girls! Young ladies they are now and not wanting to come up here for much longer if I am any judge! Och, they will be far more interested in the young men than seeing poor old Aunt Marcia! I am sure you will be pleased to see your Father again, Jessica."

"Yes I hope Giles will be at home for Christmas although I doubt it, and we will spend the time with him. It has been so good of you to have us here Marcia. It has been a most wonderful stay. You must come and spend some time in London next year."

"I've a mind to do just that lassie! In the meantime I think the Rear-admiral is mightily relieved that you solved his problem for him, and even got him another new ship to play with!"

"Yes and to crew, not only with men but officers as well! I think I have just given him a bigger headache!"

"Nonetheless you did a good job and he was very impressed, anyone could see that! There's many a fisherman can put to sea a little happier thanks to you!"

Giles looked at both of them and smiled, then sipped his coffee and drank his Brandy. He wondered what was in store for him when he returned to London.

There was snow on the ground in Whitehall. It masked the thunder of iron-shod carriage wheels which came and went along the street. Everything seemed curiously muffled even though there was only a thin layer. It was bitterly cold. As Courtenay stepped down from the coach, his breath clouded. He turned back and smiled at his wife.

"Now go back home dear, and I will be there again as soon as possible." He lent in and kissed her and then closed the door. Trafford came round from the horses.

Courtenay drew his cloak around him. "Let's hope it is warmer inside Alex. Off to the Mediterranean or the Caribbean, eh?"

Trafford smiled. "Well somewhere in-between sir. Not too hot, and not bloody cold!"

They entered the Admiralty building and after a few moments were striding along the corridor which led to Crompton's office.

Trafford turned to Courtenay as his Captain slipped out of his cloak.

"I had better make myself scarce Sir Giles. His Lordship will not want me hanging around!"

"Nonsense. You will remain here until I have finished. There is a good fire over there."

The doors to Crompton's office swung inwards and his Secretary saw Courtenay and smiled briefly. He stood to one side as Courtenay straightened his uniform coat, and walked into the room.

There was a blazing fire on one side and Crompton was coming round the side of his desk near it as Courtenay entered. He had his right hand outstretched, and he shook Courtenay's hand warmly.

"Good to see you again Sir Giles. Sit you down. Claret? No, I know, some Brandy. Warm your bones. God what awful weather. Bet you wish you were somewhere warm eh? I know you hate this kind of weather! Trafford outside? Yes? Thought he might be!" Crompton poured two generous measures, raised his glass to his young companion and studied him carefully. "How was Scotland? What is all this I have been reading. eh? Thought you were on leave, not galavanting around the North Sea fighting French privateers!"

"Someone had to do it my Lord and there was no-one else!"

"Porter should have done it. Used to be a good Captain I seem to recall. He could have done it if needs be. Your idea I suppose? Well executed from what I hear. Did you have trouble with the Revenue men?"

"Some. One of them damn near wrecked the whole plan by hauling down the French flag and running up his own colours before we were ready to engage! He told me afterwards he was frightened I was going to open fire under French colours! Damn the man! Still all's well that ends well and we suffered relatively few casualties."

"What about the sloop Giles?"

"I recommended it be given to the First-Lieutenant, Pardew. Rear-admiral Porter judged him too young and too junior, but he fought well and he can handle the ship."

"H'mm. Heard about that as well. He gave it to someone else. A son of a friend who happened to be home visiting. Some damned jackadandy who will probably make everyone's life hell!"

"I am sorry to hear that. Young Pardew deserved a chance to see what he could make of it."

Crompton tilted the Brandy glass to let the rest of the amber liquid slide over his tongue. "Well, that's life. Now. Slight change of plan. Nelson wanted you as you know, but it will have to wait. Admiral Lord Keith is in command of the Mediterranean Fleet and he is due some reinforcements. A small Squadron is being sent out to join him at Gibraltar under Vice-admiral Sir Angus Browne, whom I believe you may know?"

"I served under him in the *Claymore* as a Midshipman and then Lieutenant."

"Good. He does not, unfortunately, enjoy the best of health and I fear that the command may only be temporary before he is recalled to London. He is due for further promotion in any event but I know he wanted a sea-going appointment and he welcomed the opportunity. I am sure he will be pleased to see you. I have heard from James Fenwick by the way. Everything is in order. There are no problems and *Pegasus* is at Plymouth awaiting your return. Now before you dash away to that beautiful young wife of yours I am sure she would not begrudge me taking you to lunch at my club. In any case there is something I want to discuss with you in private."

Courtenay smiled. He always enjoyed lunch with Crompton. He was a lover of good food and fine wines.

"So what did his Lordship want Giles?" Jessica was asking him later, sitting close to him on a comfortable sofa in her Father's house.

"Oh he wanted to tell me about a new addition to the Spencer-White Naval clan. Pardon me I forgot, he is of course now Lord Cairns. He rejoices in the name of Marmaduke Spencer-White and I understand he is one of Cairns' youngest nephews, and one of his favourites. He is not long commissioned and seems to have secured the appointment as Cairns' Flag-Lieutenant. He is far too young really and will not have the faintest about his job, but Cairns does not have an appointment yet so he will doubtless have some time to learn. From what Crompton told me the young man is adept at the tables, good with a sword and pistol. He also fancies himself with the ladies."

"As long as he keeps out of your way Giles, that is the main thing. You will be at sea anyway and he will be at home!" She cuddled her Husband. "I am going to miss you so much my darling."

"What time are we supposed to be dining with your Father?"

"He will be working until about seven. I have arranged we will meet him at about half-past at Greens." She hesitated, smiling, "That gives us two hours or so before I have to get ready Giles. Do you think…"

"……that there is anything we can do to keep ourselves amused for those couple of hours Jess?" He bent his head and kissed his wife.

Three days later, the night before Courtenay was due to return to his ship, he and Jessica were present at a Reception being held by an old friend of her Father. They had just come off the dance floor and were quietly toasting each other with glasses of champagne when a tall slim officer in the uniform of a Flag-Lieutenant stopped beside them. The young man wearing the uniform had a smirk on his face. He bowed slightly, looked Jessica up and down.

"Excuse me ma'am," He had a very rich plumy manner of speaking, "would you care to dance with me? I am a good dancer. I have watched you dancing with this officer and there is much I am sure I could teach you." He smiled in a way that made Jessica's skin crawl.

Courtenay turned to him before Jessica had time to speak. "I will thank you, Lieutenant whoever you are, to mind your manners when you speak to my wife."

The man was clearly unimpressed he was speaking to a post-captain, and continued with the lazy smile on his face. He was about to say something when their host Lord Hadley, appeared.

"Ah Jessica my dear, there you are. I have been trying to have words with you all evening." He looked at their faces and stopped. Courtenay turned to him coldly.

"Perhaps my Lord, you would be so kind as to introduce this *person* who appears to be masquerading in the King's coat?"

Hadley suddenly looked most unhappy. "He is not masquerading Sir Giles, he is a Naval officer. May I introduce The Hon Marmaduke Spencer-White, Flag-Lieutenant to Vice-admiral Lord Cairns." He turned to Spencer-White. "This, Lieutenant, is Captain Sir Giles Courtenay and Lady Courtenay." He was acutely aware of the tension. "Is there something wrong?"

"Only if you consider that a *gentleman* telling a Lady that she cannot dance well enough for him is wrong my Lord!" answered Courtenay very calmly. He should have guessed who it was. No other person, no other Flag-Lieutenant, would dare to behave towards a more senior officer and a Baronet at that, unless he was certain of very powerful support. He realised in an instant what this was about.

"Jessica, I do believe it is time to retire. My Lord I thank you from my wife and myself for your kind invitation. Goodnight to you." He took Jessica's arm and steered her away. They were awaiting their coats when Jessica's Father appeared.

"What the devil is going on? Giles? What has happened?"

"Spencer-White, or perhaps I should say Lord Cairns, has sent his latest Flag-Lieutenant here to insult not only me but your daughter in the hope I would call him out. It is as well I was warned by Lord Crompton only a few days ago that Cairns has picked himself another killer to help him, only this time the man is one of the family whelps! It is better if we leave Sir Geoffrey before words are spoken."

"I will come with you."

"There is no need Father," said Jessica. "You stay. Lord Hadley will be most displeased if you leave as well."

Sir Geoffrey's brow furrowed. "He is most annoyed even now. I heard him asking that young man what on earth he thought he was doing annoying his guests. Spencer-White just laughed at him. It is as well that Cairns is not going to be your Flag-officer Giles. I have told him I am most displeased that he should invite such a person and I have said I am leaving." He suddenly smiled. "In any case you two are far better company than most of the people here. I am beginning to see the charm in living where your parents do Giles! Come, let us go home and we can dispose of a decanter of port and a cigar or two, what say you, Giles?"

Giles Courtenay was very fond of his Father-in-law and smiled his acceptance, then even more broadly as a picture of his dear wife smoking a cigar came into his mind!

The following day Courtenay was supervising the packing of his bags when there was a knock at the door of the room he and Jessica shared. The Butler, Hedges, stepped into the room with a silver tray upon which there was a single card.

"There is a Naval officer downstairs Miss Jessica, who says he would like to speak to you." Hedges had not got out of the habit of calling her that and never used 'your ladyship'. He turned as Courtenay spoke.

"Does he have some fancy gold braid on his left shoulder Hedges?"

"Why yes sir, how clever of you to know!"

Courtenay smiled. "Very well Hedges, leave it to me."

"Now Giles he came to call on me, and I will therefore deal with it!" said Jessica. With that she picked up her skirts and bustled out of the room. Hedges looked impassively at Courtenay then followed. Courtenay also followed but only to the top of the stairs where he could hear but not be seen.

Jessica walked slowly down the winding staircase. The officer was in the hallway. It was Spencer-White as Giles had said it would be.

"Good morning Mr Spencer-White." she said calmly. 'I am surprised to see you here. How did you know where I live?"

"It was not difficult Lady Courtenay...I do work for an Admiral and your Husband is a Naval officer. I have come to offer my apologies over my behaviour of last night. It was unforgivable and I do ask that you accept my apology."

"I have always been taught to accept apologies Mr Spencer-White, and therefore I will do so. And now if you will excuse me I am rather busy at the present."

"I know your Husband will soon be away, Lady Courtenay. I am sure you will be lonely......bored perhaps. A Lady such as yourself, well, I am sure you enjoy the social life which London has in such quantities. Perhaps I could attend on you and escort you..."

"I am afraid what you have suggested is impossible sir and in any case I would not dream of accompanying you anywhere!"

"Well, Lady Courtenay, if you change your mind you have my card."

Jessica looked at the card in her hand, looked at the smiling man and tore the card into four pieces. "Now I do not! Good day to you sir!" With that, Jessica turned her back on him and walked back up the stairs. The Flag-Lieutenant looked at her for a moment, then realised the door was open and turned and went through it.

Jessica saw her Husband at the top of the stairs. "The cheek of that man! Wanted to escort me to balls and receptions when you are away so that I would not become bored! Seduce me more like! How I kept my temper I do not know!"

Courtenay was very serious. He was worried, but he could not let the worry show.

"Well done! That told him! You will not see him anymore I'm sure! Now, your Father said he would be back shortly?"

"Yes he had to deal with a couple of matters but he wanted to be here when you go. Giles, I am going to miss you so much!" She put her arms around him and hugged him and she felt him gently kissing her hair.

"I shall miss you as well dearest."

"No you will not! You will have your ship and your men. They are the lucky ones, having you! You just make sure you take no risks. Oh what am I saying, take no risks! Just be careful."

"I shall. Now there is something I need to have a word with Trafford about dearest. I shall return in a moment."

About ten minutes later Trafford let himself out of the door, ran down the steps and turned in the direction of Whitehall and the Admiralty. Five minutes later Sir

Geoffrey returned. Before Jessica saw him Giles took him by the arm and led him into the morning room.

"Sorry about the subterfuge but there is something I need to discuss with you, and where I need your indulgence."

They sat. Sir Geoffrey poured two measures of Brandy for them and Giles told him what he had in mind. At the end of the conversation, Sir Geoffrey nodded and said very seriously, "Yes Giles, of course that is alright my boy. Capital idea."

There was the sound in the hallway of baggage being put on the carpeted floor, and Giles Courtenay knew it was time for him to leave his wife and return to his ship.

A couple of hours later he and Trafford were seated in a fast coach taking them on the first leg of their ride to Plymouth.

"All arranged Sir Giles. Had a word with Joe Harrington. Remember him from the *Amazon?*"

"Of course. Good man. Well done Alex. I am most grateful to you."

"If that man comes a'sniffing, he'll have an unpleasant surprise!"

The Bosun's mates calls trilled, the Marines presented arms with a stamp of their booted feet and as Captain Sir Giles Courtenay stepped through the entry port of his ship, *Pegasus,* he lifted his hat briefly and then turned to smile at his waiting Senior Lieutenant.

"Good Morning James. I thought we were supposed to be part of a new Squadron here. Has it been delayed for some reason?"

"Good morning sir. No, there has been no delay. The Squadron was here until yesterday but I understand the Admiral received an order to proceed as soon as possible and he therefore directed the Squadron to leave. I was sent a message to the effect that the Admiral realised you were not due to return until today and he therefore requested that you follow as soon as convenient and meet with him at Gibraltar."

"I see. I wonder what made the Admiralty direct him to leave earlier James. I was only there the other day!"

"Well, sir…."

"I know, I know. Well, come aft with me whilst Trafford is fussing around with my chests and you can tell me who we have lost and who you have been able to hold on to!"

Fenwick smiled. "Aye aye sir!"

He followed Courtenay off the cold maindeck, beneath the poop and into the illusion of warmth between decks. He knew Courtenay hated the cold weather and would be glad to get back to the warmth of the Mediterranean, but equally he knew how sad he was at leaving his wife. Into the cabin where Trafford was busy with Kingston, the cabin servant, stowing things away.

"Ah, Kingston," said Courtenay. "Some Brandy for the First-Lieutenant and myself. Might warm us a little." He turned to Fenwick, slipping out of his cloak and laying it across the back of his chair.

"If Browne wants us to quit Plymouth as soon as convenient he means now, rather than later! Is everything ready?"

"Yes sir. All ready. We only need the tide and we can leave."

"Very well. What about my officers?"

Fenwick paused for a moment, gathering his thoughts. "We have lost Mr Beare. He has been appointed First of a frigate.' He took a fine goblet of Brandy and sat down. "We still have Mr Stevens and Mr Henson. Mr Stevens, believe it or not, is senior to the two new officers we have been given, so he is now Second, God help us! Our new men are Roger Burton, whom I have made Third Lieutenant and Arthur Kingman, who is Fifth. Mr Norris has passed his examination and asked to remain and as junior Lieutenant. Is that in order sir?"

Courtenay smiled over the rim of his glass. "Excellent. Put McBride in charge of signals. Have we still managed to retain Owen Davies?"

"Yes sir, despite efforts by the Port Admiral to put him into a three-decker!"

"Good. I shall see him later. I also met with Mr Oates' brother-in-law when I was in Scotland but that is a tale I shall save for supper one night!"

"I er, *heard* of your little expedition sir." Fenwick smiled broadly. "You were supposed to be on leave!"

"And you Mr Fenwick, sound just like that man Trafford! How is your Mother?"

"She is well thank you." He put the glass down and stood. "I shall leave you now sir, as there are still a few things I have to do and I wish to be able to up-anchor as soon as the tide turns."

Courtenay watched him as he left the cabin, then slid an envelope out of his coat pocket. He could smell her perfume, light and subtle, as he slit it open. Trafford paused for a moment to watch as his Captain's face softened. He watched as two sheets of paper were unfolded and then there was a sharp intake of breath.

"Are you alright sir? I mean, is there......" He stopped. There could not be anything wrong. The Captain had brought the letter with him from London. He had heard Lady Jessica say he was not to open it until he was in his cabin.

Courtenay turned and looked at him. "We are having a child Alex! She did not tell me!"

Trafford smiled. "I suppose she thought if you knew before you left you would not want to come sir. She knows how much you miss the sea."

"Yes, but she should have said something! Now I have to sail off and be away for months, possibly longer, and I will not be there!"

"Can I offer congratulations sir?"

"What? Oh, of course you may Alex. Thank you! I wish to write a letter quickly. Will you make sure it gets ashore before we sail?"

Trafford smiled. "No trouble sir!"

"And then Alex we will take a drink together!"

The quarterdeck of his Britannic Majesty's ship of the line *Pegasus,* of 74 guns, was a hive of activity. The hated middle watch from 4am to 8am was just ending and the morning watch which would run until 12noon was about to begin.

It was bitterly cold. Winter in the Bay of Biscay was never a pleasant experience and this morning was no exception. It was almost Christmas and there was sleet in the air. Kingman, the new fifth Lieutenant, stamped his feet and flailed his arms for the hundredth time since he had come on watch at 4am and willed his relief, Stevens, to come and take over the watch so that he could go below, have a hot drink, and catch some sleep. He stopped stamping his feet as there was a cough from the quartermaster which meant the Captain was up and about. Courtenay appeared beside the wheel and looked sidelong at the men on the wheel, who studiously avoided his gaze.

"Morning lads." He said, and smiled to himself. He had heard the cough and was pleased. "Good morning Mr Kingman. Are we still on course?"

"Good morning sir. Yes, ship is on the larboard tack. Wind steady from the noreast, course sou, sou west sir."

"Good." Just then the bell in the ship's belfry started to ring, to sound the end of the watch. Courtenay smiled, remembering only too well his days of being officer of the watch between 4am and 8am.

Martin Stevens appeared on the quarterdeck and Courtenay left him and Kingman to discuss the details of taking over the watch. Stevens saw him, smiled briefly and touched his hat, then took up position near the binnacle where he could watch the ship's course. The helmsmen changed, and Davies appeared.

"Morning sir."

"Morning Mr Davies. Do you think the wind will hold?"

"Reckon so sir. Might back a'piece but should hold to get us clear of Biscay."

"Good. I am going to breakfast." Courtenay turned and walked beneath the poop and the men on the quarterdeck visibly relaxed.

In his cabin, Courtenay once again opened the letter from Jessica, the one which told him he was to be a Father. How she had known so quickly he did not know. He had been with her for a few weeks after returning home at the end of October. He smiled. She knew. Women always did. He would now have to worry and care for another person. He smiled briefly. His parents and his sisters would be delighted. Jessica would want for nothing and never be short of company. For once, he found himself cursing the life he had chosen to lead. If he had not joined the Navy…..then he smiled at the thought he may well have become a lawyer as his Mother had hoped. A Lawyer! Fat chance!

The ship was rolling a little but not to a great deal. In his old *Seagull* or even the frigates, the motion would have been bad. He was lucky in that he had managed to keep most of his crew. Some had gone and there were some new men, most gallows-birds from Plymouth and Torbay Assizes but they would blend in soon enough. He had had the men at gun-drill almost as soon as they had weathered Rame Head!

He sat back in his chair, savouring his second cup of coffee, cupping his hands around the mug, when he heard a low rumble and a hail from the masthead. He was on his feet grabbing his hat and cloak when there was a roar from the Marine sentry outside his cabin.

"Midshipman of the Watch *Sir!*"

McBride entered. He was older, more confident now.

"I am sorry to disturb you sir. Mr Stevens sends his compliments and the masthead look-out has sighted a ship on the horizon. Also sir…."

"Aye Mr McBride. I know. Gunfire!"

"Yes sir."

"Where is this sail Mr McBride?"

"On the starboard bow sir."

"Very well. Lead on young man!"

FIVE

Martin Stevens, the ship's Second Lieutenant, turned and touched his hat as he heard his Captain's footsteps on the deck behind him.

"Gunfire sir, to the south-east the look-out reckons. He has sighted one sail sir, which I cannot understand."

"Take a glass Mr Stevens, and get aloft if you please. Give me a full report."

"Aye aye sir!" Stevens grabbed the glass which Midshipman Hughes held out to him and headed for the starboard ratlines. He swarmed aloft and soon was yelling down.

"Deck there! *Three* ships of the line sir, firing into each other by the look of it!"

"Can you make out their colours yet?" Courtenay yelled back.

"Not yet sir, just a moment. Yes! One ship bears our colours sir, with an Admiral's flag at the fore! The others are Frenchies!"

"Trouble sir?' Fenwick had arrived on the quarterdeck, together with the Master who took up his usual spot by the wheel.

"H'mm. Would appear so James, but I am wary of a trap as always. Mr Stevens says one of the ships is one of us and wears a Vice-admiral's flag."

Fenwick turned an inquisitive eye on his Captain. "Vice-admiral sir? Could it be?"

"Yes, I suppose it could. Vice-admiral Browne only left Plymouth the day before us. There might have been a storm, you know as well as I what Biscay is like. The Squadron may have become scattered. Those two Frenchies could have slipped out of LaRochelle in the same storm. Could be anything but we will not take any chances. Beat to quarters and clear for action. Mr Davies, I will have the courses set if you please." He looked up at Stevens and simply waved him down.

With increased canvas and the wind favourable, *Pegasus* leant forward into the troughs and soon was throwing back over the beakhead an impressive bow-wave. Also, very soon the gunfire was louder and the ships were visible from the quarterdeck.

"James, is that the Flagship?" asked Courtenay with his glass levelled at the three ships locked in combat.

"Aye sir, that's the *Suffolk.*"

"Excellent. Now, she has a Frog to her starboard and the other is about to engage to larboard. He is closer. Have the Gunner clear away the bow-chasers and start firing at that one. Soon as you care, Mr Fenwick!"

"Aye aye sir."

Courtenay turned to see McBride by his signals. "Mr McBride. I wish you to bend on the following signal which you will show on my command. '*General signal. Enemy in sight. Prepare for battle. Form line of battle astern of me.*'"

Fenwick smiled "Trying to kid the Frogs there are more of our ships around?"

"That Frenchie alongside wears a Commodore's Broad Pendant. He knows damn well that Admirals do not usually go footling around on their own especially not in Biscay, fairly close to the French coast. I am sure he would not be surprised at all at such a signal. He does not know we were not with the rest of it. For all he knows we were with the Admiral!" He broke off as the look-out shouted down again.

"Deck there! Sail to the east sir!"

Telescopes swivelled in the new direction. Davies saw it first.

"Sloop, sir. Or one of their corvettes?"

McBride, having had the signal bent on, ran to the other side of the deck with his signals glass and could be seen mouthing the signal which even as they looked, the sloop was flying.

"Sir, she has made her number. She is the *Honeysuckle* sir, Commander Hanson."

"Acknowledge Mr McBride, and then get that signal flying."

There was a *bang!* from the bows as the first, then the second bow-chaser sprang into action. Waterspouts appeared very close to the French ship.

They watched as the sloop kept coming towards them, and then finally Courtenay gave McBride a final signal order.

"Tell *Honeysuckle* she is not, repeat not, to engage. She is to stand off and act as appropriate."

Fenwick grunted. "One shot from a French pea-shooter and she would roll over!"

"Yes, and she is the Squadron's eyes. Vice-admiral Browne would not thank me for losing her!"

They were now closing rapidly on the embattled ships. Courtenay had not ordered the guns run out as yet. He did not want to show his hand.

"Alter course two points to larboard Mr Davies."

"That second ship is setting her courses sir!" called Fenwick. "Her Captain clearly does not like the odds now!"

Courtenay watched the ships and said nothing. The French Captain might be well be setting sail to intercept their headlong rush. But he was doing no such thing. Courtenay watched with something approaching disbelief as the French Captain worked his ship away from the others, and with courses set started to draw away.

"We will take the Frenchman on his starboard side. Mr Fenwick, in a few moments you may run out the larboard battery. Clear the starboard battery and arm the men. As soon as we are alongside we will board her. Mr McBride, you will keep a weather eye open for that other Frog ship. If her Captain decides to return you will let me know instantly, understand?"

"Aye aye sir."

Pegasus drew closer and closer. Then she was sweeping across the stern of the British Flagship, with some of her crew waving to her. She crossed the bows of the French ship, and the wheel went hard-over with the sails being trimmed immediately to compensate for the change of course.

"As you bear Mr Fenwick, division by division."

The first division on both decks fired, closely followed by the next guns as they found the ship crossing their gunports. A double ripple of orange tongues ran down the side of the British ship and her balls crashed into the side of the French ship which only had a handful of ports open.

"Get the courses off her Mr Davies and put the helm over!"

The mainsails disappeared and as Fenwick dropped his hand there was a broadside from the *Pegasus* . Smoke funnelled inboard and made several of the men cough and choke, but than she was sidling up to her French opponent and grapnels were flying as Oates' men tried to keep the ships together.

Courtenay was down the larboard ladder in an instant, Trafford behind him. The men from the starboard battery were climbing onto the gangway and roared their support as Courtenay turned to face them momentarily.

"What are you waiting for lads? Here's another prize for the old *Pegasus!* Follow me!" He climbed across the gap with his crew following en masse. They dropped onto the French decking and soon there was bitter hand to hand fighting. The men from the Flagship recovered and were seen climbing over from the other side. Courtenay had just run his sword through the chest of a French officer when the Tricolour came fluttering down, the French Commodore realising he was completely outnumbered.

"That was quick sir!" panted Trafford.

"He was sensible Alex. Between two British ships, his friend run away? No chance! This way he gets the opportunity to fight another day if he can be exchanged. Now, let us see if we can find the Admiral."

The Flagship was in quite a bad way. Her starboard side had been battered in the fight,. but Courtenay sensed the stubborn resistance of the British sailor as he climbed over a shattered bulwark and dropped down onto splintered decking.

A dishevelled officer appeared in front of him and touched his hat.

"Barnes sir, Second Lieutenant."

"Courtenay. Where is the Admiral, and your Captain?"

"The Admiral is in his cabin sir, being attended upon by the Surgeon. He took a splinter in his leg but I understand it is not serious. Captain Mason is supervising repairs. He asked that he be forgiven for not meeting you but the Senior and two of the other officers have been killed, and….and…."

Courtenay touched his arm. "I understand Mr Barnes. The ship is far more important than greeting visitors! I shall find the Admiral. Alex, my compliments to Mr Fenwick and ask if he would arrange for a party of our lads to be sent over to help out with repairs." Trafford nodded and turned away. Courtenay looked after him for a moment then turned and climbed the ladder to the quarterdeck.

There was a sentry outside the Admiral's cabin already. He pulled himself to attention when he saw Courtenay's twin epaulettes appear in the gloom and opened the door. Courtenay walked slowly through and heard voices from where the sleeping compartment would be when the screens went back up.

Admiral Browne was sitting in a chair and another man was finishing tying a bandage around his lower leg.

Browne looked up as he heard footsteps. His face creased into a smile.

"Well well. Captain Sir Giles Courtenay." He held out his hand as the other man, clearly the surgeon, stood up and stepped back. "How are you sir?"

"I am well sir, but more to the point how is your wound?"

"Oh, nothing to worry about despite what the old sawbones here says! Just a small inconvenience would ye not say Mr Jeffers?"

"Aye, provided that you look after it and rest a while. If you go galavanting around I'll not answer for the consequences. There could still be an infection you know."

Browne smiled. "I will remember your advice. Now off with you and see to the men." He turned back to Courtenay.

"You haven't changed too much Giles. I have followed your progress of course. A post-Captain now, and a Baronet no less. Richly deserved, even if half what I have read is true!" He turned again and bellowed for his servant. "Smith! Some brandy for myself and Captain Courtenay!"

"I have arranged for my senior to send over some men to help out Sir Angus. My Marines are securing the prize. Once we have the immediate repairs effected we can make sail for Gibraltar. May I ask what happened sir?"

Browne smiled then winced as pain shot through him. "Of course you may. There was a bad storm Giles. One of the worst I have ever seen at sea. My Squadron had to fend for itself and we got scattered." He paused to collect his thoughts. Courtenay smiled inwardly at the use of his first name. Browne had not forgotten. "When day light came so did two French 74s. Must have got out of LaRochelle, I reckon. One of them was still deciding what to do when you turned up."

"I am sorry I did not arrive in time for *Pegasus* to join the rest of the Squadron sir, but I was not aware that you were leaving a day early." The servant put a silver tray down on Browne's desk with a decanter and two fine glasses. Browne nodded to the desk and Courtenay poured the brandy.

"Och, I knew you would not be there. For some reason the Admiralty wanted me to leave with what of the Squadron there was earlier than planned that's all." They both looked up as there was a hail from the masthead. "I'll wager that's the rest of the Squadron!"

"We met up with your sloop as we were heading in to engage sir. You have a frigate somewhere as well?"

"Yes, the *Redoubtable.* Should be at Gibraltar or on her way back by now." He broke off as another officer entered. He was clearly Mason, the Flag-Captain. "Ah there you are Mason."

Mason was a stern-looking man in his forties, with grey hair and a small scar under his left eye which dragged the skin down a little to one side.

"Mason, this is Captain Sir Giles Courtenay of the *Pegasus.* Giles, this is Captain Frederick Mason, my Flag-Captain." Courtenay noticed that Mason looked up quickly at the use by the Admiral of his first name. "Giles Courtenay served with me on the old *Claymore* as a Midshipman and then Lieutenant."

Mason smiled at Courtenay, but not warmly. "I am pleased to meet you Sir Giles. Sir Angus did of course say your ship would be joining us once you had returned from leave. You are most welcome."

Courtenay gave a slight bow. "Thank you sir. I am pleased to be here. If you will excuse me Sir Angus?"

Browne nodded and smiled. Courtenay left the cabin and was soon back on his own quarterdeck. Fenwick approached him, pausing for a moment as he watched his Captain looking over at the Flagship.

"How is the Admiral sir?"

"Fine James. Just a small splinter wound. Have you sent our men over?"

"Aye sir. Mr Oates has gone with them. I will go myself if I may and see what is needed, then we can get things put to rights as soon as possible and get on to Gibraltar. I suspect *Suffolk* is going to need some dockyard repairs."

"I see the rest of the Squadron has appeared?"

Fenwick smiled. "Yes sir. They look as if nothing has happened!" That was true enough. The other two 74s had appeared from the starboard quarter, in a neat line ahead and were now running down on the ships which were hove-to, the first ship with a string of flags flying requesting instructions.

Gibraltar. The seat of the Royal Navy's power in the Mediterranean Sea. Christmas had come and gone. The four liners of Vice-admiral Browne's Squadron had been languishing in the harbour for a number of weeks. *Suffolk* had undergone weeks of repairs before her captain was satisfied she was ready to stand in the line again, and then she had been warped out of the dockyard into the harbour and had taken her place amongst her kith and kin, ready for whatever orders Lord Keith should give them, and Courtenay did not think they would be long without such orders. Keith was in command of the Mediterranean Fleet although not all of it was gathered in Gibraltar. There were some store-ships and the usual coming and going of brigs and mail-packets.

One such mail-packet had brought some letters for the Squadron and some for Courtenay. There were several from Jessica, all reassuring him that she was well and some from his family. They were all looking forward to welcoming the new member of their family.

Courtenay was toying with his breakfast one day soon after the New Year, the beginning of the new century. He was thinking more about Jessica and his unborn child than the Squadron which was now ready for whatever orders it was to receive. He felt guilty that he was here, commanding this powerful ship of the line, Lord and Master of well over 600 souls, doing the job he loved whilst at home over a thousand miles away, his wife was expecting their child and having to make do without him. He knew she would have all the help and assistance she could possibly require. Her father, Sir Geoffrey, and his parents and sisters would make very sure of that. It was just that he ought also to be there…..He stopped his thoughts with a cold smile. Jessica had known exactly what she was doing when she chose not to tell him until he was on board his ship.

There was a knock at the screen door and the Midshipman of the Watch entered. Mr St. John Smythe.

"Good morning Mr Smythe." smiled Courtenay. They all shortened his name. Imagine trying to call all that in a storm at sea! The Midshipman had simply smiled the first time and accepted it. He had very little choice in the matter.

"Good morning sir. There has been a signal from the Flag. Captains of the Squadron to repair on board for conference at four bells on the forenoon watch."

"Very good Mr Smythe. Carry on. Ask the First-Lieutenant to arrange for my barge to be ready fifteen minutes before."

"Aye aye sir."

Trafford padded in, quiet as ever. "Conference Sir Giles? D'ye think the Vice-admiral has had some orders at last?"

Courtenay smiled. "Who knows Alex? However, I am sure that all will soon become clear and you know me. As soon as I know what we are at so will the ship's Company."

At ten minutes to four bells in the forenoon watch, Courtenay stood at the entry port, and acknowledged the side party. It was odd to see a different Marine Officer in command of the ship's detachment. Captain Morris Connell, a dour Scot with a broad accent so bad Courtenay heard tell his Sergeant had to relay orders because his men could not understand a word he uttered, saluted with his sword, and the muskets of his men came to the present. Calls twittered, Courtenay smiled and nodded to Fenwick and then went down into his barge. He had barely sat down in the stern when Trafford was roaring his orders and the barge pushed away with the crew dropping their oars into the clear water. Five minutes later he was standing to climb up the side of the *Suffolk.*

There was a repeat of the exercise he had witnessed on his own ship, then he was lifting his hat to Mason. The man smiled briefly then led the way to the Admiral's cabin. Courtenay was the first to arrive. Browne greeted him warmly and his servant offered a tray with finely-cut glasses containing claret. He took one, and whilst the Admiral was talking to his Flag-Lieutenant, looked idly out of the stern windows. He heard more boats coming alongside and soon the cabin was quite crowded.

Vice-admiral Browne stood in front of his desk and Courtenay noticed with concern that as he walked across the decking he was limping quite badly. He would have thought a slight splinter wound would have healed by now.

"Gentlemen, we have all met before but you did not have the chance to meet the Captain of the *Pegasus,* which joined us in the midst of the Bay of Biscay!" There were smiles from everyone save Mason. "Sir Giles Courtenay comes to our little Squadron with a fine record and a lot of experience. We are glad to have you Sir Giles." He waved his hand around the gathering. "Sir Giles, this is Harper of the *Andromeda,* Silvers of the *Omega* and Commander Hanson of the sloop *Honeysuckle.* You would have met the Captain of our frigate, *Redoubtable,* but I had to send him off and when I give you the news I have had, and details of the orders I have received you will appreciate why. Now then, you all know of course that as from the First of this month, Ireland has joined the Union. A courier brig has brought a supply of the new Union Flag and each ship will of course have its own. Whether that will help the situation in Ireland God only knows. I hope it does. Very well. As you all know Lord Keith has been blockading the island of Malta for some time. He has with him Rear-admiral Nelson and a number of ships but as always he could use some more. That is where we are bound gentlemen. Malta. Now, I hear the thoughts you have in your minds. Dreary blockading duty, but this is not the same as being off Ushant or LaRochelle in a winter storm. There is a real threat that the French will be able to slip through our blockade and bring supplies to the garrison and the people. At the moment also they are denied any news as to what is happening on the mainland. We need to keep it that way. We will check convoys, individual ships. Any enemy ships will be intercepted and stopped. I trust that you are ready, and I daresay eager, to leave?" There was a nodding of heads. "Good. We weigh anchor at two bells in the afternoon watch. A toast gentlemen?" He raised his glass and looked at the most junior Captain, Hanson of the sloop. Hanson stood and raised his glass.

"Death to the French!" There was a chorus of approval and they all drunk deeply. As the other Captains were filing out, Courtenay hung back. Browne saw him, and turned to him after folding away a chart.

"Something not clear Captain?"

"I could not help but notice you are limping, sir. Is that wound troubling you?"

Browne smiled and placed a hand on Courtenay's shoulder. "It is not clearing up as fast as I would have liked Giles, but it will be perfectly healed very soon. Thank you for your concern."

"A pleasure sir."

"How are your parents and your Aunt Marcia by the way?"

"They are very well sir. I was with Aunt Marcia shortly before Christmas."

"Be sure to give her my best regards when you next write. And I hear congratulations are in order. I understand Lady Jessica is with child?" He was smiling. "Do not seem so surprised Giles, you know very well that a Squadron is a very small place!"

"I am surprised you did not find out earlier sir!"

"I did, but there has not been the opportunity for us to have a discussion since we arrived! You will pass my most heartfelt best wishes to her as well?"

"Delighted to obey sir."

"Good. Carry on Captain Courtenay. We shall speak again when the opportunity arises."

Courtenay replaced his hat, touched it, and left the cabin.

Two days later the Squadron was steering east nor'east on the starboard tack, a stiff sou' westerly coming in over the starboard quarter. *Pegasus* was at the end of the line of ships and McBride spent most of his time precariously hanging onto the ratlines, balancing the big signals telescope as he tried to keep a watch for the Flagship's signals. When the Fifth Lieutenant, the new officer called Kingman, had tried to point out that any signals from the Flag would be repeated by the ships down the line McBride had looked at him for as long as he dared, and then summed up the matter.

"Excuse me sir, but not in this ship. *Pegasus* does not wait for anyone to repeat orders to us. Captain Courtenay will want to know what the Flag is signalling as soon as the hoist is run up to the gaff. Excuse me sir."

Trafford had overheard the conversation and relayed it to Courtenay. He had simply smiled and nodded. Pride in the ship and what it had achieved.

Pegasus was astern of *Andromeda* with *Omega* ahead of her, the Flagship *Suffolk* leading the line. Their frigate *Redoubtable* was to windward and slightly ahead of the Squadron with their sloop still further ahead. Courtenay walked out from beneath the poop, automatically looking at the binnacle to check the ship's course then strolled to the windward side, his longish hair whipping in the breeze coming in over the quarter. It was a warm day even though it was only January, but this was the Mediterranean Sea, and it was a far cry from January in England. He turned as he noted McBride hanging out over the side of the ship more than usual, balancing the signals telescope, and was not surprised when the youngster turned back inboard and reported a signal from the Flagship.

"Flag has ordered *Andromeda* to make more sail sir. She is lagging behind *Omega* somewhat."

"Very well. Carry on Mr McBride, and well done for seeing the signal so promptly." The youngster blushed beneath his tan as he moved away.

On the sail to Malta the Squadron saw nothing apart from the odd Arab trader and a smart brigantine flying the Stars and Stripes of the United States of America. Courtenay had watched the brigantine as it had sailed past on the opposite tack and even levelled his glass at it to study it the better. His lips pursed in a smile as he wondered how many of the crew were 'Americans' Most of them he surmised, were probably British deserters. It was a ticklish point. The Americans were sensitive about the men who served their ships.

Trafford had read his thoughts. "Reckon there's many a Captain grinding his teeth at the thought of the prime British seamen crewing that Yankee sir!"

"Like enough Alex. It is a pity we cannot entice men to serve in our ships in other ways than the Press!"

Eventually the Squadron reached Malta and made contact with Lord Keith's ships who were blockading the Island. Vice-admiral Keith was in the *Queen-Charlotte* with Rear-admiral Lord Nelson in support in *Foudroyant.* There was one other 74 in sight, the *Audacious.* As soon as Browne's Squadron was in signalling distance the signal was hoisted from the *Queen-Charlotte* for Browne to go aboard and the Squadron hove-to, the Captain of each ship wondering what they were going to be asked to do. Courtenay took a glass from the rack and trained it on Nelson's Flagship which was not more than a few cables away. He paused for a moment as a slight figure came into view on the quarterdeck. He had seen Nelson before, after the Battle of the Nile and he knew instantly it was him. Browne returned to the *Suffolk,* and shortly afterwards the Squadron got under way heading for the south of the Island, before heading around to the east to Valetta which was being blockaded by two other 74s. Once off the ancient harbour Browne hove-to again and signalled his Captains aboard for a conference.

"Very well gentlemen. I had an interesting meeting with the Admiral. It seems that according to a spy network on the Island he has discovered somehow a small ship slipped between our patrols a few days ago, and brought news that there had been a revolution last year. This has, it seems, had the effect of cheering the defenders and they are now in great heart. We will continue to enforce a blockade and ensure no supplies whatsoever reach there. We can be certain also the French will attempt to raise the siege. Lord Keith's spies have heard the French garrison is daily expecting a Fleet from Toulon which will crush our forces and give succour to the inhabitants. We have patrols looking after Toulon but ships do escape from time to time, we all know that! It is, however, highly unlikely that any force of the size contemplated would be able to break out without being seen and brought to action, unless the covering force suffered a large amount of ill-luck! We will patrol between here and Sicily. We have plenty of water at the moment but we will replenish our supplies as and when required, so if the opportunity presents itself gentlemen, at your discretion, I have no objection to your watering your ships. I will not keep the Squadron together all the time. I will divide it into two divisions. In that way we can cover a greater area. I will take *Andromeda* and *Redoubtable* with me and *Omega* and *Pegasus* will act as the other division, with *Honeysuckle* maintaining contact between us. For the moment however, we will remain together. Very well, return to your ships where, no doubt, you will tell your crews what you believe they ought to know. I believe it always helps if the ship's crew knows why they are doing what they are but I must leave that decision to you individually as my Captains. Thank you gentlemen."

One by one they filed out and Browne limped over to the stern windows. Eventually he saw the dark red painted barge from *Pegasus* pulling towards the ship, Courtenay seated in the sternsheets. As if Courtenay sensed the inspection he looked around, but in the glare from the blue sea he could not make out Browne just inside the cabin. Browne turned and almost lost his balance. He swore and rubbed his leg where the wound was positioned. It was getting worse by the day. He was resisting all efforts by the Surgeon to carry out a further examination because he suspected he knew what the man would say. He looked once more at the red barge, then limped to his desk, sat down and started to look again at the chart.

SIX

The two 74s were cruising along easily on the larboard tack, a fine breeze coming up from the larboard quarter. For the hundredth time since he had come on watch, Owen Davies, the Sailing Master of the *Pegasus,* looked up at the hard-bellied sails above him and then at the weathervane, which was the tell-tale for the wind direction, and rubbed his chin.

Courtenay was standing by the larboard nettings and saw the action. He smiled, strolled over to the wheel and stood beside the Master.

"Is there something wrong Mr Davies? The wind is fair, we are making good speed, not that speed is essential to our purpose of course, but I have the feeling that you are worried about something."

"Aye sir. You know this Sea, you have been here on many occasions. You know as well as I that these conditions can change almost instantly. Ahead of us sir, is Sicily. I just do not want to get caught on lee shore there!"

"And you will not Mr Davies, rest assured. We will be changing course soon to head towards Pantellera, and then from there we head back towards Malta. You know all this!"

"Aye sir, but by my reckoning we ought to be changing course very soon now. The *Omega* shows no sign of getting ready to alter course sir. Just a mite worried that Cap'n Silvers might have decided to poke his nose a little more closely into Sicily, that's all."

"I am sure that will not be the case Mr Davies. Perhaps he is waiting for the next turn of the glass." He nodded towards the half-hour sandglass which showed there was still time to go before the half-hour. He smiled at Davies, nodded to the helmsmen and then went back to his position by the nettings. Trafford came out from under the poop and strolled to join him.

"Kingston has made some fresh coffee Sir Giles. Would you like me to bring you some?" He broke off as he noticed that his Captain appeared to be thinking of something else. "Is there a problem sir?"

"What? Oh, no not really, at least not yet. Owen Davies is worried that Captain Silvers has not yet ordered a change of course." He ran his fingers threw his hair. "He is right. We should have changed course by now. Yes Alex thank you, a mug of Kingston's coffee would be appreciated. I shall come down to the cabin." He nodded to the officer of the Watch, Kingman, and followed Trafford below the poop.

One hour later Captain Silvers had still not ordered the change of course. Courtenay had been looking at the chart and trying not to get worried as the Island of Sicily drew ever closer. There was a knock at the door with the usual bellow from the Marine Sentry and Fenwick stepped over the coaming.

"Hello James. Are you coming to tell about something in particular or can I make a guess?"

"I think you can guess sir. There is still no sign of Captain Silvers altering course to the east'rd. We should have done so some time ago by my reckoning."

"Aye, and by Owen Davies' reckoning as well. Very well I shall come up."

However when they arrived on the quarterdeck they saw Davies lowering his glass and the Midshipman of the Watch, Smythe, reading a hoist on the *Omega*. Smythe turned, saw his Captain and straightened before formally reporting.

"Signal sir, from *Omega. Tack in succession. Steer nor' east.*"

"Very well Mr Smythe. Well Mr Davies, there you have it. Late, it would seem, but prepare to tack to follow *Omega.*"

"Aye aye sir!"

Three hours passed, the watch had changed, and the two ships were still making a good speed through the blue water. The wind moved a little further round to the south, which helped them. Courtenay was again on deck, worrying news for the new Third Lieutenant, Roger Burton, who paced nervously around the binnacle and the wheel. Courtenay noted all this and smiled inwardly. They both suddenly looked upwards as the mainmast look-out yelled down from his dizzy perch.

"*Deck there!* Sail to the south! Might be more'n one sir!"

Courtenay waved to the man by way of acknowledgement, and threw himself into the ratlines with a glass although he knew he would not be able to see anything from the deck.

Fenwick appeared. "*Omega's* look-out must be asleep sir!" He looked around as McBride clattered onto the quarterdeck and took his station at the signals.

"I agree. Mr McBride. Signal *Omega. Strange sail to the south. Request permission to investigate.*"

"Frenchie, sir?" asked Fenwick. Courtenay turned to him smiling.

"Now James, what do you think? We know there are French ships in Sicily, we also know there are no other British ships in the area because the rest of the Squadron is elsewhere."

Fenwick thought about it for a short moment. "When you put it like that sir, not much doubt is there? Trouble is they are to the south and we can't sail close enough to get down to them. What course are they on?"

"Waiting for the look-out there, James."

"*Deck there!* Two sail o' the line sir! Sailing more or less east!"

"There you are James. They are more or less on the same course as us and unless that wind backs a'piece we are going to have trouble closing with them. Ah, I do believe *Omega* is signalling!"

McBride did not need the signal book. "*Omega* directs us to lay as close to the wind as we dare sir, to lay on a converging course with the strange sails."

"Very well Mr McBride. Acknowledge." Courtenay turned to Davies. "You heard Mr Davies. Close as you dare."

Courtenay walked away to the nettings to get out of the way of the men as they ran to the braces to trim the sails. They could not edge much further round. The French ships, if *they were* French ships, would be in the same position if, as Courtenay suspected, they were really heading for Malta. A thought crossed his mind. If only Silvers had ordered the change of course at the right time they may well have found themselves meeting up with the French ships. Now, a chase was in prospect.

Very gradually, the ships converged, although the amount of time it was taking was maddening. The wind did move back to the sou'west, which meant that all the ships had to tack, and then it moved more to the west. Darkness fell, without it being possible to identify the ships as definitely French. Courtenay was worried the Frenchies might slip away in the night, but he reasoned that if they were going to Malta, and they were now heading more or less in that direction, they would not be able to slip away anywhere during the night, because they would still have to turn back to the Island at some stage.

Dawn broke on an anxious ship. Fenwick was already up and about by the time Davies came on deck, and both of them had been beaten to it by Courtenay. Even McBride had eschewed some precious sleep and study time to be at the signals so that as soon as it was light enough, they would see any hoists from the leading ship. Courtenay watched as the lad climbed into the starboard ratlines, turned and stepped down carefully. There was a flag hoist on *Omega.* Courtenay recognised it rfrom his days as a signals Midshipman.

"From *Omega,* sir. *Enemy in Sight. Prepare for battle!"*

"Thank you Mr McBride. Mr Fenwick. It will be a little while before we are to yonder Frenchies. I would suggest you send the hands to breakfast before you clear."

"Aye aye sir." Fenwick turned, beckoning to a Boatswain's mate.

Courtenay turned away, and then back. "Care to join me in a cup of coffee James?"

"Delighted, sir!"

And so the two British 74-gun ships of the line sailed unerringly towards the two French ships which were of similar size. The distance between them was gradually decreasing. This was because not only were the British ships possibly better sailers, but because the French may have been locked away in harbour for some time and their sailing qualities were not as well-honed as the British crews. Whatever the reason *Omega* and *Pegasus* were slowly, gradually, overhauling them.

Fenwick sent the hands to quarters after they had been fed a good hot meal but he hoped that it would not be too long before they could bring the French to action since otherwise the meal would be a forgotten memory. The men went leisurely but efficiently, knowing that they still had time to ready themselves and their equipment, make sure the first balls were the best they had, lay out some weapons in case they had to board. Courtenay had his sword on his belt, and two pistols thrust through it just in case. To the crew he looked his usual self, calm, relaxed, composed.

Many, many miles away from the warm seas where her husband was facing battle with the French, Lady Jessica Courtenay was peering through the misty window of her coach as it was driven slowly through the London streets. It was day, but very dark. There had been snow flurries all day. It had been and still was bitterly cold and she would be glad when she got home and could sit in front of a roaring log fire. She had been to see an old school friend who did not live that far away. She had left it later than she had intended but she had been enjoying her friend Jennifer's company, and her friend had been very pleased to see her, plying her with many questions about her husband and his feats at sea.

She huddled in her cloak, with a thick blanket pulled around her, and although she willed the coachman, Albert, to drive faster she knew he was going as fast as he possibly could. The road was icy, despite the straw which the richer families put down to dampen the noise. She was not far from home. Just around the next corner and then at the other end of the street.

Up on the top of the coach on his seat Albert the coachman was concerned about the state of the road and the cold, and did not see the four men who were silently slipping along in the wake of the coach waiting for the right moment. What they had not seen was that there were three other men on the other side of the road, hugging the shadows and doorways.

Two of the men in the road started to trot, cursing silently as they slipped in the icy conditions, but eventually they drew level with the coach and then one of them moved further ahead. The other two were all ready on the other side of the coach.

Suddenly, the one who was ahead turned and held up his hands in front of the horses, shouting 'Whoa there!' as he did so. Albert hurriedly reined in, and as he did the other man climbed up and held a pistol towards him.

"Not a word mate. Jus' keep quite, like, and no harm will come to you."

As he said that, the other two men reached the side of the coach and one of the men put his hand on the door-handle. Inside, Jessica had heard the shout and was thrown forward as the coach came to a sudden stop. Her right hand felt under the blanket and as she looked out of the window she saw a man with a ragged beard and staring eyes looking et her. Stifling an impulse to scream, she drew back against the cushions, and the door was wrenched open.

"No use struggling Lady Jessica, we got your man under our control. You're comin' wiv us!" He reached in towards her.

As all this unfolded the other three men were unnoticed One circled around behind the man holding the horses and the others stealthily crept up behind the men at the coach door, and who were reaching in for Jessica. The man holding the horses never knew what hit him. He had time for a short scream, which ended abruptly as his throat was slit. The man on the box turned for just a moment as he heard the noise. "Fred?" was the last word he uttered. As he turned his head, Albert withdrew from his cloak a pistol which he cocked and fired at the man's head. The ball took him in the right temple and threw him off the box to lie, kicking for a moment, on the icy cobbles.

The man reaching in for Jessica snarled as he heard the shot and then looked down as he saw his intended victim had drawn a small pistol from her cloak and was pointing it at him.

"Get away from me!" she shouted, "and do not be under the illusion that I would not use this. My husband has taught me well in the use of a pistol." There was a muffled noise from outside and the fourth man reeled away, hit over the head with a club. The man reaching for Jessica snarled again and raised a pistol. Jessica pulled the trigger of her own pistol, and the ball entered the man's right eye, blasting it and a piece of his cheek-bone away. He howled in pain and dropped back onto the cobbles.

Albert was off his box in an instant. The three men who had been shadowing the coach were standing near the horses as Jessica was helped down from the coach.

"Are you alright my Lady?" asked one of them, obviously their leader.

"Yes, thanks to you. Who are you by the way? You appear to be seafaring men, by the look of you!"

"Bless you my Lady. My name is Harrington. I served with the Cap'n in the *Amazon* before I had an accident which meant I was of little use. I well remember you my Lady, when we rescued you from that Island! These lads are friends of mine. The Cap'n, well, he asked Alex Trafford to get some lads organised to keep an eye on you. I think he felt something might happen and he was fair worried about it."

"I see. What of these, these villains?"

"The two at the front are dead. Your Albert here got one of them. We clubbed one of them over the head because we needed someone to tell us who arranged this. They had been following you for a while and we were followin' them, but they didn't know it, if you see what I mean my Lady?" Jessica smiled and nodded. "Unfortunately we hit the bas……man too hard. He's dead. But the one you shot, he's still alive….just."

They bent down over the man, whose face was covered in blood. He was moaning. Harrington took hold of him by his collar and dragged him up.

"Who arranged all this matey? You're done for, you know that? No point goin' to your maker without making an effort to make up for what you done is there? Who put you up to it?"

"Sp……..Spencer-White, he did, the bastard. Told……..told us……there were no guards on the bloody coach……bastard…….bastard, he's done for me!"

Jessica looked down. "Which Spencer-White? The Admiral?"

The dying man opened his remaining eye and looked up her. "Didn't think you would use that bloody pistol……didn't want to do it ma'am…….don't make war on women……wrong…..it was that bloody Marmaduke Spencer………"

107

Harrington laid the man on the ground. "Sorry my Lady, 'e's gone."

"He has still told us who arranged all this. I will tell my father. Can you arrange to have these men taken away? Good. Then when you have done so please come to the house. Cook will make something warm for you. Have you a place to sleep?"

"Bless you my Lady, but we do have rooms. A good hot meal would be acceptable though!"

Jessica smiled through chattering teeth. "Then do as I have asked. You will be very welcome and I am sure my husband will reward you when he returns home."

"My Lady," said Harrington, "it was an honour to serve with him. You being safe and sound is reward enough."

"My Lady, I do think you should get back in and let me get you home. It will not do you any good to be out like this in your condition." butted in Albert in a worried tone.

"Stop fussing Albert. In my condition for goodness sake!" But she allowed herself to be helped back into the coach.

Meantime, back in the Mediterranean the two British ships were gradually getting themselves into a position where they could open their attack on the French liners. The French ships had their starboard batteries run out and Courtenay knew this was going to be a broadside battle. He had little qualms about who was going to win. Unless a lucky shot struck something vital he felt that given equal terms a British ship would almost always win. In fact, any British ship was expected to take on two enemy ships and still win!

There was a sound like rolling thunder, accompanied by two lines of orange flashes as *Omega* opened fire with her two gun-decks. Almost simultaneously the rear-most French ship opened fire and a thick bank of smoke started to form. A quick look told him that all *Omega's* masts and sails were untouched. The French fired high, to bring down masts and spars, which would cripple a ship. The British fired into the hulls of the ships. That meant more crewmen killed or injured and encouraged an early surrender.

"Mr Davies." said Courtenay conversationally. "As soon as you are able I would like you to estimate the distance between the French ships." He turned to McBride. "Bend on Flag 40 if you please, Mr McBride, but do not hoist until I tell you."

Fenwick looked at him. "Going to pass through between the ships sir? Is there room?"

"I have no idea, but Mr Davies will tell me as soon as he knows. Now I do believe we will be able to open fire shortly James."

They turned back and saw they were about to overreach the first French ship. Courtenay also knew they would face a broadside or two. The guns fired, division by division, then reloaded and awaited the order for a broadside. Balls slammed into the French ship and whole sections of planking were thrown high into the air. The French broadside was ragged, not at all like the controlled firing from *Pegasus,* and although some balls slammed into the hull most were aimed high. Most of them also missed, although there were one or two severed lines and two blocks fell from above and bounced in the nets stretched above the decks.

Fenwick raised his sword and brought it down. A broadside ran down *Pegasus'* side and all the balls slammed into the side of the French ship. The French fired again, and Courtenay could feel his ship taking punishment. There was a heavy pall of smoke over the fight, and from time to time Courtenay could see orange tongues as the ships ahead of him fired at each other.

"Well, Mr Davies?" Courtenay asked.

"Aye, should be enough room sir."

"Very well. Mr McBride, you may hoist the signal."

The flag run up to the mizzen gaff and broke to the breeze. Flag 40. *I am about to pass through the enemy's line*

Pegasus was surging ahead of the French ship. Her side was pitted with shot holes and some of her sails were little more than rags. Courtenay watched the French ship, knowing she was still very much alive with plenty of fight left in her. As his ship left the French one behind and came up towards the leading one Courtenay turned to Davies. "Very well Mr Davies, put the helm down. Alter course three points to larboard!"

The spokes of the wheel spun and he watched as his ship's bowsprit started to come round. Gradually, very gradually, it seemingly brushed across the taffrail of the enemy ship, although in fact it was still well away from it.

Courtenay watched the ship they had just passed, concerned he had cut the corner too finely, and even as he did the larboard guns were firing into the ship's bows. With her sails in rags, she was losing way and he breathed a sigh of relief as he realised they were clear.

"Standby, the starboard battery. Starboard carronade, as you bear!"

The carronade crew up in the bows waited with their charge, and as the bows of their ship started to cross the stern of the enemy ship the Captain of the gun jerked the lanyard, and the huge ball was fired at the enemy's stern. It exploded just above the lower row of windows and made a gaping hole in the stern,. blowing in all the windows on both decks. *Pegasus* surged through the gap, firing on both sides, but division by division, her starboard battery fired through the stern of the ship. The deck of a 74 gun ship of the line in action is open from bows to stern. Anything fired from a ship crossing the stern of another, or 'raking' as it was termed, would go straight down the whole length of the gundeck. Solid iron balls were bad enough. Grapeshot was murder. Gun after gun fired through the shattered stern of the French ship. Even as *Pegasus* came out from under the stern, and turned to run down her larboard side, the mizzenmast teetered, and then crashed down over the starboard side. On the other side *Omega* had got ahead of the French ship and was going to wear ship to bring herself back into the action. However, the ship now lying on *Pegasus's* starboard side was in a terrible state. Her mizzen hung over her starboard side like an anchor. Her sails were in tatters, blood was running down her side, and she started to pay off.

"Got her steering sir!" Davies happily reported.

"Broadside, Mr Fenwick."

"Aye sir!" He turned to the rail, and barked his orders. The starboard battery erupted in orange flame and smoke and since the guns had been double-shotted, some seventy balls struck the French side like an avalanche. The ship heeled slightly to starboard under the onslaught. The guns were hauled in, sponged out, reloaded and run out. Here and there a gun fired from the French ship. She had been caught unprepared by *Pegasus* cutting across her stern, and raking her. Courtenay was willing her Captain to surrender and save further bloodshed when the Tricolour was seen to be fluttering down.

"Now then," muttered Courtenay "where is that other ship?" He ran up the ladder to the poop and looked aft. He could see that the rear-most French ship was tacking away from the conflict. He was not really surprised. The odds it faced were now overwhelming.

Omega showed no sign of wanting to chase her.

"Well Mr Fenwick, I suggest you take some men and two squads of Marines and take that Frenchie's surrender, if you please, although it would appear we will have to share the prize!"

Fenwick grinned broadly. "Aye aye sir."

"Mr Stevens? Go below and ask the Surgeon for a report on casualties."

As all these tasks were being carried out, the mainmast look-out who had stuck to his job throughout, called down there were three ships of the line in sight, but also added he knew the leading one to be the *Foudroyant.* Rear-admiral Nelson had arrived with his ships. Unfortunately he was just about in sight at the time *Pegasus* and *Omega* completed their capture and the little Admiral would therefore take the lion's share of the prize money.

Winter passed into Spring. Lord Keith departed to Leghorn with his ship, Rear-admiral Nelson indicated to their Lordships of Admiralty that he was ill, and retired initially to Palermo. Vice-admiral Browne therefore became the most senior officer on station but he had very few ships at his disposal and with which to enforce the blockade of the Island. *Pegasus* found herself on many occasions alone on patrol, a fact which suited Courtenay and his crew perfectly. During these lonely patrols they intercepted a number of ships all of whom were clearly bound for Malta. On the occasions *Pegasus* made contact either with the Flagship or with their sloop, Courtenay found this story being repeated by the other ships of the Squadron. It seemed their blockade was working, especially when Browne received a detailed report from one of Keith's spies on the Island who was living with a Maltese family whose loyalties were more with Britain than France. The man came off shore once, in a small boat at the dead of night, and made contact with the *Honeysuckle* sloop, which vessel transferred him to the *Suffolk.*

By a happy coincidence, *Pegasus* had completed a patrol to the north-west and had returned for further orders. Browne had signalled that Courtenay should join him.

When Courtenay entered the Admiral's cabin, he was distressed to see that his old Captain was very clearly in a poor state of health.

"Sir, it distresses me to see you in such obvious pain. Is there nothing the surgeon can do for you?"

"Sit you down Giles. Yes, there is something he can do. He can cut off the leg. He assures me that eventually I will feel a lot better! I have other problems as well, as I am sure your friend Admiral Crompton told you about!"

"Not in detail sir, no."

Browne smiled. "In any case, I wrote to the Admiralty a while ago to say that I was too ill to continue to run the Squadron. You just missed the courier brig but I have some letters for the Squadron, including for you and Flags will give them to you shortly. The same courier brig brought orders for me to return home and that a replacement Flag-officer is on his way. Vice-admiral Lord Cairns. Do you know him.?" He watched his old Midshipman's face change to one of scarce-controlled anger. "I can see that you *do* know him, and by the look on your face you do not approve?"

"He and I have, er, a kind of feud sir. It is a personal matter sir."

"Yes, and I daresay the Court-martial you unjustifiably went through last year had something to do with it! I wish I had known Giles, I really do. I may have been able to do something about it."

"I doubt it sir, but you are most generous."

"H'mm, well you take care of yourself. Now, I thought you might like to meet the man who has been making himself very useful on Malta for us. I think it would be a good idea if you did, because I think at some stage it will be necessary to make a move on the Island and he will be invaluable in advising as to landing sites. It is important that you get to know him, just in case you are involved." There was a knock at the door and Browne's Flag-lieutenant stepped over the coaming with another man, in civilian clothes, behind him. Courtenay turned and his face broke into a broad smile.

"My God, Piers Tandy! What on earth are you doing here? I thought you were in the Caribbean!"

"I see you two have met previously!" observed Browne unnecessarily.

"Giles Courtenay and myself are old friends Sir Angus. We have shared many an adventure together, and last year he saved my life. I am so sorry I was not at home for that damned Court-martial Giles, but I understand it went well. How is Jessica?"

"She is with child, and I understand in good health Colonel Tandy!" broke in Admiral Browne. "I daresay you and Captain Courtenay can catch up on old times later, but in the meantime may we have a discussion about the island, do you believe?"

Later, as Courtenay was waiting for his barge Tandy was explaining his presence.

"I was in the Caribbean Giles, but my Masters decided in view of my ability to mix in with the locals, it might be a good idea to have me here, so that I might keep a close watch on the situation and advise as to the best time for an invasion. You know the sort of thing and I daresay your ship will be in the thick of it as usual!"

"*Colonel* Tandy?"

"Ah well, a little gesture of thanks for my services, which is more than that which you were given. You know that Cairns is on his way here?"

"Yes. He has a new Flag-lieutenant. A relative who rejoices in the name of Marmaduke Spencer-White."

"What!" Tandy roared with laughter.

"Apparently he is even deadlier than Harding with pistol or sword."

"Harding much preferred his victim not to know he was there and to have his back to him from what I have heard. You did a good job there Giles, but you will need to watch your back even more now. As always I shall do what I can. I think that Cairns does not know of our friendship?"

"Not as far as I am aware Piers. When do you return to Malta?"

"Tomorrow."

"My wishes for your safety go with you. I hope I shall see you again shortly."

Courtenay lifted his hat to the side-party and made his way down into his barge.

"That Major Tandy up there, sir?" asked Trafford as soon as Courtenay was settled in the sternsheets and the barge was idling away from *Suffolk's* side.

"Colonel Tandy now, and not a word to anyone you understand?"

"No fears Sir Giles. I can guess what he is doing here! I just hope we keep away from him!" Courtenay hid a smile from the barge's crew as they bent to their looms and made the barge skim across the calm blue sea to his ship.

The mail arrived as promised, and after Courtenay had dealt with the official letters which demanded his attention he turned to a number of personal letters. There was the usual one from his parents, one from Jessica, and one with handwriting he did not recognise. He slit that one open first, curious to know who it was, and as Kingston walked in quietly and placed a fresh pot of coffee within easy reach, he realised it was his father-in-law, Sir Geoffrey. He poured a mug of coffee and started to read. With the first few words, the coffee mug dropped onto the floor, spilling coffee everywhere, and prompting Kingston to rush in wondering what on earth was happening. He saw his Captain staring at the letter in his hands and was about to speak when Courtenay held up his hand.

"Leave me Kingston, you can clear this up later."

'*My dear Giles,* (the letter began) *I know not exactly where to begin this letter. Let me first of all allay any fears you may have that there is anything wrong with Jessica. She is well, and greatly looking forward to the birth of your child, as indeed we all are. However, the day before yesterday, something quite unimaginable happened, just a street away from where I am writing this letter to you.*'

Courtenay read on, the letter unfolding the story of the attempted abduction, or murder whatever had been the intention.

'*Alex Trafford must be thanked for engaging the services of Joe Harrington and his friends. Needless to say, they have been handsomely rewarded, and I have found them*' *somewhere they may call a proper home where they will never want for anything. In short, they have joined the household! Your wife is a brave, resourceful young lady, quite different from the daughter I thought I was bringing up when we made that passage to Ceylon. It must be your influence upon her! Rest assured that she is well, and I am sure that in the letter I know she has written to you, she will mention nothing of what happened, since she does not want anything to deflect you from your duty. She made me promise that I would say nought, but I cannot allow this incident to pass. As to Spencer-White and Lord Cairns, well, I fear they will never be brought to book, since they had already sailed before the incident, and of course, there is not a shred of proof which would stand up in any Court of Law which would show that Spencer-White was behind this outrage. Although I suspect he should not have done so, Admiral Crompton has told me that Cairns is sailing to your area, to take over command of the Squadron. Please be very careful. Do nothing rash. In the end, justice will prevail; the truth will out.*

Your father-in-law,

Geoffrey.

Courtenay dropped the letter on his desk and slammed his fist on top of it with a crash. There was a frightened shout from the sentry at the door, but Kingston was there in a flash and Trafford was right behind him. He looked at the letter and saw that his Captain was as white as a sheet, his teeth clenched and his eyes mere slits in his face.

"Captain sir, is there something wrong? It isn't Lady Jess…..?"

Courtenay looked up slowly. "No she is well thank you, although no thanks in that direction are to be given to Lord Cairns and his nephew. Alex, will you pass the word for Mr Fenwick?"

"Aye sir." He opened the screen door and relayed the instruction to the Marine sentry. Then he turned back to see his Captain shakily pouring a glass of brandy. He crossed the decking in two strides. "Let me, Sir Giles." He poured a measure and Courtenay swallowed it in one gulp.

"What is wrong sir? Is it bad news from home?"

"You remember I asked you to engage the services of some men to keep an eye on my wife?" Trafford nodded. "Well you made a good choice, and one for which I and Jessica will eternally be in your debt. When James Fenwick gets here I will tell you both, because you both need to know." There was a brief knock at the door and Fenwick stepped over the coaming.

"Sir?"

"Sit down James. Alex, a glass for the First-Lieutenant. I think he is going to need it!"

"Sir, you cannot possibly allow this to go unreported!" exploded Fenwick after Courtenay had finished telling the two of them what had happened.

"There is no proof James. The only man who said anything is dead and Cairns made damn sure neither he or his nephew were around when the act happened. They were all ready at sea! There is no proof, as my father-in-law has rightly said, that will stand up in a Court of Law. No, at the moment they will escape justice but it will not continue. At some stage something will happen, and then we will have them."

"And Cairns is coming here sir?"

"Yes. I think he has very few friends in Admiralty but he does still have friends and influence at Court, and now that he is a Peer of the Realm…..well. I am sure he used this new-found power to get himself appointed in charge of the Squadron when news reached the Admiralty that Sir Angus is ill."

"Perhaps Nelson will come back and take over sir?" ventured Trafford.

Courtenay smiled grimly. "Hardly. I doubt he will return for a while at least, and in case he is still junior to Cairns. He would have to do what he was told even if he did not agree!"

"So what do we do sir?" asked Fenwick, accepting a little more brandy from Kingston.

"We keep our Counsel, as my Father would say. We watch and we wait and we will hope that the opportunity will arise when the truth will appear. I suspect that Cairns will deny all knowledge and he will get away with it anyway. James, have you heard from your Mother?"

"Yes sir, I have. Apparently she received a letter from Cairns' lawyer suggesting a quiet divorce and offering a settlement if she will agree. It was generous, I understand. There has been no other contact I am relieved to say."

"Good. I know my Father has people he knows keeping an unobtrusive eye on the school and the house, just in case."

"I wonder when Lord Cairns will arrive sir?" asked Trafford

"Difficult to say Alex. I daresay they managed a fairly quick passage to Gibraltar, but it will depend upon how they are getting here. They could arrive tomorrow!"

In fact, it was a week before Vice-admiral Lord Cairns arrived.

The mainmast look-out saw the frigate approaching with a Vice-admiral's flag flying at the foremast truck. The Squadron for once was together off the west coast of Malta. The only ship missing was their sloop, the *Honeysuckle,* patrolling to the north west. Nelson's old command and her two supporting ships were away to the north east of the Island itself, patrolling closer to Sicily.

Courtenay heard the hail from the masthead, guessed who would be on board the frigate and contented himself with a second cup of coffee. He saw nothing to rejoice in at the arrival of Cairns and his Flag-Lieutenant.

Without any fuss the flag of Vice-admiral Sir Angus Browne was struck and the new flag hoisted. Command had passed. Courtenay did go on deck to see his old Captain lowered down the side of his former flagship to the frigate, which spread her sails almost as soon as the bosun's chair had been emptied of its human cargo and was soon making off to the west. Her Captain was no doubt eager to get out of sight of Cairns before he could overrule the orders he already had. Browne must have been in a bad way if he allowed himself to handed down to the frigate in such a way. Courtenay looked hard at the flagship. He half expected a signal hoist to appear immediately, summoning all the Captains to a conference. An hour passed, then another. He came to the conclusion the Admiral was in no hurry to meet with his Captains.

In fact nothing was heard from the Admiral for two days, during which the ships remained where they were. Then, mid-way through the morning watch the *Suffolk* hoisted a signal. McBride was there as usual.

"From Flag, sir. *Flag to Pegasus. Standy to receive Flag-Lieutenant.*"

"Very well. Acknowledge Mr McBride, if you please." He turned to Fenwick. "Now then, why cannot the Admiral send his messages by letter or flag, James. Why send his precious Flag-Lieutenant?"

"No idea sir, but we will soon find out because the boat is already on its way!"

As he was speaking, the Admiral's barge appeared around the stern of the *Suffolk* and was pulling swiftly for *Pegasus*.

"I will be aft James. I will leave you to greet him."

"Aye aye sir."

"Admiral's Flag-Lieutenant, *Sir!*" barked the Marine sentry. Kingston darted across the deck to the screen door.

"No need to hurry Kingston, it's only the Admiral's Flag-Lieutenant come to pay a call you know!"

Trafford, seated on a small stool in a corner and industrially polishing Courtenay's sword, laughed. The door was opened and Marmaduke Spencer-White stepped carefully over the coaming. He was superbly attired in an elegantly cut uniform with a fine sword at his side. His stockings were clearly of the finest quality and he wore a pair of black shoes with buckles which suggested they were real gold. He walked haughtily across the decking and stopped in front of Courtenay's desk. Courtenay had not move. He did not stand up and hardly took any notice of the officer in front of him for a long moment whilst he looked at the chart open in front of him. At last he looked up, fixing Spencer-White with a cold stare.

"Well Mr Spencer-White, to what do we owe this honour?"

"I have come sir from Lord Cairns, with orders for you and your ship." He laid an envelope on the desk. "My instructions are to ensure the orders are received by you personally and that you understand them."

Courtenay picked up the envelope and a knife which lay on the desk. He slit open the envelope. "I had best read my orders then, Mr Spencer-White, so that you may go back to your master and report that I have both received and understood them." Spencer-White went to sit down without invitation. "I do not recall inviting you to sit, Lieutenant?"

Spencer-White blushed and remained standing. Courtenay looked past him as the door opened again and Fenwick came into the cabin removing his hat as he did so. Courtenay smiled at Fenwick and then went back to reading his orders.

At length he looked up at Spencer-White. "Is that all? Did the Admiral think that I would not understand my ship is to patrol between the western end of Sicily and Cagliari?"

"Lord Cairns wanted to be certain that you understood you are to patrol that area sir until you are relieved."

"I understand well enough Mr Spencer-White. What am I supposed to do for supplies? I have over six hundred and fifty souls aboard this ship to think about who need to be fed and watered on a regular basis."

"Were you not well provisioned before you left Gibraltar sir? The Admiral was led to believe that all the Squadron was well supplied."

"That was weeks ago Mr Spencer-White, weeks ago." Courtenay was containing his anger with an effort. "Believe it or not my men do need to eat!"

"I am sure you will manage Sir Giles. You understand your orders?"

"Yes Lieutenant, you may report that I do understand, only too well! I will not detain you further. Me Fenwick, see the Flag-Lieutenant over the side if you please. I regret he will not have time to be entertained in the wardroom." As Spencer-White turned to go, Courtenay added smoothly, "Even though I am sure Mr Spencer-White would be eager to hear news from home." The Lieutenant stopped.

"I have not long left home sir. Usually it is a person such as myself who brings news from home."

"Yes, I am aware of that Lieutenant. But in this case, news from home arrived before you did. How much did those four cutthroats cost you Spencer-White, or did your Uncle pay them? I had a very interesting letter from home, from my father in law, who told me about the cowardly effort by four men to attack a helpless woman with child, I may add, to either kidnap her or murder her. I confess I know not which was intended because none of the men survived." Spencer-White turned slowly to face him, his features controlled.

"I know nothing about that to which you refer sir. This is a scurr…"

Courtenay slammed his fist down on his desk and stood up. "Don't you dare lecture me Mr Spencer-White. You may be interested to know the last man to die named you as the person who had paid him and his friends! You of course were conveniently not there at the time because you had already sailed. Did you not think news of this would reach me?"

"I have no idea what you are talking about sir, but I would advise you to be very careful. There are witnesses. You have no proof that either I or Lord Cairns was involved in this most unfortunate episode"

"Yes, unfortunate because it did not succeed Lieutenant. No I have no proof as yet. But when I do obtain such proof I will see you dance on your precious Uncle's mainyard, by God!"

"I would once again counsel caution Sir Giles. There are two witnesses to your threats!"

"Threats Lieutenant? They are no threats. They are promises! A little warning for you. You did not know that I suspected something may happen the moment I was safely out of the way and I therefore….let us say, took precautions? Keep away from my wife Spencer-White. Do not go anywhere near her if you ever return to England alive, or I will kill you!"

Spencer-White fell back. He looked around the cabin. Fenwick and Trafford were motionless and blank-faced. "There are witnesses here Captain Courtenay, that you have threatened to kill me. You have also besmirched my good name."

"Witnesses? Where? What did they hear or see?"

Fenwick spoke clearly. "Never heard any threats sir. I think the Flag-Lieutenant is tired after a hard voyage from home. I would suggest a spell in the maintop or a good sleep, sir. How about you Trafford?"

"Never heard a thing sir. Been polishing Sir Giles' sword. Got a good edge and point on it now, as well. Could do some real damage with that sir!"

"Well Lieutenant, there you are. As to besmirching your good name I was not aware you had one to begin with!"

"Sir, I intend to send my second…."

"For a duel Lieutenant? I can see you are conversant with the Kings Regulations which expressly forbid a junior officer challenging a senior one to a duel. It is a Court-martial offence. Get out sir, before I forget about the Regulations and call you out myself! Remember what happened to Matthias Harding!"

Spencer-White left in something of a hurry, and indeed in so much of a hurry he tripped over the coaming and measured his length on the decking, his sword clattering away. Courtenay came to the screen door where Fenwick was tut-tutting. Courtenay glanced sideways at the Marine sentry. The man was trying hard not to laugh. There would be a good tale told in the Marines' barracks later!

"Are you all right Mr Spencer-White?"

The man got up, brushed himself off and made for the door leading out onto the quarterdeck. His face was bright red with humiliation. Fenwick followed him trying to keep a straight face.

"Perhaps he should have taken a spot o' water with it sir?" asked Trafford after the door of the cabin had closed.

"Perhaps he should." replied Courtenay thoughtfully. "Kingston! A glass of claret! To wash away a filthy taste!" he said quietly.

He looked around and smiled at Trafford. "Pass the word for the Master, Trafford. We have work to do!"

SEVEN

His Britannic Majesty's Ship *Pegasus* was close-hauled on the larboard tack, the wind coming in from almost amidships, her yards braced right round. She rode the swell in her usual dignified way, her bows thrusting aside the blue water to leave it creaming along her flanks. She was part-way between the western end of Sicily and Cagliari on the island of Sardinia. She had been on this patrol now for two weeks. Fortunately, Courtenay had been able to secure some supplies from a small fishing village on Sicily, but apart from being able to replenish the ship's water supplies it had hardly been satisfactory, and Courtenay had had no alternative than to put his crew on rations. He was glad that at least there was plenty of fresh fruit.

Their orders had made their objective perfectly clear. They were to patrol the gap between Sicily and Cagliari, keeping a close watch for any enemy ships, merchant or otherwise, which might try to slip through the gap and then south-east to Malta. Troubridge and his ships were to the north. The rest of the squadron was to the south but scattered apart of course from the Flagship. Cairns made it clear he was going nowhere. *Suffolk* sat off the Island, Cairns being fortified with the supplies he had brought for himself, only moving out to sea when a wind appeared which drive the ship onto a lee shore.

It was just after two bells of the forenoon watch. The hands had long since had breakfast, and Courtenay had lingered over his last coffee, looking morosely at his chart, knowing very well there was very little chance he would be able to prevent anyone slipping through. The wind was against it today in any event. He knew only too well why his ship was where it was. Cairns wanted him out of the way so that if anything did happen *Pegasus* would be elsewhere. On the other hand he was equally well aware that if he did meet with any ships, the chances would be that there would a number of them, and they would be outnumbered. He was under no illusions that Cairns would be perfectly happy to see him dead or captured by the French. He was equally determined it would not happen,

He got up, walked slowly to the salt-stained windows and then heard the hail from the masthead. Trafford was in the cabin in a flash taking down Courtenay's sword from the rack. Courtenay as usual was clad in shirt and breeches, and his longish hair was held loosely in place with a piece of black ribbon, a present from his wife.

It was just a minute or so for Courtenay to get to the binnacle and to look up at the mainmast look-out, but Stevens, the Second Lieutenant, had beaten him to it.

"Sail almost dead ahead sir. Topsails have only just shown above the horizon, but Cooper swears they are those of a liner."

"H'mm" replied Courtenay, rubbing his chin. "Not likely to be one of ours from that bearing, Mr Stevens."

"Frog, sir?"

"More than likely." He turned. "Ah, Mr Smythe. Good morning to you. Get aloft with a glass and tell me what you find."

Smythe made it to the maintop in just a few moments. The news he yelled down came as no surprise to Courtenay at all. There were two ships of the line ahead of them and there was little doubt they were French. But there was something else and Courtenay noticed Smythe having one last look before he came back down via backstay.

"Sorry sir, but just as I was going to come down I had one last look and there was a *third* ship. Think it was a 74 as well sir."

"Thank you Mr Smythe. Well done."

Courtenay turned and started pacing the deck. He saw Fenwick and Davies arrive on the quarterdeck but ignored them as he thought. Three to one. Even *Pegasus* could not be expected to take on three French liners and survive. Even if he could take two of them on the third could easily cross his hawse or stern, and rake the ship. He would not run….straight away, but a thought was germinating in his mind.

"Mr Davies. Whereabouts are Captain Troubridge's ships supposed to be?"

"To the north of Malta sir. I believe they were patrolling between the Island and Sicily, sir."

"Those ships up ahead are not going to be able to sail where they need to go with the wind the way it is at present, and we are in the way of their advance."

"But there are three of them sir!"

"What would you do Mr Davies? Run?" Courtenay was a little angry.

"I suppose I would sir, since we are so heavily outnumbered, but then sir, with respect I am not you!"

Courtenay smiled and touched his arm. "No you are not. I have no intention of sacrificing this ship and our lads just because the Admiral decided to place us somewhere vulnerable without proper support."

Fenwick broke in. "We are supposed to have the sloop for messages. Where the hell is she? We've not seen her since we began our patrol!"

"Deck there! Three ships o' the line sir, all flying the French Flag! Rear-admiral's flag on leadin' ship!"

"Well," said Courtenay, "there you have it. Mr Fenwick, clear for action and prepare for battle if you please. I will have the larboard battery loaded with double-shot and a charge of grape. And run up the Colours, if you please."

"What do you intend to do sir?"

"Do? We are going to fight!"

Fenwick went about his duties and Trafford moved to stand next to his Captain.

"We really takin' on that lot Cap'n? Or have you got something up your sleeve?"

"Oh, I think we may give the French a bloody nose but I have no intention of doing either what they, or our Admiral, want!"

Pegasus and the French ships continued to grow close. The men on the British ship were ready for anything. The guns were loaded, decks sanded, the gun captains had selected the best roundshot they had available and there were spare cartridges of powder at each gun. The powder-monkeys stood ready with their carriers to replenish these supplies once the fighting began.

Courtenay was still dressed as before. Fenwick and Davies looked on anxiously as the French drew closer and closer. Courtenay had been watching the leading ship through a glass. She was not handling that well. Her sails were not drawing as they should. Whereas the sails on his *Pegasus* were full-bellied and hard, and the ship was moving well, every so often the sails on the French ship would flap. Courtenay merely smiled. He was not necessarily convinced the French Admiral was on the leading ship. He had seen the trick before. As soon as the action starts, the flag comes down on the leading ship, and a new one goes up on the second ship, showing the Admiral was aboard that one, and could see what was happening with the first broadsides. For what he had in mind, it mattered not.

"Mr Davies, lay off a course if you will to take us to Captain Troubridge's patrol area. Then await my instructions."

"Aye sir."

The gap narrowed. The men grew tense as they realised the French were getting closer. There was a *bang!* and a few moments later a waterspout rose off the starboard bow. There was another, but again the aim was bad.

Fenwick turned to Courtenay, asking the question with an upraised eyebrow. Courtenay smiled and shook his head. The French Captain was giving his gunners the chance to build up some confidence by firing his bow-chasers. Courtenay intended to wait until he could use his artillery to the maximum.

Closer and closer. It seemed to Courtenay they were going to lock bowsprits, although they were in fact still a hundred yards away. The gun-captains were fingering their lanyards, waiting for a target to appear in their gun-ports. A little move here, an adjustment there.

The bows of the French ship started to cross with those of *Pegasus*. The French started to fire as its guns were bearing. It was haphazard fire. Some balls whimpered overhead, although one or two did slam into *Pegasus' side*. Courtenay paced the deck and then heard musketry starting. A squad of Marines under their Sergeant stepped up to the nettings, aimed their Brown Bess muskets and fired a volley. Even as Courtenay watched, three men were swept away from near the bows.

Fenwick turned to watch his Captain. He knew very well the need to get in a good broadside, and so did every last one of the gun-captains.

"I think a broadside when you are ready James!" said Courtenay.

Fewnick turned back, judging the moment, feeling more French iron slamming into the hull. A length of rope dropped onto the nettings spread above the gunners and the quarterdeck. Then there was a larger object fall. It was a seaman who had been aloft. He had no head.

"For God's sake get rid of that!" barked Davies.

Fenwick's sword dropped and *Pegasus* was thrown over to starboard as her larboard battery erupted in orange flame and smoke. The weight or iron, the guns double-shotted, swept into the side of the French ship like an avalanche, and the grape which went with it found flesh and bone as the small iron balls slapped through the gun-ports and sprayed amongst the crews. The British crews feverishly dragged in their guns. A man stepped up with a rammer soaked in water and thrust it down the barrel. Out came the rammer, down went a charge with a wad, then a ball, and another wad. Run the gun back up to the port and await the order to fire.

The French were still firing, but haphazardly. As Courtenay's ship started to clear the French one, another savage broadside ripped across the narrow stretch of water and Courtenay, coughing on the smoke which was blowing across the decking, could clearly hear cries and screams.

He turned to Davies who was tending to one of his helmsmen who had been struck by a musket ball. The man died even as he tried to help him. His place was taken

131

by Davies himself.. "Very well Mr Davies, standby to wear ship. We will cross the Frog's stern and then wear again and steer down his other side."

"Aye sir. What then?"

"Then Mr Davies, you may lay the ship on that course you calculated to take us to Captain Troubridge. Do you *really* want me to take on the other two as well?"

Davies forced a smile. "I was beginning to think you were going to sir!"

"I intend to maul the French flagship so badly they will come after us, especially if they see us run. If we can run far enough we may be able to bag all of them! Now standby, Mr Davies!"

He turned again to watch how they were progressing. They were almost past the French ship and up ahead he could see the other two of a similar size, with their larboard batteries run out, ready to take on this impudent British ship who thought it could beat all of them!

"Now Mr Davies!"

"Ready ho! Off tacks and sheets! Put the helm down, there!" He threw his weight on the wheel as the spokes spun. The ship was having to turn through the wind and be laid on the starboard tack. The bows started to come around. As the ship started to lose the wind she slowed, but the bows were coming round. As her bows passed the stern of the French ship the larboard carronade blasted out its message and the aim was true. The windows in the stern, and the ornate woodwork on it, disappeared as the massive ball blasted a hole. The mizzenmast teetered and then fell, fortunately to larboard, crashing down amongst the quarterdeck gunners, cutting down her helmsmen and smashing to fragments her wheel.

"She's paying off sir! Must have taken her steering!" yelled Fenwick. Division by division, *Pegasus'* guns were firing into the smoke and the stern of the French flagship. Courtenay had no idea of its name, as this had been blasted away in the onslaught.

Then she wore again and sailed down the other side. A number of guns were run out and firing, and *Pegasus* took some balls in her side, but another full broadside from the larboard battery silenced the remaining guns.

"Cease firing Mr Fenwick if you please. Set the courses and let us see if our ruse has worked!"

The French ship was a shambles. Her mizzen was gone, shrouds and stays parted on her main, and she was listing to larboard by the bows. Courtenay watched her closely as his own ship gathered speed and moved away. He ran up the ladder to the poop and smiled as he saw the other French ships spreading more sail and coming after him. They thought he was running. He ran lightly back down to the quarterdeck.

"They appear to be following James. Let us give them a merry chase!"

"Shall I set the studding sails sir?"

"Not yet, just set all sail to the Royals and see what happens. I don't want them to lose heart and decide they cannot catch us. They were going somewhere and my guess is that it was to try to slip through into Malta. I wonder if there was a food convoy around somewhere, and they were supposed to meet up with then? I hope I have dented their egos more than a little by singeing their Admiral's beard and they will feel honour bound to catch up with us impudent and perfidious British! Perhaps they will forget for a short while what they are supposed to be doing."

Hour after hour, *Pegasus* reached to the east, with the wind still coming from the south. All eyes were on the French ships astern, with all their sails set although not drawing that well. Unnoticed by the French Courtenay actually reduced some of his sail plan, so that in fact the French were keeping up quite well although he knew at any time he wanted he could simply re-set his sails and his ship would walk away from the Frenchmen. Davies cast many a concerned eye at his Captain, but he had served with him now for too many years to be overly worried. Courtenay knew what he was doing; that was good enough for Davies. Stevens, the Second Lieutenant, strolled the quarterdeck on his watch as if he did not have a care in the world. The mainmast look-out left the French ships to others and concentrated on everywhere else. The Frogs were in view, other ships were not.

Courtenay raised his telescope and looked again at the French ships following. He smiled as he saw the second ship yawing slightly and a signal hoist immediately appeared on the leading ship, which presumably was now carrying the senior Captain. McBride was with him, and he saw the smile.

"They are not very good with their sail drill Mr McBride, would you not agree?"

"Aye sir. Very bad. May I ask you something sir?"

Courtenay lowered his glass and looked at the Midshipman. He was tanned, quite tall, and slim. Good looking. He would be popular with the ladies when he got his commission.

"Now Mr McBride, you ought to know me better than that by now. What is it?"

"Sir, you have very surreptitiously reduced sail on more than one occasion. I assume for some reason this is to enable the Frogs to keep up. Are you trying to lead them away from somewhere sir? *Pegasus* could outrun those tubs in no time at all!"

"Very astute Mr McBride. Where do you think they were going?"

"There is only one place around here sir. Malta."

"Yes. And where is Captain Troubridge's Squadron?"

"To the north of…..You are leading them into a trap sir?"

"I most sincerely hope so Mr McBride, otherwise we are having a long sail away from our patrol area for nothing!" He smiled, and went lightly down the larboard poop ladder.

Fenwick was there, chatting to Stevens. He turned and smiled at Courtenay. He was not wearing either uniform coat or hat either.

"Still in the same place sir?"

"Aye. Just about keeping up. Where do you think we are James?"

"Just to the north of Pantelleria sir, and to the south of Marsala. I would say that we are just about in Captain Troubridge's area."

"Excellent. Let us hope the French are not aware of our dispositions otherwise they will turn tale and run!"

But the French kept coming. *Pegasus* was now well away from her patrol area and Courtenay was in serious trouble if the Vice-admiral discovered the fact but he countered that thought in his mind by the fact he was leading French ships away from their destination, and if……

"Deck there! Sail dead ahead to the east, sir!"

"Ah," said Courtenay. That should be *Culloden!"* Fenwick and Davies exchanged glances.

Fifteen minutes later the mainmast look-out yelled down the leading ship was indeed Captain Troubridge's *Culloden* with his other two ships following.

"Mr McBride. When we are within signalling distance you will make our number and then signal the *Culloden. Enemy in sight!*"

It was not long before the signal hoist was fluttering in the breeze, with an answering signal from Troubridge.

"Sir, signal. *Culloden to Pegasus. Welcome back. Take position ahead of me.*"

"Acknowledge. Mr Davies, standby to wear ship. We will turn in a moment when we are closer, and tarry a while to allow the others to catch us."

Stevens had been watching the French astern. "Sir, the French are wearing ship!"

"I would have been a mite surprised if they had stayed to trade blows with four of us! The French don't like those kind of odds at all!" replied Courtenay. "Now, I wonder what Troubridge will do? General chase, or just make sure the Frogs disappear?"

"Sir, *Culloden* is signalling. *General chase.*"

Courtenay smiled. "There is our answer. Very well Mr Davies, wear ship if you please and then set all sail. We will show those Frogs what sail drill is all about!"

The four British ships, no longer required to stay in a rigid line of battle, set all the sail they could safely carry and very soon were catching the French ships. *Pegasus* was well in front of the others but she did have the advantage of her position to begin with. It did not take at all long to overhaul the French. Courtenay was disgusted. As the four British liners caught up with their foes, the two French ships simply hauled down their colours. They often fired one or two guns before surrendering, *pour honneur de pavilion,* but these two did not even bother to do that. As *Pegasus* ranged up on the larboard quarter of the rearmost one, with *Culloden* not that far behind, the tricolour came down, and the ship started to heave-to. The other one soon followed suit.

Courtenay sat in his cabin, looking out of the stern windows at the sea beneath the counter. It was a week since the fight with the French ships and Troubridge had offered to take the prizes back to the rest of Cairns' Squadron, with a full report as to what had happened. He had realised Courtenay was well off-station and had suggested he returned there as soon as possible. He had heard a lot about Cairns and did not like one bit what he had heard. Courtenay listened and said nothing, and Troubridge realised there was a lot more to it. *Pegasus* was now back on station, sailing back and forth, not that anyone expected any other ships to try and break through the blockade so quickly after the others.

There was a bellow from the Marine sentry that Davies was outside, a knock at the screen door, and then the Sailing Master stepped over the coaming into the cabin. Courtenay turned and smiled. Davies raised one eyebrow.

"You sent for me sir? Is there something…..?"

"Have a look at the chart Mr Davies. Do you remember once before when we were off the French coast, I asked you to estimate from where a French convoy would appear? Well I have a feeling those two French ships we saw last week were going to meet up with some store-ships of some kind. The French are desperate to get supplies through to Malta. Where do you think they might come from?"

Davies stooped over the chart, rubbing his chin. Kingston hovered nearby with a glass of rum, which Davies took and swallowed. "I reckon sir, that if they were sailing from Toulon they would head almost due south down the west coast of Sardinia, almost to the North African coast, but not too close of course, and then they would turn to the east."

"They would hope to make a junction with their escort before they met up with Chebecks?"

"Yes sir."

"Good. That's what I think. Very well Mr Davies, I think we will sail a little further to the south when we are on that leg of our patrol. Not for too long. Nothing to get the Admiral excited about. Perhaps just a day or so."

"They still might slip past sir."

"Yes, but then again they might not! Carry on Mr Davies."

The Master left and Courtenay was once again with his thoughts.

During the forenoon watch two days later, the gun crews were being exercised, one division competing against another when there was a hail from the masthead.

"Deck there! Strange sails to the west sir!"

Courtenay was in the lee nettings in an instant, telescope to his eye, searching for the sails. He could see nothing. He turned and looked at the officer of the watch, Burton.

"Fancy a climb Mr Burton? I want to know if they are the supply ships we have been searching for."

Burton grinned and was soon half-way up the ratlines. It was not a few more moments before he was levelling his glass. Courtenay waited impatiently on the quarterdeck, tapping his foot on the pale decking. Fenwick arrived, hatless and coatless like his Captain, eyes raised to the masthead. He looked enquiringly at Courtenay. He knew his Captain would never rush the officer aloft. He wanted a proper report, not what the officer thought he wanted to hear. Even so…….

"Deck there!" Burton was yelling down. "Looks like a convoy sir! Half-a-dozen merchant ships and a corvette sir! Wearing French colours!"

"Good!" said Courtenay. "Run up the colours Mr McBride. Mr Davies, set the courses and all sail to the royals. Lay off a course to intercept."

The hands were piped to the sails, and with a favourable wind the distance soon dropped away. The French corvette could be seen altering course to investigate their appearance, but suddenly the French Captain hauled his wind, put up his helm, and the small ship, about the size of a British sloop-of-war spread more sail before speeding away, leaving its charges to their fate. Signal flags appeared on the corvette.

Courtenay grunted as he looked through his glass. "Telling them to scatter. I hope for their sake they do not stray too close to the African shore. Very well let us see what we can take gentlemen! Beat to quarters and clear for action Mr Fenwick!"

Before the merchantmen had the chance to put much distance between themselves and the *Pegasus* she had caught up with them. To encourage the others, as she ranged up on one of them Courtenay ordered a half-broadside, upper deck 18 pounders only to fire into it. The French flag came down as the balls slammed into the ship's hull. Two other ships surrendered immediately but two others made a run for it. Courtenay put the two launches over the side with double banked oars and a full boarding party, and although he fretted because he wanted to go he had to watch as Fenwick and the Fourth Lieutenant, Henson, went after the ships. Eventually, the two ships hove-to as well. There was just one ship left, which was last seen sailing due south.

"A fair catch gentlemen," commented Courtenay later when sharing a glass with his officers, "and one which I believe we need to get back to our Squadron as soon as possible. The supplies will come in useful, after we have, er, *liberated* some of them for our own use!"

Pegasus rode the easy swell just off the Malta coast. She stood guard over the supply ships she had captured and around which were a cluster of boats from the Squadron. Courtenay had almost been able to feel the scrutiny as his ship had tacked gracefully towards the squadron's anchorage with the flagship *Suffolk* apparently not having moved since the last time Courtenay had seen her. He was certain that Cairns had watched their approach. They had hardly hove-to when there was the signal flag for 'Captain to repair on board immediately'

Courtenay had been made to stand in front of the Vice-admiral's desk whilst he read through the report.

"I heard from Troubridge about the capture of the French two-deckers of course, Courtenay," Cairns was saying smoothly, "and it was bad enough that you were off station, but I suppose I cannot altogether blame you. You showed initiative and that enabled us to rid ourselves of two more French ships. However you were again off-station when you intercepted the supply ships. You seem to make a habit of being off-station do you not, *Sir* Giles?"

"It would certainly seem to be the case my Lord." interjected Marmaduke Spencer-White, standing next to his Uncle. For just a fleeting second, Courtenay saw a look of annoyance on the Admiral's face but it went as soon as it had arrived.

"It seemed logical sir that those French 74s were around for a reason. We know that the French are desperate to supply the garrison on the Island. I have seen a copy of Colonel Tandy's report……"

"Yes, yes, I know what he has said Captain. The price of everything has risen dramatically, even rats for God's sake!" He paused and looked at Courtenay carefully. "I understand you and the Colonel are quite well acquainted?"

"Yes sir. We have shared a number of adventures together."

"Yes I seem to recall he managed to get himself made a prisoner when we were in the Caribbean last year. You effected one of your 'escapes'"

"That was by chance my Lord. I was there to rescue some French Royalists."

"H'mm. Well I will overlook you being off-station Courtenay, because you have served our cause well." Courtenay hid his surprise. There was grudging respect in the Vice-admiral's voice. Then he spoilt it. "However, there will be no further escapades of that nature. One of the other ships can take over your duties. I may have a job for you which involves your Colonel Tandy, since you know him so well. Very well you may return to your ship."

Courtenay stepped back from the desk and turned, but not before he had seen the sneer on the Flag-Lieutenant's face. He looked the man calmly in the face as he was about to leave. "Does something amuse you *Mr* Spencer-White?"

Cairns broke in. "Carry on Captain Courtenay, if you please!"

That was a week ago. Ever since, they had done nothing except sit at their anchorage consuming stores. The officers kept up the men's spirits with all the usual competitions, but the ship's company could not understand why they were in a way, being punished for the success they had had. After all they had helped to take two French

141

liners, and a number of supply ships. The cargoes had provided the Squadron with sufficient to last them a few more months without returning to Gibraltar. Here they were, sitting doing nothing when they should have been turned loose on their patrol looking for more pickings.

Eventually there was a signal for them to stand by to receive the Flag-Lieutenant, and fifteen minutes later Spencer-White appeared, as urbane and sneering as ever. He marched into Courtenay's cabin, where Trafford was standing in a relaxed fashion near the stern windows. The Flag-Lieutenant sneered in his direction.

"Really Captain Courtenay, do we have to have your man here whilst we discuss my Uncle's orders?"

"It would not do any harm at all *sir,* if you showed Sir Giles some respect." spat Trafford ."You seem to forget he is a Baronet!"

The Flag-Lieutenant almost gave a mock bow, but the sneer went from his face. "And my Uncle is a peer of the Realm!"

"Yes," said Courtenay, "but *you* are not. Where are the orders I assume you brought for me, or is this a social occasion?"

Spencer-White passed over the sealed orders and Courtenay signed the receipt for them. He looked up. "Yes Lieutenant, was there something else?"

"My…the Admiral said he thought I might be of use to you in carrying out your orders," there was a pause, "sir."

Courtenay smiled broadly. "Did he indeed. In other words, he does not trust me to undertake the task with which I am being entrusted without going off-station? Remember what happened on the last occasion his Flag-Lieutenant came to see what I was about?"

Spencer-White swallowed hard. "The Admiral considers I am need of some further education in certain matters."

Courtenay was smiling even more. "Well in that case Lieutenant, I suggest you find somewhere to seat yourself in the wardroom until I have read my orders and decided how to put them into operation. Carry on if you please." Spencer-White left.

Trafford smiled. "He is not likely to be too popular in the wardroom Sir Giles!"

"I know. The French have a tasteful expression for it. *Quel domage.*" Trafford looked blank. "What a shame." Trafford laughed softly. "And now," continued Courtenay, "I had best see what the Admiral has in store for us."

EIGHT

The officers of His Britannic Majesty's ship of the line *Pegasus* were gathered in Courtenay's cabin, together with a smattering of the senior warrant officers. Henry Oates, the Boatswain, stood next to one of the Master's mates, Jed Smith, arms folded across his broad chest. It was almost dark, the light fading quickly. On Courtenay's desk was a chart. Davies knew it well. It was of the Island of Malta and he had looked at it almost every day for some weeks.

"Very well gentlemen, we will take both launches and the cutters. Captain Connell will provide a detachment of our Marines, and all told there will be one hundred of us. The battery is situate here," he pointed to a spot on the map not far from Valetta. "and the Admiral would like us to rid the Island of it. It seems that, despite what we have been told of the Island slowly starving to death there is enough spirit amongst the French gunners to keep this battery firing, and sometimes they hit something!"

"Why does the Admiral want to bother with it sir?" asked Stevens, staring quizzically at the map. "They are not going to bother us if we are out of range, and from all accounts the Island will soon be starved into submission."

"I have no idea Mr Stevens, but he wants us to get rid of the battery and this is what I intend to do. If getting rid of it means the Island may surrender sooner than later, so much the better, not only for us but the Islanders as well. I am sure they did not wish to starve and knowing the French if there is any food of any description available, they are taking it and leaving the people with nothing!"

"I understand that sir, but even so……"

"So we will land in this little cove here, just to the east of the battery."

Oates rubbed his chin and cleared his throat. "Not goin' to be an easy landing sir. As you know full well, there are no beaches on the Island, just rocky bays. The lads will have to be dead careful goin' in, and backwater long enough for everyone to go over the side like."

"Thank you Mr Oates. I agree that is a problem, but I am sure you will ensure that your very best men are in the boats for that purpose."

"I've detailed off the men sir, and Mr Smith here will take one of the boats 'imself."

Courtenay smiled. "There. We are in safe hands gentlemen." There was a round of smiles. Oates and Smith looked at each other and grinned. "There will be a guide waiting for us. From there we will move towards the battery. Silence is paramount. Wrap rags around anything which may make a sound. Muffle the oars. Muskets and pistols are to be left unloaded until we are almost at the battery. That," turning towards the Marine Captain, "does not apply to your men of course, since they will be our advance guard. I require them to move ahead of the rest of the men and ensure our way to the battery is clear. When we arrive in force any sentries can be disposed of and then we will take the battery. Any questions?"

There were none.

"Very well. I think a drink is called for." He looked over at the screen door as Oates and Smith made to leave. "Mr Oates. I see no reason for Mr Smith and yourself to leave us? I am sure you would like a tot?"

Oates nodded and smiled. "Well, thank you sir. Right kind of you."

He raised a full measure of rum to his lips, looked over the glass rim and saw Fenwick looking at him. He thought for a moment there might be some resentment at the Warrant Officers drinking with their Captain but Fenwick smiled pleasantly and nodded to them, raising his own glass.

"Now gentlemen," Courtenay was speaking again, "I will lead the operation with Mr Stevens as my second in command. Mr Fenwick will remain here in command of the ship. Mr Davies insists on accompanying us on this occasion. There will be a Midshipman in each boat and Mr Fenwick will deal with that, but not Mr McBride. I want him to remain with his signal party."

Fenwick smiled. "He will be mightily disappointed sir. I think he was looking forward to some action!"

"I am sure he will get his fair share in due course!"

He nodded to them as they filed out. All, of course, except Trafford and Fenwick. Courtenay looked at the latter and sighed.

"And what pray are you going to say, James? That you should be leading rather than me? You know that is not the way I do things. Honour and danger are something a Captain should share with his men."

Fewnick smiled. "Oh I know I will never persuade you not to go sir, but what about the Flag-Lieutenant? Is that right, his Admiral has ordered him to accompany you?"

"Yes, and I think he did that to make sure I went and did not leave this to someone else!"

Fenwick faced him squarely. "He wants you dead. How do you know that when there is all the usual confusion of a fight in the dark you will not be laid low by Spencer-White? A blade is a blade after all!"

"Beggin' your pardon sir, but I will be with the Cap'n!" interjected Trafford.

"I know that Trafford, but even you cannot do the impossible. You might be fighting for your life yourself!"

"Do not worry yourself James. Aside from Trafford here, Piers Tandy will be on hand. He is the guide. He can blend in with any background that man! Forewarned is forearmed, remember? Keep your friends close and your enemies closer? I am on my guard. And he will know it!"

Fenwick smiled grimly and left it at that.

Pegasus' cutter drifted in slowly between two large rocks, Trafford at the tiller struggling with the current, and the men at the oars desperately trying to prevent their looms being smashed to pieces. Smith was in the bows, leaning over a swivel gun which had been shipped there just in case. He peered through the gloom, then turned and looked back at his Captain.

"Just a mite to larboard Cox!" Trafford shifted the tiller and the boat swung slightly. A few more seconds, then Smith held up his hand and brought it down. It was the signal. They were as close in as they dare. Smith jumped over the bows into waist deep water, followed by several other men to hold the boat steady. A dozen Marines were off the boat in an instant, working their way up over the rocks and forming a rough picket line. Trafford turned and showed a shaded lantern astern for the next boat, one of the launches with more Marines, to come in. There was just room for two boats. Courtenay dropped into the water and then climbed up onto the rocks. He looked round to see the launch backing out as Marines came ashore and another boat taking the space left.

He turned and saw Connell in the gloom. Behind him a figure materialised. Piers Tandy. "Good evening Piers. This is Captain Connell. You will guide his men towards the battery. Very well Captain, you know what to do. We will pause here for a few moments whilst the rest of the men get ashore. That will give the chance to get your men out ahead and scout."

Piers Tandy nodded and grunted. "It is a little climb out of this cove Giles, and then easier going across the headland. The battery is on the other side. Well dug in but they will be asleep at this time of day! There are two sentries."

"I am sure they will cause our gallant bullocks no trouble, is that not correct Captain?"

"Aye sir. We will move out now sir. I will send a man back as a guide." In a moment he had disappeared., following Tandy.

It took a little while for all the seamen to gather. The boats would lie off the shore a little, ready to come back in on the signal. When everyone was ashore Courtenay turned to Stevens. "Take charge of the second half of the men. Mr Stevens. Keep them quiet and on the move. Mr Smythe will be our link."

"Aye aye sir." Stevens did not appear to very happy.

Courtenay looked at him again. "What is the matter?"

"Nothing sir. Just a little nervous. Enemy shore and all that!"

Courtenay gripped his arm. "Come along Martin, the men are depending on us!" Stevens smiled grimly.

Trafford came alongside Courtenay as they started climbing over the slippery rocks. Spencer-White was almost immediately behind them having been placed in one of the other boats, and unbeknown to Courtenay, one of the Boatswain's Mates, Stoddart, was right behind the Flag-Lieutenant. He was carrying a cutlass and had a pistol thrust through his belt together with a tomahawk. As he climbed across the rocks he was keeping his eyes on the white breeches and bony backside of the officer in front of him.

Eventually they climbed out of the cove. Connell had left some of his men behind in a picket line under his Sergeant.

"This way sir" said the Marine. He turned and melted away and Courtenay followed more by instinct than anything else. Trafford padded silently after him, with Spencer-White striding along behind him. He had not yet realised that Stoddart was right behind him.

They marched carefully over short grass and through some low scrub, following the Marine who re-appeared from time to time to make sure everyone was following. After about half-an – hour Courtenay saw Tandy appear out of the darkness and held up his hand. The men stopped, looking around in the darkness, fingering their weapons.

Tandy said very quietly, "We are almost there. Your Marine Captain has his men spread out in a picket line across the top of the headland near the slope which runs down to the battery. Six guns, look like some of our 18 pounders."

Courtenay nodded. "Yes I think they are ones the French captured from us. Any sign of life aside from the two sentries?"

"No, all quiet, but one slip, one clink of metal...."

"Yes Piers, I know. Very well. I will come and have a look." He turned and looked into the sneering face of the Flag-Lieutenant. "Still with us Mr Spencer-White?" He looked past him at Stoddart, grim-faced, and then to Midshipman St John Smythe. "Mr Smythe, go and find Mr Stevens and bring him here if you please."

The Midshipman scuttled away and returned in just a few moments.

Stevens touched his hat. "Sir?"

"We are nearly there. I am going with Colonel Tandy here to view the battery. Take charge until I return. Mr Spencer-White will accompany me."

"Aye aye sir."

Tandy turned without a word and led the way to where Connell waited with his men. Courtenay dropped to his knees as they got near the top of the slope down.

"Grass and scrub sir. Some rocks, but not many." Connell was saying. "Not much cover if anything goes wrong!"

"Then Captain, nothing must go wrong!"

He peered over the edge. He looked down towards where he knew the battery would be. Tandy lay down next to him. "Why does the Admiral want this battery destroyed Giles?"

"Been firing at our ships and getting a little too close. Giving the Frogs heart, encouraging their resistance, you know Piers. An example needs to be set. Encourage them to give up and surrender. What do the Frogs say? *Pour encourage les autres?*"

Tandy's teeth were white in the gloom. "I see. Are you sure he isn't just trying to get rid of you?"

"My God, you sound like James Fenwick!"

Tandy smiled again. "Ah, there is one of the sentries. The other one is at the other end."

Connell slid over. "I have sent one of my men to the other end sir. When Flowers here whistles, the two sentries will be, er, disposed of."

Courtenay turned to the Midshipman. "Mr Smythe, go and fetch Mr Stevens and the rest of the men. Tell them to be very quiet."

Spencer-White spoke for the first time. "What does he mean Sir Giles, disposed of?"

"The sentries will have their throats slit." He heard the man swallow hard.

Stevens appeared, being very careful not to make the slightest noise and laid down beside his Captain.

"All present sir," he whispered.

The Marine called Flowers looked at his officer, then made a warbling noise. From below them there was the briefest sound and then a warbling noise came back.

Connell stood up. "Very well sir, time to go if that is in order?"

Courtenay stood, pulled out his sword with his right hand, and a pistol with his left. He thumbed back the cocking mechanism.

"I agree. Quietly now. Let us get right amongst them before they realise what is happening!"

The mixed formation of Marines and sailors moved down the slope. The Marines moved rigidly in a line, muskets at the ready bayonets fixed. The seamen in more of a ragged line, with a variety of weapons. They were almost at the battery and could see a small row of tents when someone, somewhere amongst the many men, kicked a stone which bounced against a rock. In the quiet of the night it was like a pistol shot. A man appeared from a tent, then another, and then another appeared from behind what appeared to be a roughly built furnace.

"At 'em lads!" yelled Courtenay, and the men charged into the battery. Courtenay was conscious of Trafford at his right shoulder and Tandy at his left. Spencer-White was not in sight. His men charged amongst the French soldiers screaming murderous yells. The first French soldiers who appeared were slaughtered where they stood, shot either by the Marines or slashed and stabbed to the ground. More men appeared and Courtenay found himself locking swords with a Sergeant of Artillery. The man twisted his sword, locking hilts, and tried to use his weight to push Courtenay off-balance. Courtenay allowed him to do so and stepped aside. He was about to run the man through when the Sergeant screamed shrilly, but only for a second. Tandy had got to him first with his sword and Trafford finished it with a savage cutting stroke across the man's neck. His head went bouncing across the hard ground on which the battery had been placed.

Courtenay turned to face another opponent and parried away a wild slash before forcing the man back against the press of men who were now hacking and slashing in the darkness. The man slashed again, was blocked and then failed to guard himself in time to stop Courtenay's blade sliding into his chest. Blood fountained down his tunic and he dropped away with hardly a sound, to be trodden underfoot by the others fighting.

Courtenay was worried the noise might bring other soldiers from nearby.

"Captain Connell! Send some of your men to the east to make sure no-one comes along to disturb us!"

"Already done sir!" the Marine yelled back. "Oh no you don't, my friend." A man had tried to get beneath his guard with a running lunge. He stepped aside and pushed the man over. As the man fell one of the Marines thrust downwards and impaled the screaming man with his bayonet.

Trafford was trading blows with a French soldier who looked a good six inches taller but he was not the cutlass fighter Trafford was, and in just a couple of moments Trafford had slashed the man across his stomach, causing him to drop to his knees, holding himself. His sword fell to the ground as he used both hands to keep his insides in but Trafford calmly slashed him across the throat with a backhand slash and the man toppled over.

Connell was yelling "I do believe the Frogs have surrendered sir!"

The French soldiers were throwing down their weapons.

"Very well Captain. Secure the prisoners. Mr Stevens, get to work disabling the guns. Smartly now, I want to be away from here within the half-hour." He looked around as the Lieutenant hurried away. "Have you seen Mr Spencer-White, Alex?"

Trafford grinned. "Nary a sign Sir Giles. I reckon he has found a little place to hide!"

Just then, Spencer-White hobbled up. "Sorry sir. Stepped into a pot-hole. Twisted my ankle."

For a moment a smile played on Courtenay's mouth. Another member of the same family had used a similar excuse years ago when he had been a Lieutenant in the *Claymore*. "Really? Well, you have missed everything here Mr Spencer-White!"

There were a few sniggers from men nearby. Courtenay could sense the Flag-Lieutenant's discomfort.

"I suggest you help Mr Parsons, the Gunner, to get rid of the guns."

Parsons appeared beside them. "Shame about them guns sir. Good 18 pounders!"

"Yes I know Mr Parsons, but there is no way we can take them with us. See that they are all spiked."

"Aye sir."

Tandy took Courtenay by the arm and led him away from the others. Trafford watched Spencer-White for a few moments, then followed although stood out of earshot.

"Can your men find their own way back to the cove Giles?" asked Tandy.

"I am sure we can manage Piers! Why?"

"Well, it will be getting light soon and I have a fair way to go to get back to where I am staying. I am safe there among people who will hide me in case there are problems. I would like to be there and out of sight before daybreak."

Courtenay held out his hand. "Then I'll not detain you Piers. It was good to see you again. Take care of yourself."

"And you Giles." Tandy looked over to Trafford. He raised an arm, turned and disappeared into the murk.

Stevens appeared. "Guns all spiked sir."

"Very well Mr Stevens. Get the men ready to move out. I want to be back to the cove and away before the light finds us again!"

His Britannic Majesty's ship *Pegasus,* was once again at anchor off the Island of Malta. Some of the ships were now a little further inshore thanks to Courtenay's raid on the battery, not that there was a lot of thanks from the Vice-admiral. Spencer-White had gone back to the Flagship, and Courtenay, distrustful to the last, sent Martin Stevens with his report to give it to the Flag-Captain and thus make sure it found its way to Cairns without being tampered with. Quite what the Flag-Captain thought of it he did not know. He cared not.

Weeks dragged into months. Everyone knew the Island could not hold out any longer, and then mercifully it was over. The French soldiers on the Island capitulated and the siege was over. Cairns was notified as to the surrender on 4th September, and immediately decided he would return with his Squadron to Gibraltar. He presumed that after that he would be ordered home. Courtenay in the meantime was fretting over news from home. He had not received any letters from Jessica or his family despite a courier brig appearing off the Island on many occasions during the siege.

Cairns last act was to order that *Pegasus* enter the harbour of Valletta and remain there until relieved. Then he ordered the rest of the Squadron to set sail.

Cairns' actions were not however to have much effect. Barely had the Squadron been lost to sight over the horizon when a ship from Troubridge's Squadron dropped anchor in the harbour. At the same time a brig entered. A bare two hours later the brig left and Courtenay had a visit from the Captain of the other 74. He was a pleasant man named Hudson.

"I thought your Admiral had taken himself off the minute he found the Frogs had surrendered, Sir Giles?"

"So he did. He ordered my ship into the harbour until relieved."

"I see. Did something wrong did you, to incur such displeasure?"

"You could say that."

"H'mm. I have sent a letter to Captain Troubridge. He is now the senior officer in these waters and I suspect he will order me to relieve you. We will all be going soon anyway. There will be a new Squadron out here shortly. My ship could do with a scrape,

I can tell you. The weed on her bottom must be about twenty feet long by now!" He had lifted a glass of claret, looked at it keenly, smiled at Courtenay, and drunk it in one gulp.

"That hit the spot. Time for another my dear fellah?"

Within a few days the brig was back and Courtenay had his orders relieving him and ordering that he return to his Squadron if possible, but otherwise to report to the Admiral at Gibraltar.

As *Pegasus* slowly approached her anchorage Courtenay noted the Squadron was there, but only just. Clearly, preparations were being made to up-anchor.

"Standby to let go the anchor Mr Davies," he ordered automatically. The guard boat with the blue flag was in place and the anchor went down. The sails quickly disappeared and were furled up with their gaskets as neatly as if they were on review at Spithead.

Courtenay turned seeking out Trafford, but he was already down on the boat tier seeing to the removal of the lashings holding the barge in place, as a preparatory to hoisting the same out. Kingston appeared with his dress coat and best hat. Courtenay smiled his thanks. Half an hour later he was with the Port Admiral.

"Ah, Sir Giles. I did not expect to see you just yet. Your Admiral told me he had left your ship guarding Malta!" Vice-admiral Lord Porterfield was plump but gave the appearance of being quite agile. He had a heavily wrinkled face which was burnt the colour of teak, thereby showing many years of service in the tropics.

"That is so My Lord. Captain Troubridge relieved me by ordering one of his ships to take over."

"I see. Well, your Squadron is about to leave as you can see. Did Lord Cairns not send for you?"

"No sir. I will return to my ship and seek to follow him but I am in rather dire need of supplies. There was little on Malta for the people who live there let alone the ships."

Porterfield thought for a moment. "I am sure in the circumstances your Admiral would understand Sir Giles. I will direct you remain here until you have been able to re-provision."

"I am grateful to you my Lord. Has there been any activity around the Spanish coast recently?"

"Not a lot. However, I think something is being planned soon. That is where your Squadron is being sent and I will give you the details so that you may follow. I am sure your Admiral would appreciate the presence of another 74."

"My Lord, I am a little concerned there has been no mail for my ship for some time. I know the Courier brigs have been arriving safely but there has been nothing for my ship." He saw Lord Porterfield raise any eyebrow.

"That is odd. The other day one of my aides found some bags of mail. They were all for your ship. I was going to arrange to send them on but it is just as well I did not. One moment Captain." He walked to his desk and picked up and rang a small bell. A door opened immediately and an immaculate Flag-Lieutenant appeared.

"Have you those mail bags for *Pegasus?*"

"Yes my Lord. I have them here."

"Good. Give them to Sir Giles immediately."

Courtenay stood up. "I am grateful sir. My wife is expecting our first child, and in fact should have had it by now, and I have not had any news for some time."

Porterfield smiled. "Yes, it is very worrying is it not? I was away when my wife had our first. Still-born. The next time, I was lucky enough to be there! I wish her well Sir Giles."

Courtenay was soon back aboard *Pegasus,* with the bags of mail. Fenwick's eyebrows nearly went into his hairline when he saw them.

"And where, may I ask sir, did they appear from?"

"No idea James. The Admiral's staff 'found them'. If I were a betting man I would say the Admiral withheld the mail and when they got back to Gibraltar had his nephew dump them somewhere they would be found."

"By God sir, that is going too far! That is keeping other people out of their mail as well!"

"Do you think he cares James? Of course not. Now get the mail sorted, for the mens' sake."

"I will let you have anything for you immediately sir."

Courtenay clutched Fenwick's arm. "See to the lads first."

Eventually, Trafford returned to the cabin holding a small number of letters. One was from Courtenay's parents, the rest were from Jessica. Trafford stood back, smiling, as he saw his Captain snatch up a paper knife and slit open the first letter. He read it in silence.

"A son. A *son,* Alex! By God, I have a son!"

"And what about Miss Jessica sir. Is she......."

"Miss Jessica is fine Alex. She assures me all went well, she is in rude health and she wants me to not worry about her or the baby as they are both well cared for."

"That's just great sir. When...?"

"July. My God Alex, my son is already three months old! I should be there with her!"

"She knows you want to be sir. She also knows you have a job to do."

Courtenay looked at him. "Yes, yes, but, well, I should have been there!"

"Mind if I pass the word sir? I mean, word soon got around about her ladyship and some of the men have met her if you recall?"

"Yes of course. Owen Davies met her when we were in *Aphrodite.* I agree. She would want them to know. Tell them she is well and being cared for."

"Er, has she named the baby, like, Sir Giles?"

"What, oh not in this letter. I will have to read the others!"

He sat down on the stern seat with the unopened letters in front of him, re-reading the one he had opened.

At dawn the following day, *Pegasus,* under topsails and jibs moved slowly away from the anchorage and turned her beakhead to the west. The remainder of the Squadron had already been ordered to join the flag of Vice-admiral Sir Harvey Plummer off Ferrol. Courtenay recalled reading in his reports that Sir Edward Pellew had been active in the Bay of Biscay with his Squadron and although ships were obviously gathering for a purpose it seemed more were required. It was obvious to Courtenay that their Squadron needed to be going home. One or two of the ships needed the attention of the dockyard, including *Suffolk,* the Flagship, and it was to be doubted how much longer they could be of assistance. Also, he was anxious to get home and make sure Jessica and their son were safe and well. Jessica had named their son Edward. Courtenay had nodded his head when he read that letter. An excellent choice.

As they changed course and headed along the coast of Portugal towards the Bay of Playa de Dominos, Courtenay could not help but think that home was so near yet so far. From where they were due to meet the rest of the Squadron, to Plymouth or Portsmouth would not take long with a fair wind.

As the mainmast lookout peeled down that he had the gathering ships in sight, Courtenay sprang into the lee ratlines with his glass levelled.

Fenwick came and stood next to him.

"Quite a gathering James. Several liners, more frigates than I have seen together in one place for many a long time and God knows how many other craft." He looked again "And a number of transports."

"Transports sir? That means some kind of landing, I would imagine."

McBride was calling. "From Flag sir. Making our number. *Captain to repair on board when convenient"*

"Very well. Acknowledge if you please. Call away my barge James."

"Aye aye sir."

"Strange thing James. There is no sign of the rest of our Squadron!"

"What?" James Fenwick went to the side and raised his own glass. "Damme sir, but you are right! Where the devil has Cairns got to?"

"I would imagine that I will soon have the answer to that question James!" He watched with an approving eye as Trafford supervised the hoisting out of the barge, and as it went over the side, the barge crew appeared in their matching shirts.

Two hours later he was back. He ran lightly up the gangway ladder from the entry port and walked under the poop to his cabin. Fenwick followed him. There were curious stares from the Officer of the Watch and his Midshipman assistant. In time they would all find out what they were doing. Once in his cabin, Courtenay discarded his hat and slumped down in his chair, throwing a sealed packet onto the desk. He looked up and saw Fenwick watching.

"Sit you down James. Orders. It seems the ships are gathered here for the purposes of aiding an attack on the shores of the bay, to destroy the defences in the harbour, and to enable us to get at some Spanish ships which are hiding in Ferrol. There is a big first-rate of 112 guns lying there, with a smaller 96 and some 74s. If the harbour defences can be destroyed we can attack them with impunity. The transports have a large body of troops ready to disembark. With the soldiers, there will be a detachment of Marines and some blue-jackets."

Kingston appeared with some coffee and Trafford came silently into the cabin after seeing to the replacement of the barge on the boat tier.

"And what of our Squadron sir? Did the Admiral not come here?" asked James, sipping his coffee.

"Oh yes James, the Squadron arrived. It seems that Cairns made the Vice-admiral here, and who is marginally junior, go to him and told him that none of his ships were fit for the duty, and that they all had to return to home waters for repairs to be carried out. Plummer had little chance to refuse. However before he left, Cairns told the Admiral that we would be coming along and that we were in far better condition and could doubtless supply any number of Marines and sailors."

"My God what a confounded nerve!"

Courtenay smiled gently. "Exactly, but what we have come to expect from this man. Plummer is a man unfortunately without much imagination or foresight. He has taken what Cairns said at face value and has decided we will provide all our Marines and one hundred sailors. The idea is to land along the bay, scale the Heights and take control of the same, which will then give us a good position over the harbour. Our men will provide the scaling ladders and help to drag the field-pieces which will also be landed up the Heights. We will use the Marines to protect our men. I will take command, with Captain Connell as usual with his Marines." He stopped and looked up. " I can see again that you have that disapproving look on your face, James!"

"Have you thought sir, that this might be just another ploy to cause you harm? For all we know Vice-admiral Plummer is a friend of Cairns'!"

"Rest easy James. He is not. He was very angry that our Squadron was withdrawn for what he thought to be spurious reasons, but Cairns is senior. He needs some of our fighting jacks to help the soldiers. I assured him he will get them!" He stopped and looked at the chart he had unrolled. "Ask Mr Davies to come aft James. Never fear. All will be well. I will just be going ashore to stretch my legs with the lads, that is all!"

Fenwick's shoulders sagged. "If you say so sir, but I am very unhappy. I should go."

"And what if something should happen James? I will not then have a Senior on whom I can rely to take command of the ship to get her home. No, your place is here. You will get your chance of command, do not worry. It does not depend, in my view, on your continually placing your head where it will be in mortal danger of becoming separated from your shoulders!"

Fenwick grinned. " Not sure that I actually want it sir!"

"Stuff and nonsense. You will want it when the chance arrives, rest assured. Now, if you would pass the word for the Master?"

The barge grounded on the soft sand of the shoreline at the dead of night. All around more boats were also beaching. Marines sprung over the gunwales of the barge and sprinted up the beach to fan out in a picket line whilst the rest of the boats came inshore. There were Marines from other ships as well, but each detachment had been detailed to a particular part of the landing force. Courtenay's men had drawn a regiment from the 121st Foot, complete with their Colonel who was the senior officer ashore.

Lieutenant-Colonel James Fitzroy Rosemalecocq was a tall man of commanding presence and Courtenay was not in the slightest surprised he had been given command of all the soldiers. He was that kind of man. He had been rowed ashore at the same time as Courtenay, and he now squelched along the sand, drawn sword in one hand, the other resting on a pistol butt.

"Ah, there you are Sir Giles. All your men here?"

"Good morning sir. My Marines are at the top of the beach in a picket line. Most of my men are here and the rest are arriving now. We will be ready to move out shortly."

"Good. Marvellous. Well done. I will go along the beach and make sure everyone else is ready as well. I will send my runner to let you know when to move. Clear?"

"Yes sir."

"Your men will go ahead with your Marines as cover and start getting the ladders up. The field pieces will be here soon. Can your men get them up the heights?"

"I believe so sir."

"Good. Until later then Sir Giles!" He strode away with two orderlies half-running to keep up with him.

It took a few hours for all the men to get ashore. Roosmalecocq had five thousand troops with him as well as Marines from the ships and some of their seamen. Courtenay was on the left flank of the main body of men and the Colonel sent a runner along just before dawn to let him know that he could start moving his men up. Some of his men loped past him with field piece wheels over their shoulders, climbing to the top of the beach and then the slight slope which led to the higher ridge slightly to their right and in front of them. That was where the Colonel wanted to place the main part of his force. The Marines were already moving up towards the bottom of the ridge, and so were some of the *Pegasus'* crew with their scaling ladders, which would be needed to overcome some of the climb. Sheer legs would have to be constructed to lift the field pieces, although the wheels could easily be hoisted.

As light began to flood the sky Courtenay looked around a little anxiously. It had all taken far too long. They should really have been at the foot of the ridge by now, out of sight, and where they could move the artillery up without detection. He fully expected to hear shots but there were none. He marched among his men, Trafford next to him and Midshipman Smythe behind him. Surprisingly, they reached their objective by mid-morning without any problems.

Captain Connell was waiting to greet him.

"Marines in place sir. They will be able to cover us in respect of any unwelcome visitors. May I ask sir, how many men the Spanish have here?"

"Of course you may Captain. The Colonel is told that there are about 5000." Connell pursed his lips.

"About the same number we have sir, and we are fighting on their ground. Good job the Marines are here to make up the difference!"

Courtenay smiled. "As you say Captain. The Colonel obviously has his men over to the right. Our job is to hold the flank. He intends to entice the Dons out, destroy them, and in that way leave the way clear for our ships to destroy whatever is in the harbour. We will then apparently withdraw."

Connell scratched the side of his rather large nose. "Seems like a sledgehammer to crack a nut sir but I suppose we will endure!"

Courtenay looked at him for a moment. "You sound like Nicholas Strathmore!"

Connell smiled. "I shall take that as a compliment sir. He is a fine officer and a good friend"

"I think all you Marines are the same!"

Connell grinned and touched his hat before following his Sergeant.

"Mad as hatters sir, all on 'em!" muttered Trafford, but he was smiling.

Courtenay was about to open his mouth when the first shots were heard. The men were working erecting hoists and attaching ropes to the field pieces which led to the sheer legs which were on top of the ridge and froze for a moment but Henry Oates, the Boatswain was there, cursing at them and yelling.

"Who told you dozy lot you could stop work? Ain't you 'eard gunfire before?"

There were more shots but the work lifting the guns to the ridge continued. The edge of the ridge nearest Courtenay's men ran steeply down towards a gully and then opened out into more of a plain between two rows of hills. It was not that wide but not an easy place to defend. Courtenay strode down the gully and looked out over the plain. There were rocks strewn across the landscape and various fallen trees.

"Alex, ask Mr Oates to join us if you will."

Oates was there in an instant.

"Mr Oates. How is the lifting of the guns proceeding?"

"Fine, sir. Them Army lads have made some good positions for 'em, and they'll be quite well 'idden."

"Good. Get some of our men and start moving those fallen trees across the end of the open space there. Use those rocks as part of the breastworks you will make."

"Right sir."

Connell came up. Courtenay told him what he had in mind. "Good idea sir. Them Dons will probably try and slip some men down here to outflank the Colonel's position. What do you have in mind?"

"We draw them in as close as possible. The sailors will be out of sight behind those boulders and the trees. Your men will of course be on show. I want them fairly close, because after they have fired a volley and they are reloading my lads will jump them. That will give your lads a chance to reload and come in behind us. It does however, depend upon how many there are!"

Connell nodded seriously. "It most certainly does sir!"

By the middle of the afternoon, Colonel Roosmalecocq had his men in place and Spanish troops could be seen forming up just below the ridge. The Colonel had the commanding position and although the ridge was steep on the rear slope the climb was gentler on the other side. Courtenay was supervising his men creating the breastworks when more sustained firing could be heard. One of the Colonel's runners arrived red-faced and trying to get his breath.

"Colonel's compliments sir, and are your men in position guarding the flank?"

"Tell him yes. I am just finishing the defensive position and we will move into it within the hour." The runner vanished.

Connell marched up. "All ready sir. Looks pretty good, actually!"

Fallen tree trunks joined several large rocks together and although Connell had his Marines drawn up as if on parade on one side, the sailors under Oates' leadership were moving silently into their positions. Courtenay eyed the position, then deliberately strolled down to it, climbed over a trunk and strode out onto the plain. Trafford followed warily, hand on his pistol. All was quiet. They continued to walk out for a while as if taking a stroll then turned and walked back. Courtenay was pleased to note he could not see any of his blue jackets at all.

Back behind the position, Courtenay smiled at Connell. "Excellent. One hundred yards out, and I could not see a man."

All was quiet for the rest of the day and provisions arrived from the beach. Fires were lit, food cooked, and a close watch kept for any enemy infiltration during darkness.

Courtenay stretched out on a blanket and tried to sleep but he could not. When he did finally fall into a doze it was almost dawn. The Third Lieutenant, Burton, had come ashore during the late afternoon with some more men. He was asleep, hat covering his eyes as the first trays of dawn started to steal over the eastern range of hills. Courtenay sat up rubbing his eyes. Trafford held out a mug of coffee. Courtenay nodded to the sleeping officer.

"I wish I could sleep like that Alex!"

"Not a care in the world Cap'n!" said Trafford quietly.

"Is that right Trafford?' asked Burton, his eyes still hidden. "Is there any more of that coffee I can smell?"

Trafford grinned. "Aye sir."

Burton pushed the hat away and looked at his Captain. "What now, sir?"

"We wait, Mr Burton. Our job is to guard the flanks whilst the Colonel draws out the Spanish troops and destroys them. He does not want any unpleasant surprises whilst he is doing so!"

"I see sir." He took a mug of coffee. He smelt it, raised one eyebrow at Trafford and drank with appreciation. It was half-full with rum. "If you will forgive me sir, I will go and make sure our defences are still in order."

"Take off your uniform coat Mr Burton. You won't look like a Naval officer then, and give the vapours to any Don with a glass looking at the defences and only seeing what to him look like soldiers."

"Yes sir."

Almost promptly at 8am there was a heavy burst of firing from the ridge and thereafter almost continual volleys for nearly an hour. The Colonel was not worried about ammunition. More supplies had been landed during the night and brought up to the positions. Courtenay and Trafford ran down to the breastworks and sat down behind one of the tree trunks. A quick look showed him everyone was in place. Some had muskets, others cutlasses or tomahawks and some had pikes. Courtenay took out his sword and laid it on the ground then checked each of his two pistols. One went back in his belt, the other was put on the ground with his sword.

"Listen lads!" he called quietly along his line of men. "We will remain hidden here for a while in case the Spaniards try to outflank the Colonel. If they do, we will allow them to get close. The Marines will give them a volley. They will reply and then whilst they are reloading we will give them a charge. Plenty of screams and curses lads. If you can't kill 'em, frighten them to death!" There were smiles and nudges and grins.

More firing from the ridge, and more yelling. The firing faded away and a runner slipped in beside Courtenay.

"We're beating them off sir! Colonel says he has been told about a number of Spanish troops moving off in your direction sir. Says to watch your front."

"We are ready." replied Courtenay.

They waited for another hour. The men all had a plentiful supply of water, which was just as well as it was very hot. He allowed the men to sleep, every other man awake and keeping watch. There was renewed firing from the rear of the ridge then Trafford moved slightly and whispered, "They're comin' Sir Giles."

Courtenay twisted round and peered through a gap between the trunk and a boulder. Then he could hear the tramp of marching feet. He turned back. He need not have worried about the Marines. Connell had them standing in two smart lines behind the defences, one rank standing and the other kneeling. He had seen them as well. Courtenay looked along the line of his men, all well-hidden.

"Stand-to lads!" All his men turned slowly and prepared their weapons. The Spanish troops were now in sight, marching in tight formation along the dusty road. Their officers saw the Marines. There were hundreds of the Spanish soldiers, a handful of Marines. Trafford looked at Courtenay and raised an eyebrow. He said nothing. Courtenay cocked his pistol and waited as the tramping feet grew closer.

NINE

Connell, at the side of his double row of Marines, watched the Spanish troops. They gradually grew closer and closer until there was a short command and they stopped.

"Ready Marines!" barked Connell. He had no intention of allowing the Spaniards to get in the first volleys. He wanted to hit them first so that at least in the front ranks there would be many casualties.

"Take aim! Make every shot count, my lads!" He waited for a moment, then as he saw the Spanish soldiers start to raise their muskets, *"Fire!"* A volley blasted out catching the Spaniards by surprise. Holes were torn in the front ranks and there was confusion as men dropped screaming. There was the blast of return fire but nary a Marine was hit, because the moment they had fired, in accordance with Connell's earlier orders they dropped to the ground. There was a ragged volley but the musket balls simply hit thin air.

Courtenay was up before the sound of the volley had gone. Connell was already ordering his men to reload but Courtenay was vaulting over the tree trunk, and raising his sword, turned towards the Spaniards, still in a certain amount of confusion.

"Follow me lads! At 'em, *Pegasus!* " His men surged out of their hiding places after him as they charged towards the enemy. Connell led his men forward, reloading

171

complete, ready to pour in more volleys if necessary. In the meantime Courtenay was only a bare few yards from the Spanish. Some of them had reloaded and there were one or two shots, but before any effective amount of muskets were ready *Pegasus's* men charged into the packed ranks.

Courtenay slashed at a fancily dressed officer who tried to defend himself with an elegant sword but was hindered by the press of men. Courtenay slashed him across the stomach, watched briefly as blood splashed down in his breeches and then turned to the next man. His sword took him through the chest and he had to tug the keen blade free from the screaming soldier. Trafford was right next to him pushing away a man he had cut across the shoulder before using his cutlass hilt to hit another soldier across the jaw. A slash across his exposed neck and blood fountained across the short grass under their feet.

All around there were screams and shouting. Then the Marines waded into the fray and the Spaniards started to break. Some started to run away, throwing down their weapons, equipment, anything which would enable them to run faster. Courtenay turned to see why and his eyes lighted in a large number of British Redcoats running out of the gulley towards them.

His men stared around in disbelief as the Spanish cut and run, leaving dead and dying all around. Courtenay looked on as a Spanish officer stopped trying to prevent his men running and lifted his hat in a mock salute preparatory to turning away and joining his men, or so Courtenay and Trafford thought. Even Connell was looking elsewhere with a huge grin on his face.

Courtenay looked away from the Spaniard for a moment and when he looked back he saw the man had raised a pistol, and just as he witnessed this the man fired. Courtenay felt as if a horse had kicked him in the side and looked down as blood pumped out of the wound and down his dirty breeches. Then the pain hit him, he felt ground beneath his knees and then there was nothing.

"Cap'n!" called Trafford as he saw Courtenay stagger and then go down to his knees. "Jesus, he's been hit!" Connell turned round, saw everything, and the Spanish officer turning away with a sneer on his face and start to run to catch his men. He snatched a musket from one of his men, took very careful aim and fired. He first shot just missed but a Marine tossed him a second musket and this time the ball hit the fleeing officer squarely between the shoulder blades. He collapsed into the dirt and did not move.

Trafford was turning Courtenay over. "Oh God, he's been shot in the side."

Connell was there again. Burton came running over with a lot of *Pegasus's* men behind him. "Move back lads, don't crowd!" he ordered. Connell bent down. He turned to Trafford.

"Looks as if the ball went straight through, Trafford. There's blood on his back as well. Let us hope that is the case. We need to get him some help, *now!*"

"Where sir?" said Trafford ."The Surgeon is on the ship. The army have one but I daresay he is more involved with his own men right now!"

A strange officer appeared. "That was a damn fine show, what! Drove the Spaniards mad with fear! My God....what is wrong?"

Connell stood. "Who are you sir?"

"Captain Walters, 121st Foot."

"Have you a surgeon?"

"Well of course we have, what do you think we...."

"Can you send for him. Our Captain has been wounded."

"Immediately." The man beckoned to his orderly.

Connell kneeled on the ground again. Trafford had ripped off Courtenay's shirt and was trying to stem the flow of blood.

It seemed an age before the Surgeon came, but in reality he came very quickly. He bent to his task and after binding the wound firmly, stood up.

"I can't be certain here, but since there appears to be both an entry and an exit wound I think the ball must have gone straight through. Trouble is we don't know what damage it may have done on the way, and whether there is any cloth caught in the wound which might breed infection."

"Can we move him sir?" asked Trafford.

"Yes, carefully. Rig a litter. Where will you take him? All our men are on the move. Our job is done, but in any event I have to get back to the Colonel. He has been wounded and I doubt he will last the hour."

"We'll get him back to the ship sir"

"Back to the ship? He'll never make it!"

Trafford stood up, his face determined. "Oh yes he will sir. We look after our own." He turned to some of the men. "Rig a litter lads. We'll take it in turns to carry it. We'll get along faster that way. We are going back to the ship!"

Even after they had returned to the *Pegasus,* to be met by a stunned Fenwick and crew at the entry port, Trafford could not coherently recall how they had managed it so quickly. They had rigged a litter, placed Courtenay carefully on it with his uniform coat folded as a pillow, and they had double-timed all the way down the ridge and down the slope to the beach. They had taken it in turns so that they could keep up the pace Trafford set and even some of the Marines had to run to keep up with them. They had hurriedly signalled for a boat to be sent and then with slings rigged to the litter, Courtenay had been lifted up the side of his ship. He had been dimly aware of something happening as the litter had hit the tumblehome and he had stirred from his unconsciousness. He had partly opened his eyes but the pain had been intense and he had lapsed back into darkness before the litter was lowered gently to the decking. Then he had been hurried below to the Orlop deck where the Surgeon was waiting.

O'Keefe had the looks of a renegade Irishman but he was far from that. He was of gentle tone and manner and he never touched a drop of hard drink.

Trafford thought of all this as he sat in the Cabin with a large tot of rum in his hand. Fenwick standing over him anxiously.

"What happened Trafford?"

"We had just seen off a lot of Spanish soldiers sir. The Cap'n, well he planned to jump them when they were reloading and we did it beautifully." He stopped and chuckled. "He said he wanted the lads to go in screaming and shouting, and by God so they did. They must have scared the Dons half to death before we even got to grips! We were in among 'em before they knew what had hit 'em. Captain Connell and his Marines joined in and then some Redcoats came chasing out of the gully so the Dons knew it was all up and ran for it. One Spanish officer gave the Cap'n a mock salute, then before we knew it lifted a pistol he was hiding and shot him!"

"What! What happened to the Spanish officer?"

"Dead. Captain Connell got him right between the shoulder blades." He emptied his glass. Kingston replaced it. Fenwick strode back and forth across the canvas flooring.

"You say you were told the Army's job was done?"

"Aye sir. We found out on the way down that them Redcoats shattered the Spaniards and they all turned and ran, them that was alive of course. There is nothing left now between those ships in Ferrol, and the Squadron!"

"Good. I will send a signal to the Flagship asking if we may be released to join the rest of our Squadron. We must get Sir Giles home!"

"Aye sir. Do you think the Admiral will agree?"

"We were only loaned to him Trafford, not transferred to his Squadron. If it comes to it I shall explain why! Now get off to the Orlop and find out what is happening, eh?"

"Aye sir. Thanks."

Trafford moved through the decks, hardly noticing the concerned faces of the watch below as they sat at their mess tables. One, a seasoned campaigner, reached out and took Trafford's arm. "What happened Cox?"

"Took a pistol ball in the side. Army Surgeon reckoned it 'ad gone straight through but it did God knows what damage! "

"Cap'n'll pull through Cox, 'e's a strong'un right enough!"

Trafford found himself on the Orlop. There was no sign of Courtenay. The door of the sick-bay opened and O'Keefe stood framed in the opening.

"Wondered when you would be down Trafford. I've got the Captain in here. Now tell me exactly what happened to Sir Giles."

Trafford recounted the events.

"I see. He was lucky that the ball went straight through. I can't see any material in the wound but that is not to say there isn't. All I am saying at the present is that I couldn't find any. I suppose he wasn't wearing a clean shirt by any chance?" A clean shirt could cut down the chances of infection. "Judging by the look of the one I took off, I would guess not!"

"No, sir. How is he?"

"Well I think the ball missed everything important, but I am worried about infection so I will keep him in here for now. Later we may move him to the Cabin. Loss of blood is important."

"He lost quite a bit sir, while we were trying to patch him up."

"Very well."

"Can I see him?"

"He is still unconscious at the present, which is just as well. He will be in a lot of pain when he comes around. You may go and sit with him for a while if you wish?"

"Thank you sir."

Up on the broad quarterdeck, Fenwick was staring unseeing at the Flagship.

McBride turned and said quietly. "Flagship is signalling sir. *You may proceed when ready. Our thanks for your assistance*".

"Very well Mr McBride. Acknowledge. Mr Davies, standby to up hook and get under way if you please!"

"Aye aye, sir. May I ask how the Captain is?"

"You may Owen, but I do not know at the present. Ah, here is Trafford. I am sure he will know."

Trafford walked slowly over to the weather nettings and breathed in deeply. He felt the wind coming in over the quarter and heard the men on the capstan pulling the ship up to its anchor. He turned and saw the others.

"Trafford? Is he....?"

"He is all right at the moment sir. The Surgeon says it seems nothin' vital was struck, but he is worried about the chance of infection. We will have to wait and see sir."

"Very well Trafford. Go below. You have no duties at present. Keep us informed if you will?" Davies, one eye on the men swarming aloft to loose the sails, crossed the deck and grasped Trafford's arm.

"When he wakes up you be sure and tell him we are all waiting up here for him to come back, you hear that?"

"Aye Master, I hear you!"

Trafford walked slowly beneath the poop.

James Fenwick drove the *Pegasus* like he never thought he would be able to drive such a large ship. The winds as ever were perverse, and in the end it took over a week of tacking back and forth generally getting not very far, before they finally reached Plymouth. In the time it took to get the ship from the coast of north-west Spain to home, Fenwick hardly left the quarterdeck for more than an hour or so at a time. The other officers kept their watches, and Owen Davies on more than one occasion cast a worried look in the direction of the First-Lieutenant. Fenwick would stand for many hours on the deck making sure every sail was drawing to perfect. He had even ordered Pritchard, the Purser, to check to make sure they were taking stores from the right holds so that the trim of the ship would not be affected.

Courtenay had been transferred from the sickbay to his Cabin. There was always someone with him. The Surgeon came and went, changing dressings, checking the wound for infection. He was looking at the wound one day with greater concern than usual and Trafford noticed.

"Is there something wrong sir?"

"I am not sure Trafford. Can you hold that lantern a little closer?" Trafford moved closer. Courtenay had regained consciousness a day or so ago, but he was drifting in and out of it with the pain, and when he was awake he was hardly aware of it. When he was awake, he was aware of someone holding his hand or arm. O'Keefe straightened eventually. "I have a feeling there is some infection there. It may be a piece of cloth which was pushed in deep and which is working its way closer to the surface. It happens. I think I should investigate. Would you pass the word for Stringer to bring my instruments?" Stringer was his assistant. Trafford stumbled out of the sleeping space. He knew what this would mean. The Surgeon would have to probe the wound to see if he could find anything.

With O'Keefe ready, Trafford and Kingston turned Courtenay onto one side so that the Doctor could see both entry and exit wounds. Courtenay moaned with the pain of being moved and his eyes flickered open. O'Keefe signalled that he should be laid back, and as he did so he saw Courtenay's eyes fixed on his face, more alive than they had been for the last two days or so.

"I am glad to see you are with us again sir."

Courtenay opened his mouth to speak, but it was little more than a croak. "How long have I been like this Mr O'Keefe, and what happened?"

"You were shot with a pistol ball and it went through your side. It does not appear to have struck anything important and the exit would is satisfactory, but I think there is some cloth in the entry wound and I think you have started some infection. I need to probe the wound sir, with your permission."

Courtenay felt his hand being gripped. He looked up and saw James Fenwick. "My God James, you look as if you haven't slept for days!" He dropped back exhausted. He looked at O'Keefe firmly. "You will do what you have to Mr O'Keefe."

Trafford and Stringer bent over Courtenay to hold him firmly as the Surgeon prepared his instruments. Courtenay tensed and then felt like screaming as he felt the probe sliding into the wound like fire. He didn't know how he managed not to utter a sound, it was just pride. It felt like hours, the fire spreading through his body in waves but then the pain subsided and he looked up, his body now covered in sweat, to see O'Keefe grinning.

"Found it sir!" He held up a piece of blood-covered cloth. "Right sir, if you will bear with me whilst I apply some stitches and then we will have a fresh bandage."

"How long Mr O'Keefe," Courtenay said through gritted teeth, "will it take for me to recover?"

"I wouldn't like to say sir. If you take plenty of rest, hopefully not too long but you have been seriously wounded and you have lost a lot of blood."

Courtenay looked at Fenwick. "You look as if you could do with some sleep. Where are we James?"

"Not far from Plymouth sir. Should be there in the morning. We closed with a home-bound courier brig yesterday and I sent a message ahead for the Port Admiral and Lady Courtenay."

Courtenay managed a smile. "Not much of a home-coming but at least I appear to be in one piece!" He nodded to O'Keefe. "Thank you Mr O'Keefe."

"Perhaps Kingston could make you some soup sir. It will do you good."

Courtenay looked round at Trafford. "Thank you too, Alex. I was waking up from time to time although everything was a blur, but I felt you were there."

Trafford grinned. "That I was sir, that I was. Me and Mr Fenwick, and Kingston."

Courtenay drifted off into sleep again.

O'Keefe turned to Fenwick. "Why don't you get some sleep James? Who is on deck?"

"Martin Stevens and Owen Davies."

"Well then. The ship is in safe hands. They will need you in the morning fresh and awake."

Fenwick yawned and smiled. "Perhaps you are right." He knew though that he would get precious little sleep during the night.

In the grey misty dawn, *Pegasus* approached Plymouth Sound. There were several men o'war at anchor and as Fenwick completed a look around the anchorage with his glass he could see some more ships in the Hamoaze.

"Plenty of shipping Mr Davies." he commented to the Sailing Master. "Get the courses off her then, and get the anchor party ready."

The maindeck was a hive of activity as men bustled back and forth and topmen sped up the ratlines in response to the Boson's pipe to take in the sails. The ship edged into the Sound under topsails, and Fenwick watched as the usual guard boat stopped near two other 74s with the blue flag showing.

"There is our anchorage. H'mm. Not too bad. Fairly close to the shore. Still a long swim though. Very well Mr Davies, standby to anchor."

The ship moved very slowly up to her anchorage, her sails disappearing swiftly and neatly, the men only too well aware of the fact that the Port Admiral would have his telescope on them judging their performance.

With the anchor secure Fenwick walked beneath the poop and entered the Cabin. He walked into the sleeping space. Courtenay was propped up with some pillows, looking pale and bathed in sweat, even though outside it was very chilly.

"At anchor sir." Fenwick formally reported.

"Well done James," Courtenay said slowly. "Now if Trafford and Kingston can help me get dressed, somehow I am going to get down the side of the ship and go ashore. I had best report to the Port Admiral."

"With all due respect sir, you are not fit enough to do that. I will report to him. I have sent word ahead anyway and I am sure when we get to the quayside we will find a comfortable coach waiting for you. You need to be at home sir, in the warm with Miss J……Lady Courtenay caring for you."

Courtenay managed a smile. "Bloody hell Mr Fenwick, you sound like a Post-captain already!" Fenwick smiled back but he knew only too well what his Captain was going to try to do. He would not leave his ship in a bosun's chair. He would try to climb down the side into his barge if the effort killed him.

"Right then, come on you two, topsails and jib!"

Slowly, they managed to get Courtenay dressed as he sat on the edge of his cot. Supported by them he stood up, and nearly fell over. He held onto the cot with one hand whilst Kingston slipped his uniform coat on. Trafford stood by with his cloak. Fenwick could see that Courtenay was testing himself to see if he could stand. After a few moments he managed a couple of steps. The bandage around his waist and chest was tight but seemed to be containing the pain. He tried a couple of steps but nearly fell again as the ship moved slightly.

"Rough out there James?"

"Bit of a lop sir. Here, take my arm if you will. Try a few more steps?"

Courtenay held onto Fenwick's arm and they ventured out into the cabin itself. Courtenay felt a semblance of strength returning to his limbs but he wondered how he was going to get down into his barge. He banished that thought from his mind.

"That's better James. Legs are beginning to work again."

"I will go and see to the barge Sir Giles." said Trafford, and flashing a concerned look at Fenwick, left the cabin.

A few moments later Fenwick and Courtenay stood at the door leading out onto the broad quarterdeck, now almost deserted. Courtenay let go of Fenwick's arm and stepped out onto the deck. He walked very slowly, his right arm close to his body. There were many men going about their tasks on the yardarms, in the ratlines, and on the maindeck. Very slowly, he worked his way down the ladder to the entry port where the side party was drawn up. The line of Marines was there ready and all the men working suddenly stopped to watch their Captain.

"The ship is yours James. If you can get away, come and see me to let me know how things are going?" Fenwick smiled and nodded.

Accompanied by the slap of hands on musket butts and the twittering of pipes, Courtenay touched his hat to the quarterdeck and to the side-party, turned and went through the port. As his head disappeared from view men swarmed into the ratlines. It

183

was as well they could not see his face. He was racked with pain, his face sweating as if it was the tropics rather than a cold day in Plymouth Sound, and he wondered blindly how long he was going to be able to hold onto the guide ropes.

Trafford, watching from the barge, almost started up the wooden steps but he saw his Captain pause for just a moment as if gathering his strength again, and then slowly work his way down. He still managed to time it right so that as a swell lifted the barge slightly he stepped into it. He sank into the sternsheets.

Trafford breathed a sigh of relief. "Shove off there! Out oars! Give way together! Put your backs into it lads!"

As the barge sidled away, the oars went down into the water and as the stroke picked up and Trafford moved the tiller to curve the boat away from the ship's side there was a thunderous cheer from the crew of the *Pegasus*. Courtenay's head came up in surprise. Sweating hard, he managed to stand up and turn to look at his ship. He lifted his hat and waved briefly to his men before allowing Trafford to help him sit back down again. Trafford draped Courtenay's boat cloak around him to try and ward off the cold.

"Won't be long sir. Soon be home."

At the quayside, Courtenay managed to climb out of the barge but he looked up at the slime covered steps and wondered how he was going to climb them because he knew his strength had gone. Then there was a noise at the top and she was there. She had a long dark cloak wrapped around her, with a fur-lined hood, and she was looking down at him with concern. It changed to a warm smile as she saw her man and that gave him the strength to climb gingerly up the steps. Trafford was there in an instant.

"Lean on me sir, "

Courtney looked at him for a moment then nodded, and allowed his coxswain to help him up the steps. He reached the top, slick with sweat, only for Jessica to throw her arms around him as she had done at Gibraltar, and hug him to her. In the background, and through what appeared to be a mist, Courtenay could see his Father and another man he thought he recognised.

"Giles! Giles, what has happened to you?" Jessica cried.

He pushed her back to look at her, to remind himself of her beauty, managed a grim smile. "Got shot Jess. Some damned Don." His father appeared and Courtenay was able to thrust out his hand and grip that of his father.

"Let us get him into the carriage and get Giles home my dear." Courtenay senior was saying. "Trafford, can you see to the bags? Many thanks. We have arranged a room for you at the house if you wish. Have you any family to see?"

"Not really sir. That's right kind of you."

Trafford had not strayed away from Courtenay's side all this time. He helped him to the carriage and sensed what was going to happen. Jessica did not fully realise how badly her husband had been hurt and she was not prepared for his strength to suddenly go, but Trafford had been waiting. As Courtenay's knees started to give Trafford held him up, and somehow Courtenay managed to climb up into the carriage and drop back onto the leather cushions. Jessica followed, ashen-faced, and then William Courtenay. Lastly, the other man climbed in. William Courtenay turned to him.

"It is as well I asked you to accompany us Doctor."

The other man smiled and nodded, then gently pulled open Courtenay's boat cloak and opened his uniform. There was blood all over his clean white shirt. Jessica started to put her hand to her mouth but she stopped, turned to the Doctor calmly, and spoke in a firm level voice.

"Is there anything I can do to help Doctor? Is he going to be all right?"

"I suspect Lady Courtenay that this looks a lot worse than it actually is."

William Courtenay looked down at Trafford. "Why did he not use, what do you call it, a bosun's chair?"

Trafford smiled tightly. "He's the Cap'n. Sir Giles go down the side like a piece of cargo? Not on your life sir."

Courtenay senior smiled. "Very well Trafford, if you could see to the luggage then, and get up with the driver?"

Trafford touched his hat and the Doctor bent to his work.

Giles Courtenay spent the next three weeks confined to bed. The Doctor, who had known him from when he was a small boy, had flatly refused to allow him up and was supported by all members of the Courtenay family. Jessica had told her husband under no circumstances was he to get up until the Doctor said he was fit to do so, and it was not until the latter part of November that he was finally allowed up and then under strict instructions that he could go no further than to sit in front of the fire in the drawing room.

As soon as he had been settled in their bed and Jessica was certain that her husband was going to stay there, she brought their son to see him. Courtenay was not well enough to sit up and hold him but he was a determined man, and within a week he was sitting up and holding his son. Jessica would watch him, and see him mouthing the word 'Edward' over and over again.

During this time a letter arrived from Lord Crompton expressing his concern over the fact Courtenay had been so badly injured. It had been a private, rather than official letter and Crompton had not spared his feelings about the actions of Lord Cairns. He had ended the letter by wishing Courtenay a most speedy recovery and a desire to see him when he was well enough to travel. In the meantime *Pegasus* would be undergoing some minor repairs, with Fenwick in temporary command.

Eventually he was sitting in the drawing room, a rug over his knees and feeling totally ridiculous. He would often have Edward with him. The bond between father and son had formed. One morning, when the air outside was keen and frosty, Jessica walked into the drawing room with Edward only to find her Husband pacing the room, leaning only slightly on a stick.

"Giles! You should not be doing that!" she scolded.

He placed a finger on her lips and ruffled his son's hair. "Nonsense, and I won't need this damned stick much longer either! I intend to venture into the garden today Jess. The fresh air will do me a power of good. I have been cooped up in here for too long." He smiled at her. "Not that the company has not been marvellous!" She smiled back. This was the man she had fallen in love with.

Later, Courtenay walked round the garden in the freezing air with Trafford at his side. They had not seen much of each other since they arrived.

"Have you and Edward been introduced yet Alex?"

Trafford smiled broadly. "Oh aye sir, some time back. He is a fine boy. Looks just like his father!"

187

"Good. Glad you met him." They walked round for a little longer then Trafford convinced him to go back indoors.

By the time Christmas came Courtenay felt almost as good as new. His wound had healed nicely and although he had the occasional bout of pain from it, it did not trouble him. He had been for several long walks and he was regaining his strength. He had a surprise on Christmas Day in the shape of Lieutenant James Fenwick. The ship was with the Dockyard for a while to carry out the promised repairs and he had left Martin Stevens in charge. He had travelled to the small village on the outskirts of Tor Quay to visit his mother. Jessica left them alone to discuss matters and by the time Fenwick left, he had convinced his Captain that the ship was in good hands. He had looked slightly abashed as Jessica had kissed him on the cheek when he left. Courtenay had just smiled.

On New Year's Eve, Courtenay was holding Edward standing by the broad windows which looked out across the countryside. There was no snow although he knew from a walk before breakfast that it was very cold. He was thoughtful for a moment, then nodded as if he had made up his mind about something. He kissed Edward's head and turned in towards the room where Jessica was seated by a roaring log fire working on some embroidery.

"Do you think that mother and father would mind caring for Edward for a while, Jess?"

"Why, what have you in mind now Giles? I am sure they would be delighted no matter what it is."

"I feel like going for going for a ride. Perhaps only a short one but I haven't been in a saddle for a long time."

"What about your wound? It is all but healed. You do not want to do anything to put your recovery back dearest."

"The wound is healed and you know it, Jess! Time to test it with a ride. My mind is made up. Are you coming?"

Jessica dropped her embroidery onto a nearby table and jumped up.

"You try and stop me!"

"Good. I will have a word with Trafford and get three horses saddled."

A short while later Giles and Jessica Courtenay were riding slowly along a path which wound through a small copse. Behind them was Alex Trafford, looking more than a little unhappy. He could ride but not well, and hardly ever had to.

Jessica had noted both men were quite heavily armed for a short ride. Both carried a pistol, Trafford had his cutlass, and Courtenay had his own sword. Trafford had laughed shortly when Jessica had asked if there was any need for the weapons.

"Hopefully not Miss Jessica (Jessica would not have everyone calling her by her title all the time because she found it faintly ridiculous with friends) but you never knows. There are plenty o' footpads around waiting for the unwary! Best to be safe!"

They walked their horses slowly through the copse. Courtenay was happy because there had not so far been any sign of a problem from his wound although he intended to test it still further in a short while with a canter. He had suggested that they pay a visit to the house Mrs Fenwick lived in. Although officially she was still Lady Cairns she had made sure everyone locally knew her as Mrs Fenwick. James would still be there although he was due to return to the *Pegasus* shortly. Courtenay was hoping secretly they would be able to return together.

They reached the end of the copse and rode out into the open. In front of them the ground sloped down gently towards the very edge of the village, but right on the very end was the school where Mrs Fenwick taught and the house in which she lived.

Jessica was not looking at the house as they came out of the copse but she suddenly realised that her husband had brought his horse to a stop and that Trafford had trotted up beside him, peering forward. When she looked down the slope she saw the reason why. The house was clearly in view and so was the scene being enacted outside it. There were a number of men outside the house and there seemed to be a struggle ensuing. In a flash Courtenay had a smell telescope in his hand and was holding it to his eye.

"What the devil…?"

"Looks like Mr Fenwick is 'aving a spot of bother Cap'n!"

Through the glass Courtenay could see his First-Lieutenant fighting with his sword against two attackers. A third was struggling with Mrs Fenwick and a fourth was clearly trying to set light to the house. There was a whisp of smoke coming from a small porch which covered the front door.

Courtenay sized up the situation in an instant.

"Jess, stay here. Have you got that little pistol I bought you still?"

"Yes Giles, but…"

"No buts dearest. You stay here. If anyone comes anywhere near you, well you have used that pistol before so do not hesitate, but I am sure they will have their hands full with us. Come along Alex!"

They spurred their horses forward and were soon tearing down the slope at what to Alex Trafford seemed to be a breakneck speed, but even he managed to draw his cutlass. He had a quick look sideways and his Captain had his sword in his hand and was urging his horse to go even faster.

The men attacking the Fenwicks were so busy with what they were doing they did not notice Courtenay and Trafford approaching but there was suddenly a single pistol shot and that made the men look up. Courtenay also looked up, in the direction the shot had come from and saw a single horseman dressed in what appeared to be a long cloak. After that he had no time to wonder who the man was because they were on top of the attackers.

Trafford veered off after the man struggling with Mrs Fenwick while Courtenay went for the two men fighting his Senior. They were fairly proficient from what he took in, but not as good as James Fenwick, although fighting two at once was never easy. One of the attackers, a burly man with a scarred face, turned to face Courtenay waving a large sword but Courtenay was in no mood for half-measures. He simply rode his horse straight at the man. There was a scream and the man was sent flying. Courtenay held on as his horse reared, the man on the ground struggling to get out of the way but he had no chance. The horse's front hooves came down hard on the man's chest. and Courtenay heard the sound of splintering bone. There was a short scream suddenly cut off. Courtenay controlled his mount, turned it and spurred it towards the man still trying to fire the house. The man stopped what he was doing and pulled a pistol. He aimed quickly, there was a flash, Courtenay ducked and the ball went well wide. As Courtenay came up to the man, a thin stick-like person with a straggling beard he raised his sword.

"Stand damn you! I am a King's Officer and I demand you stand!"

"To hell with that you bastard!" So saying, the man drew a sword from his coat and went to strike at Courtenay. He easily parried it away and Courtenay delayed no longer. He simply plunged down with his sword and felt the blade jar on bone and then slide into the man's chest. Blood spurted and covered the man's filthy clothes as he dropped away clutching his chest.

Courtenay turned and saw Fenwick standing over one of the men, his sword still standing upright in the man's dead body. Trafford had already despatched the man attacking Mrs Fenwick and was hiding her face from what his cutlass had done to the man's neck.

Just as Courtenay was about to say something there was a *crack!* nearby and he heard a thud behind him. Jessica reigned in her horse, pistol in hand.

"I saw another of them come out of the house Giles that you had not seen. It was clear he was bent on evil intent!"

"I thought I said…" He broke off and smiled. "Just as well you are not an obedient wife Jess!" He turned and sought out his First-Lieutenant. "Are you all right James? And your mother?"

"Thanks to you Sir Giles we are both fine."

"Good. I saw a man watching all this and I am determined to catch him. So if you will excuse me…."

He turned his horse again and spurred it in the direction he had seen the lone horseman. He was not surprised to see the man had gone but he knew he would not be far. He spurred the horse on and when he reached the brow of the small hillock he saw the man not a hundred yards away. He gave chase immediately and found he was closing on his prey. At fifty yards he pulled his pistol out of its saddle holster and cocked it. As he got even closer he saw a group of horsemen appear and since the man veered towards them, it was obvious they were something to do with him. He was still gaining when the man on the horse slowed, stopped and turned, obviously with the intention of turning the hunter into the hunted. Courtenay hardly hesitated. He drew his horse to a sliding halt and waited his chance patiently. The man moved forwards and as he did, Courtenay raised the pistol, laid the barrel across his left arm to steady it and pulled the trigger. He knew it was a long shot for a pistol but he was lucky. The man suddenly clutched his left shoulder and all but fell out of the saddle. He managed to stay in it but the horsemen simply gathered around him and made no effort to come after Courtenay, who wheeled his horse and rode away at a gentle trot.

Back at the house Trafford had covered the bodies of the dead men and was about to climb into the saddle again when he saw Courtenay returning.

"Winged him Alex, whoever it was."

"I think we both 'ave a damn good idea who it probably was Sir Giles!"

"Yes we do! Alex, ride into the village and get the Constable, will you? Jeddidiah Widdecombe ought to know all about this little affair."

"Right you are sir." Trafford climbed into the saddle and moved off in the direction of the village. Courtenay looked after him for a moment then entered the house. Everyone else was in the parlour and Mrs Fenwick was setting out cups, saucers and plates.

Jessica embraced her husband. "Did you catch him Giles?"

"He caught something from my pistol dear, but I only managed to wing him. He had other people meeting him. Fortunately I think they were more interested in him than me! I have sent Alex for the constable." He turned to Mrs Fenwick, who was beaming at him. "I trust all is well with you now Mrs Fenwick?"

"Bless you Sir Giles, thanks to you and your wife and Alex Trafford there, we are fine!"

Courtenay shook hands with James. "I think we all have a good idea who is behind this James."

"Yes I believe we do. What do you intend Sir Giles?"

Courtenay smiled. "I intend that in your mother's house you shall stop being so damned formal for a start! I thought we were friends?"

"Always!"

"Well then Mrs Fenwick. How about some of your famous cake that your son here keeps boring me about when we are off watch?" He turned to the others. "And I thought we were just out for a ride!"

TEN

Sir Giles Courtenay, Bt., strode along the corridor which seemed to reach out for evermore in front of him, his heels echoing on the tiled flooring. He wondered why it always seemed whenever he was at Admiralty he had to walk to the other end of the building to reach his destination. He was due to meet with Lord Crompton, who had recently moved to an even more comfortable office with a view out over Horse Guards.

Clutching the pommel of his sword with his left hand, he pushed open a door and walked into an ante room where Crompton's secretary was working on what appeared to be orders. He smiled, and the Secretary, who of course knew him well jumped up and almost ran into the next room, returning a moment later opening the double doors for him.

Crompton was up and limping around the end of a huge desk even as Courtenay walked into the room. The doors closed behind him.

"Giles my boy, how are you? Are you fully recovered now?"

"Yes my Lord, I am very pleased to say that I am." Crompton pointed to a comfortable armchair and nodded to a decanter on the desk. "Pour us a couple of glasses, there's a good fellow." He looked at the young man for a few moments as Courtenay poured two glasses of claret. Courtenay handed one of them to the Admiral.

They toasted each other then sat down and Courtenay got the impression that Crompton was weighing up something he wanted to ask.

"What's all this I hear about your First-Lieutenant and his mother being attacked? What was it, a fanciful raid by some footpads?"

"I see no reason why there should have been such a thing sir. A little close to the village for that I would have thought. No, I have an idea that it is connected with this damned feud sir. How did you hear about this, bye the bye?"

Crompton smiled, his eyes crinckling. "You should know better than that! I have my spies everywhere! I gather you winged one of them?"

"Yes. He was obviously holding off to oversee what happened. Unfortunately his face was covered with a scarf and he wore a large cloak but I got the impression he was not a large man."

"Do I gather you suspect who it was?"

Courtenay nodded. "Yes sir, you do. Had Harding still been alive it would have been him, but he is not. However in view of what happened whilst I was abroad when Jessica was attacked…."

"How is Lady Jessica by the way?"

"Well sir, thank you and she sends her kind regards. The present you sent for Edward was most kind."

"Oh nonsense. How is he coming along?"

"Very loudly sir, when he wishes it!" Crompton roared with laughter.

"Come Giles, finish your drink and will lunch together. Where is your lady wife and your son?"

"At her father's London house at the moment sir. We are visiting for a few days but she knows that the chances are I will have to return to my ship soon."

An hour later, they were enjoying lunch at Crompton's club. To the onlooker they might have been relatives rather than senior Admiral and Post-captain. As Courtenay pushed away his plate and wiped his mouth with a napkin he saw Lord Cairns walking between the tables not far from them. Crompton saw the expression on his face and turned.

Cairns saw them and was about to turn away when Crompton spoke. "Ah, Cairns! Don't often see you about without your Flags these days? Did I hear he has had some kind of accident?"

Courtenay looked up at him sharply. The wily old bird! He had said nothing about knowing Spencer-White had been injured.

"Ah yes, well, he was hurt a little while ago. Only slightly. Damned footpads. Roads are full of the swine. Ought to hang them all as soon as a Magistrate can lay his hands on them. Not even worth the cost of a Trial if you ask me!"

"How badly was he injured, Cairns?" asked Crompton in a tone which suggested he wanted a firm answer. "When may we expect to see the young man back at your side?"

"H'mm. Took a pistol ball in the shoulder. Good job it was at extreme range. Should be back fairly soon. I am grateful to you for asking, my Lord."

"You will pass to him our felicitations and best wishes for a speedy recovery. I am sure that Sir Giles here will join me in that sentiment?"

Courtenay inclined his head in Cairns' direction. "But of course. Such an energetic young man, I have found." Cairns looked at them as sourly as he dared and bowed slightly before turning away.

"Hell's teeth my Lord, but how did you find out about young Spencer-White being injured?"

Crompton smiled. "Quite simple. Word soon gets around about someone like Spencer-White getting injured because the popular belief is that he has found someone almost as good at duelling as he is if not better! I suspected we would get the story about the footpads. Footpads indeed! We both know who the footpads were being directed by!"

"It was just as well we happened along when we did."

"Fate my boy, fate. Nothing like it. Now then, you may have one more week to make sure you are fully recovered and then I wish you to resume command of the *Pegasus*. I cannot tell you too much at the moment but something is brewing in Northern Europe, with this alliance between Russia, Sweden and Denmark."

"Yes, well that was the incident with the *Freja* last year."

"Quite right. Anyway I want you back in command of your ship. I have a mind to let you have an independent command for the time being. I will send your orders in the usual way of course."

"Very well my Lord. I shall not be sorry to get back to my ship, although....."

Crompton smiled. "I understand only too well. Do you recall when we were in Antigua together?" Courtenay smiled and nodded. "I missed my family and was very glad to be able to return but I have not held a sea-going command since and that is something I miss. Now, some pudding and one of the Club's brandies each then I must send you on your way. It is all very well for you young Post-captains to have plenty of spare time, but someone has to do the work!"

A little over a week later, Courtenay and James Fenwick were sitting in Courtenay's cabin on the *Pegasus,* with a pot of coffee and some mugs in between them. Also between them on Courtenay's desk were a few pages of parchment and Fenwick could clearly see the Admiralty crest at the top.

"So it does seem rather obvious it was young Spencer-White you winged, sir?"

"I think so, don't you James?"

"Shame you didn't kill the bugger but at least that ought to teach him a little respect!"

"I doubt that. You know the family, but I doubt they will try that again. The Constable will be keeping his eyes open and so will some of the other villagers. Your Mother has made herself very popular I understand."

Fenwick allowed himself a small smile. "It would seem so sir." He looked down at what were obviously Orders. "May I ask what is in there sir?"

"The Admiral spoke of independent command James, but what he did not say anything about was the fact he wants us to escort some grocery captains to Gibraltar!"

"Escort work sir? For a ship of the line? A tad unusual I would have thought. Will we be the senior ship? Usually, the escort is sloops and brigs and a frigate sometimes if the merchantmen are very lucky!"

"I agree. The escort is two sloops, the *Corncockle* and *Boxer,* and a gun-brig."

"I seem to remember hearing something about the *Corncockle* sir, wasn't that….."

"You know very well which ship she is. I did try to get her for you James, you know that."

"Ah, but then I wouldn't be here in this ship!"

"Enough! Have some more coffee and listen because this next piece of information was not in the Orders. It came via a letter from Lord Crompton. Our orders are that we are to rendezvous with the convoy, which comprises twelve ships, off St. Anthony's Head. Some of them have come down from Scotland with *Corncockle* and the rest were waiting at Falmouth." Courtenay got up, walked from behind the desk and started to pace up and down which Fenwick knew meant that he was getting his thoughts in order.

"You remember when I temporarily commanded the sloop *Corncockle,* I went out after a privateer which was causing problems along the Scottish coast. Well, the man who commanded that ship died in the fight. He had a son with him although I do not know what happened to him. However, it seems being a privateer runs in that family, because the Captain has a father whom it seems is quite a well-known privateer, and he commands a large ship, forty-odd guns apparently, which he uses to harass our shipping, usually in the Bay of Biscay. He is careful but he is not averse to taking on our usual escorts if they are small enough.'

"H'mm. Too big for the usual type of escort anyway. Would blow one of our sloops out of the water. How is she armed?"

"18 pounders, the Admiralty thinks. John Company is getting a little nasty. They are accusing the Navy of not being able to protect their ships but the truth of it is that he is too big for our escorts and there is no way the Admiralty can spare a few frigates!"

"One like *Amazon* would do it!"

"Yes, but there are only two on the List and their Lordships are not going to spare one of those!"

"So where do we come in sir?"

"Lord Crompton has left it to me James, but would rather like this ship, which is called the *Poursuivante* , to be put out of action. I have sent word to the Captain of the *Boxer,* being the senior of the three Captains of the escort, that we will be delayed and we will not make the rendezvous. I have said we will meet with them out at sea."

"You don't want anyone to know we are part of the escort sir."

"That is correct. If the Captain of the *Poursuivante* knew we were with the escort he would not stir from his cosy little anchorage." He stopped his pacing, rubbing his chin. Then he turned and looked at Fenwick, his eyes glinting in the lamplight. Without a word he walked to the cabin door and opened it. "Ah, Evans," he said to the surprised Marine sentry, "pass the word for the Sailing Master.'

A few moments later Owen Davies was looking at the chart open on the broad table in Courtenay's cabin.

"Now then Mr Davies," Courtenay said, "I have need of your foresight on the matter of courses."

"I see sir," replied the Master, one hand on the chart near Plymouth. "Who do you want to set a trap for now?"

Martin Stevens, the Officer of the Watch, was pacing up and down on the poop, flailing his arms to keep the bitter wind out. He stopped as he heard laughter through the cabin skylight.

Courtenay's Orders called for him to be the senior officer of the escort taking twelve merchant ships to Gibraltar, full with supplies not only for the garrison there but also for Malta. He should have met with them off Falmouth but instead, in response to the orders he had sent, the convoy with its three escorts had slipped their cables and left without waiting for *Pegasus.* The following day *Pegasus* left the shelter of Plymouth Sound, and headed out into the English Channel. It was a very lively sea that the ship's bows headed into, with spray being thrown back over even her high maindeck. Courtenay was not too happy at not being able to set all the sail he wanted but Davies felt the wind would ease later in the day and when it did, he was able to have the courses set, and *Pegasus* was able to make far better progress. He knew the convoy would be well ahead, but equally he knew that his ship would make far better time and that they would be able to catch them up all things being equal, at the point he had selected.

With the wind steady from the nor'west, Courtenay was able to keep his ship on a south westerly course to weather the French coast at the northern end of the bay of Biscay and he had arranged that he would hopefully meet up with the convoy to the south west of the Ile de Quessant, out of sight of land. He had in fact heard of the French ship and knew that she hailed from St Nazaire. He hoped that the ship was still working out of that port, because hopefully its Captain would sail from there and start looking for the convoy ahead of it to the north.

Courtenay was in his usual place on the quarterdeck, boat cloak wrapped around him, when Stevens, again Officer of the Watch, hesitated for a moment after checking the ship's course and then slowly walked to his Captain's side.

He looked up as a flurry of snow swept across the deck then turned to Courtenay.

"Course west by south sir. Making nine knots, sir."

Courtenay looked at him and smiled. "Yes Mr Stevens I know. I was on deck five minutes ago when the watch changed and very clearly heard the Fourth Lieutenant make the same report to you. Are you curious to know what we are about?"

Stevens smiled a little sheepishly. "Well I know what we are doing here sir of course, because you always explain exactly what we are doing and why but I am just curious sir, as to why we are not actually with the convoy. It is almost as if you are using it as bait sir."

"Howso, Mr Stevens?" The Second Lieutenant smiled, unabashed.

"Well sir, I have heard a rumour about this French privateer, the *Poursuivante,* and I have also heard of her. She carries about 46 guns and many men."

Courtenay looked at him gravely "And what else have you heard Mr Stevens?"

"That she prays on our merchantmen but is too powerful for our usual escorts sir. I also gather she comes from St Nazaire."

"Well done Mr Stevens. She does indeed come from St Nazaire, and she does prey on our merchant ships." Courtenay turned and looked out over the bleak cold and grey sea. "But not for much longer!" Stevens turned and went back to the binnacle.

Courtenay stared out at the serried wavecrests and his thoughts were suddenly many miles back. It was a few short days ago that he stood on the quayside at Plymouth, watched curiously by some onlookers as he said goodbye to his wife and child. His parents were also there but stood back as Courtenay cuddled his son, kissing him on the face and head. His son looked at him intently or so it seemed, then there was a small smile which nearly broke his heart. Going back to the service he loved was one thing, leaving his family…..He kissed Edward again and handed him to his mother, before turning to Jessica. She looked very cold and he knew she was trying very hard not to cry. She had steeled herself for this moment, was determined not to let her husband down but she did not how she controlled herself as she put her arms around him, as she had often done in front of members of his crew, to hold him to her. They stood like that for several moments, had a final kiss, then Courtenay stepped back, replaced his hat and ran lightly down the well-worn steps to where Trafford was waiting with the barge. He had turned, once in the barge, and raised his hat once more, then the barge was moving away from the steps swiftly and he sat down in the sternsheets.

There was a yell near him and he came out his thoughts to hear Stevens ordering the men to the braces.

"Wind's veered a mite sir!" called Davies, "best to trim the sails now."

"Aye. Do you think it will veer further?"

Davies looked up at the sails again and the masthead pendant. "Hope not sir, otherwise that will upset our calculations! Seems to have steadied." He looked at his Captain for a moment. "Is there anything I can do sir? Is your wound troubling you?"

Courtenay smiled. "No there is nothing. Unless of course, you are able to spirit us away from this damnable weather!" As he spoke an icy gust of wind came in over the quarter, accompanied by flakes of snow.

Davies laughed. "Sorry Sir Giles, unfortunately even I do not have those powers! As we drive south the weather will get better."

"I know. I am going below. Mr Stevens? The ship is yours."

Stevens smiled but he knew that as long as Owen Davies was on deck the ship was anything but his!

Courtenay had just settled on the benchseat beneath the stern windows, propped into one corner, when there was a rap at the screen door accompanied by the usual call from the Marine sentry to announce the visitor. This time it was the surgeon. Kingston opened the door and the man stepped carefully over the coaming and advanced into the cabin.

Courtenay smiled. "Good morning Mr O'Keefe. What can I do for you? Bit early for scurvy to have broken out I would have thought?'

O'Keefe smiled. "Nothing like that sir. The ship's company is in rude good health I am pleased to say. No sir, it is about your wound I have come to call. May I ask how it is?"

"You may, and thanks to you it is well healed. I was even able to go riding when I was at home."

"Is that what you called it sir?" Trafford had appeared in the cabin.

Courtenay shot him a glance that did not go unnoticed by the Irishman.

"That may not have been a wise move sir. Your wound may have healed but you should have allowed more time before any strenuous activity such as horse riding. May I examine you, sir?"

Courtenay stood up, slipped out of his coat and pulled his shirt out of his breeches. The Doctor bent and seemed to spend a very long time with his examination.

"H'mm, well everything appears to be as it should be. Is it giving you any pain sir?"

"Odd twinge, that's all."

"Good. Well I would still advise against any strenuous activity sir."

"What happens when we run alongside a Frenchie Mr O'Keefe? Do you suggest that I remain on my quarterdeck whilst everyone else does the fighting?"

"*Everyone else* has not had a ball in the side sir, and suffered a serious wound. Time to let someone else do the fighting, at least for the time being!"

"Fat chance of that sir!" cut in Trafford.

"Trafford, have you nothing to do at the moment?" asked Courtenay.

Trafford took the hint and left. O'Keefe gathered up his bag, which he had not opened, and looked at Courtenay.

"Hear tell we are after some French privateer sir?"

"You hear aright Mr O'Keefe."

"Well, mind what I said sir."

O'Keefe turned and left. Courtenay looked after him for a moment, smiled briefly and returned to his orders.

It was during the forenoon watch the following day they sighted the rear of the convoy. The merchantmen sailed that much more slowly than *Pegasus* could manage, but even then and with favourable winds it had still taken a little longer than Courtenay had estimated to catch them. The mainmast look-out hailed down that the convoy was in sight and Courtenay immediately ordered a reduction in sail. He was banking on the French privateer coming up from St Nazaire and trying to take the convoy head on. The escorts would not frighten him and he would be able to create havoc among the merchantmen. Courtenay therefore intended to keep his ship to the rear of the convoy and perhaps in a position where he would not be noticed.

Fenwick appeared next to the wheel, looked at the binnacle and crossed to his Captain's side, touching his hat as he did so.

"Well the convoy is where it should be, sir."

"Yes, let us hope that Monsieur le Frenchman is greedy enough. The sloops and the gun brig will not put him off that's for certain!"

"Clever ruse if I may say so sir, to tell *Boxer's* commander to let off a rocket if he sees the Frenchman, which is also to be the signal for the convoy to reverse its course."

"I hope the Frenchman will simply think this is some way of sending signals he cannot read! It is hardly likely to stop him coming after the convoy and hopefully he will not see us approaching among all the other sails."

All through that day they followed the convoy just keeping them in visual distance. Courtenay was constantly checking the chart and he realised that they would be about 300 hundred miles out from St Nazaire in the course of the next few hours. He pondered the thought of ordering the convoy to sail further into the Bay but that would look obvious.

At daybreak the following day the look-outs were hardly in position when the cry came down that the rear-most escort, and which was the sloop *Boxer,* was making a signal to the convoy. Midshipman Smythe was up the ratlines in an instant, telescope over his shoulder, and he was soon peeling down to the quarterdeck what the signal was saying.

"*Enemy in sight* sir!"

Just as he did there was a sudden flare from ahead, in the sky.

"That's the signal sir!" called Fenwick. "*Boxer* must have sighted the privateer!"

Smythe was still in the mainmast cross-trees and everyone looked up as he yelled down again.

"Convoy is reversing its course sir!"

Courtenay waved him down and then turned to Fenwick and Davies.

"Very well Mr Davies, set the courses. Trim every sail so that not a drop of wind is lost. Mr Fenwick, you may beat to quarters and clear for action."

The drums rolled and men scampered about in apparent confusion. Powder monkeys ran this way and that with their cartridges, and the lashings of the guns were taken off. Sand was sprinkled on the decking, not only to assist with finding grip but also to help soak up any blood. In what appeared a very short space of time Fenwick had reported that the ship was at quarters. With all the courses set *Pegasus* was leaping through the waves, seeming to lean forward under the press of sail. In the meantime the convoy was getting closer, and this time Courtenay went aloft to see if he could make out the Frenchman. He had no difficulty at all. The ship was proudly flying a huge Tricolour from its gaff and even as he looked he heard gunfire and realised that someone had opened fire. He lifted his telescope and saw that the other sloop, the one he had temporarily commanded named *Corncockle* and which was now at the rear of the convoy, had got close enough to pour in a broadside before making more sail and pulling away. The Frenchman answered with bowchasers and Courtenay looked on relieved as the opening shots landed in open water on either side of the lithe sloop. He smiled as he watched the sloop expertly dodge the next fall of shot and then she was drawing well away.

In the meantime the ships of the convoy were getting closer. *Boxer* and the Gun-brig were shorting sail though, as if they were waiting for the French ship to come up with them so that they could take it on together and protect their charges. Courtenay thought for a moment that surely the Frenchman would see his ship then he suddenly remembered that when he was a Midshipman in the *Claymore* his old Captain, Angus Browne, lately his Squadron Commander in the Mediterranean had used a similar ploy. The Frenchman was seeing what he wanted to see. A host of ships hurrying away as fast as they could with, the Royal Navy ships gathering to protect them against far superior odds. He had a final look then grasped a backstay and made his way down to the quarterdeck.

He smiled at Fenwick. "Coming up nicely James. I do believe he hasn't as yet seen us!" He went to the larboard nettings and raised his telescope. He could just about make out the French ship through the other shipping.

One by one the merchant ships were passing. *Pegasus* was now under fighting canvas, courses clewed up, topsails drawing well, Then there were the last ships, which had been originally in the lead and two waterspouts grew out of the water as the Frenchman tested the range.

Courtenay turned to McBride, in charge of the signals. "Show the colours Mr McBride."

The White Ensign streamed out from the mizzen gaff proudly as the final merchantman was clear, and suddenly there was the Frenchman, looking dark against the pewter sea. Her larboard guns were run out but she was no match for *Pegasus*. Her scantlings would not be as strong and Courtenay doubted she would carry 24 pounders like those on the lower gun-deck of his ship.

"Mr. McBride. General signal to the escort *Do not engage. Await instructions.*" There was a short pause and then everyone looked up as the balls soared up to the gaff and broke to the wind. Acknowledgements appeared like magic on the other British warships and they prepared to be spectators.

Trafford appeared on the quarterdeck, strolled to the side and looked at the approaching Frenchman. He spat over the side and took his usual place, watching his Captain.

To the French, the appearance of a powerful 74 from the throng of fleeing merchantman must have come as a terrible shock. The French privateer's reaction was almost immediate.

Pegasus was closing rapidly on her opponent but her shape suddenly lengthened.

"She's turning away sir!" said Fenwick. "She's wearing ship!" It was true enough. Suddenly faced with the onrushing two-decker and realising there was a far heavier ship around than the sloops and gun-brig, the Frenchman had decided discretion was the batter part of valour but he had left it too late. When Courtenay had lain recovering from his wound his ship had undergone a scraping. Sea-miles of weed had been removed from her copper-sheathed bottom, which was now as clean as a whistle.

"Set the courses Mr Davies. If he thinks he will show us a clean pair of heels he has another think coming!" Courtenay was smiling grimly, hands clasped behind his back. He did not need a telescope now. The enemy was clear enough. She completed her turn and he could see all her sails being set, but he could tell already that his ship was faster and that they were overhauling.

"Run out the larboard battery Mr Fenwick, if you please. Chain-shot on the upper deck, I think. Double shot with grape on the lower."

Chain shot consisted of two cannon balls, joined with a length of chain. It would rip into masts and sails alike. The 24 pounders on the lower deck would fire a terrible salvo of two cannonballs and grapeshot for good measure.

Fenwick was pacing up and down near the rail looking over at the Frenchman occasionally. Davies was muttering to himself, watching the set of the sails and the pendant at the masthead. The topsails gave a flap and he immediately cupped his hands and bellowed for the sails to be trimmed.

"Damme sir, if the wind isn't veering!"

"Ease her a point to starboard if it helps Mr Davies." ordered Courtenay. He knew his ship could batter the other at extreme range if needs be but that was not his way. There was always the chance a stray enemy ball would hit a vital spar, bring down a mast. He preferred to get in close, use the weight of his ship's broadside and board in the smoke and confusion. When he walked to the rail and looked down at the main gun-deck he saw Oates, the Boatswain had anticipated him. Grapnels were laid out ready at convenient places. The arms chests were open and cutlasses, pistols, and other homely objects with which to kill were being handed out. Oates must have felt his Captain's eyes on him because he paused and looked up. Courtenay smiled and nodded.

"I see you anticipated me Mr Oates!" he called down.

"I knows your ways by now sir!" came the cheerful reply.

Fenwick turned to him. "Nearly up to him sir. Gun by gun or....'

"Give him the whole broadside James. What would you say he is? Fifty guns?"

"About that, I would say. Doubt he carries 24 pounders though. We could stand off and pound him to matchwood, but...."

"But what, James?"

"Not your way sir! Close with him, couple of big broadsides and over we go!"

Courtenay clapped him on the arm and moved away to the side. He watched carefully as *Pegasus* overtook her enemy. "Get the courses in Mr Davies!" In an instant the big sails were brailed up again and the view of the French ship was clear. Her stern was being overtaken by the 74's bowsprit. Courtenay noticed some of the sails disappearing on the French ship and realised the Captain had bowed to the inevitable. He was not going to out-run the *Pegasus* so he would stand and fight, or would he? Many French ships faced with overpowering odds fired a blank broadside and then stood down from their guns. *Pour honour de pavilion,* they called it. If a British Captain did it he would be up before a Court-martial in seconds flat if the Admiralty laid their hands on him once he was released from prison and every British Captain knew it. Any British ship was worth two French, they reckoned.

There was a bang, a roar, and a ball from the French ship passed close overhead. The French always aimed at sails and masts. The Royal Navy aimed at the hulls. The object was quite simple. Pepper the hull with solid iron ball and fire grape across the decks. Any cannon ball which struck something turned it into deadly splinters, metal or wood. They would scythe across a deck cutting men down. Those, of course, that the cannon balls themselves did not kill, maim or otherwise injure.

There were more bangs and Fenwick looked aloft to see if anything came down. If anything did it would be caught in the nets which had been spread aloft with that object in mind. More bangs but still *Pegasus* was silent. Some cordage fell from aloft and there was a short scream as a man fell from aloft to disappear into the sea. Hit by a ball? Struck by the wind of its passing? One of the Master's Mates hurried to the starboard side and looked down at the sea. He looked at Courtenay and shook his head.

When Courtenay judged they were in the right place he nodded at Fenwick, who, with a relieved look on his face turned to the gun-deck with a whistle in his mouth and blew it. The larboard gun-ports opened as one and the whole larboard battery trundled out into the light.

"Broadside!" Fenwick yelled, and the whole battery crashed out together. Guns were hauled in, sponged out and were being re-loaded even as Courtenay and the others peered through the smoke to see what hits they had sustained. The smoke eddied away in the breeze and laid bare a sorry sight.

The chain shot had ripped away the main topmast and had shredded sails, staysails and rigging. The ship was a mess aloft and she had had her agility taken away. The hull was pitted with holes where every shot had struck home and tendrils of smoke were hanging over the deck. Pieces of bulwark were missing and a whole section between two gun-ports had disappeared. Some of the French guns were still firing and here and there a ball whimpered overhead or slammed into the side. Then Fenwick blew his whistle again and the broadside crashed into the French ship like an avalanche. The weight of metal at the distance Courtenay was firing from pushed the ship over onto her larboard side before allowing her to right. The foremast went over the side and large amounts of red could be seen on what was left of her sails where it had splashed from the deck below. The guns which had been firing had been silenced and Courtenay could only imagine the slaughter his guns had caused to the smaller ship.

"Bring her up two points Mr Davies, get us alongside!"

As the ship sidled up to the Frenchman the Tricolour came down with a rush. They had had enough. Courtenay looked at his Senior and smiled then turned to McBride.

"Signal the convoy and the escorts Mr McBride. *Resume course and station.*"

The arrival of the convoy at Gibraltar caused little excitement. It was just another convoy passing through, some supplies being offloaded, the rest going to Malta. Courtenay had orders as far as Gibraltar and no further. Crompton had made it quite clear his responsibility ended at the mouth of the Mediterranean and that he was under no circumstances to go any further. The two sloops and the gun-brig were to continue with the convoy to its destination although they were lucky because there was a frigate returning to the Island and its Captain was ordered to accompany them as additional security.

Fenwick had been prize-master aboard the *Poursuivante,* but a lot of work had to be carried out before they could make any sail. The convoy had sailed on whilst men from the *Pegasus* worked feverishly with the survivors to carry out essential repairs. She had taken three heavy balls below the waterline and so much damage had been caused to her upper decks that it was in some respects a wonder the ship was able to sail at all but some jury-masts and temporary patching repairs had at least achieved something and had enabled Fenwick to set sail, and with the French prisoners manning the pumps, the ship managed to at least keep up with the tail end of the convoy. The Privateer Captain had been killed in the first broadside, caught with chain shot and cut neatly in half. It had been a gruesome sight. About 70 Frenchman had been killed and over a hundred wounded. *Pegasus* had suffered two dead and three wounded.

The Flag Officer Gibraltar had already received orders with a courier brig that *Pegasus* was to be allowed an independent command and had vaguely suggested that she might be used to augment the patrols around the Spanish coast and up to the Bay of

Biscay. He was quite happy to go along with this and so was Courtenay. His ship patrolled along the southern coast of Spain poking its nose into Cadiz from time to time and thoroughly making a nuisance of itself. On one occasion they surprised a Spanish frigate about to sneak out of a small cove and attack two British Indiamen. The ships had gone to quarters to try and fight off their attacker but *Pegasus* had appeared like the winged avenger from around a headland, and the Spanish frigate had set all possible sail to escape. It had been a close run thing since with her extra speed following her being careened, *Pegasus* was almost as fast as the frigate. Courtenay had fired his bow-chasers at the fleeing ship then let her escape, turning and accompanying the Indiamen as far as the Straits.

Towards the end of February Courtenay received orders to return home. But not to Plymouth or even to Portsmouth.

"We have been ordered to Yarmouth Roads James." Courtenay explained over dinner that night. "We sail in the morning and we are to join the Flag of Lord Nelson, who himself is under the orders of Sir Hyde Parker. I am to receive fresh orders when we arrive but if those two gentleman are involved then something big is about to happen."

"H'mm. Yarmouth eh, sir? Never been there. I hope our Sailing Master knows the anchorage! Do you think it is anything to do with this damned Armed Neutrality of the North? Damned cheek if you ask me sir. Russia, Sweden and Denmark deciding that we cannot search their ships for contraband!"

"The Russian Tsar has not been too happy ever since we occupied Malta, James. Something to do with the Knights Templar. I think it made him angry with us so this is how he repays us! I daresay I will find out more when we arrive. Now where is that fresh cheese Kingston laid his hands on the other day?'

ELEVEN

On the last day of February 1801, His Britannic Majesty's Ship of the line *Pegasus,* of 74 guns, dropped her starboard anchor in Yarmouth Roads just off the port of Great Yarmouth in Norfolk. The usual guard boat was in place signalling where the ship should anchor but its crew was alive to what usually happened and as soon as the position had been marked the looms went into overdrive, and the small boat was clear before the anchor splashed down. There were a few wry grins from the anchor party and a grunt from Oates, supervising the laying out of the anchor cable.

Courtenay looked around him. There was quite a gathering of smaller ships and two other ships of the line. One was a smaller, 64-gun ship which he recognised as the *Agamemnon.* She was the first ship of the line commanded by Nelson. There was a 74 similar to *Pegasus* at anchor not far away. There was hustle and bustle everywhere. Small boats were being pulled to and from the shore, piled high with supplies.

Courtenay turned to Fenwick. "Best get Pritchard ashore as soon as he likes James. I have a feeling there are going to be more ships arriving soon and we need to make sure we are fully provisioned."

"Aye aye, sir. I will see to it immediately."

Burton was the officer of the watch and as he turned back to watch the shore from looking at his superiors he saw another boat approaching.

"Looks like the Port Admiral's Flag-Lieutenant is coming to board us sir."

"Thank you Mr Burton. I will be in the cabin. Come aft when you have finished, James."

A few moments later there was a knock at the screen door accompanied by the bellow from the Marine sentry announcing the Admiral's Flag-Lieutenant, and a weary looking officer stepped over the coaming. Trafford was by the wine cabinet, looking curious.

"Captain Sir Giles Courtenay sir?"

"Yes, Mr.er…."

"Simons sir. I am the Flag-Lieutenant to Vice-admiral Sir Percival Horton. I have this message for you sir. I was asked to pass it to you personally."

"Very well Flags, thank you. You have delivered it safe and sound. Is there anything else? I have a ship to provision."

"Nothing else sir. If you need to have some transport made available for you the Admiral is pleased to place a coach at your disposal."

"Thank you." Simons left, leaving Courtenay looking curiously at the canvas envelope in his hands.

"Transport sir?" asked Trafford, "Sounds like you are being expected to go somewhere."

Courtenay slit open the envelope and opened a single sheet of paper. He recognised Crompton's handwriting immediately.

"It seems I am to report to the Admiralty Alex. Best get some clothing ready. You will come with me. I think we will have to take Sir Percival up on his kind offer."

"Aye sir. Do you want me to fetch Mr Fenwick sir?"

Just then the door opened again and Fenwick stepped in.

Courtenay smiled. "No need Alex. James, I am summoned to London to see Lord Crompton. You will remain here in command of course. I have no need to tell you to get as many provisions on board as possible and see if you can twist some arms in the sail loft into letting us have some spare canvas. We can get the sailmaker to run up a spare for that topsail we lost in Biscay."

"Have you any idea how long you will be away sir?"

"Not long I would say. I have a feeling that each day which passes is going to see more and more shipping arrive. I will be leaving immediately."

Even though it was now just the beginning of March and spring was in the air it was still bitterly cold, and snow flurries were lightly covering the road, in some places managing to hide the various ruts which had been formed in very wet weather. The coach lurched and bumped along and Trafford became quite worried that it would not do Courtenay's wound any good at all. Courtenay laughed and said he was fine but he was glad of the odd respite when they were able to stretch their legs at various Inns on the way.

They passed through Suffolk and turned through Essex to run towards London. The countryside gave way to houses, then more houses and then they were running into London itself with its myriad smells, and streets seemingly full of shouting people, many pedalling their wares trying to earn a meagre living. It seemed to take an eternity to reach the Admiralty, but reach it they did, and Courtenay left Trafford in a small room near the main entrance which had a blazing log fire. Courtenay was pretty sure also that his coxswain would be found a measure of rum as well.

He was shown immediately into Crompton's office. His desk as usual was littered in parchment and plans. He rose, walked slowly around the desk and gripped Courtenay's hand warmly.

"Giles my boy, are you well? Good. Do the usual would you, and then I have some things to tell you. I will not keep you long but I have a little surprise for you."

Courtenay went to a cabinet and poured two glasses of claret. He handed one to Lord Crompton, and they silently toasted each other.

They sat down near a blazing fire in comfortable leather chairs. Crompton held his hands to the fire for a moment and then turned to Courtenay.

"I would imagine you are wondering what the devil you have been brought to Yarmouth for, eh?" He laughed shortly. "For what I think is possibly the first time the Royal Navy is going to act as a bully boy, what do you think of that eh? This damned Armed Neutrality of the North as it is called. Russia, Denmark and Sweden. Something has to be done to put a stop to it. Denmark is the most vulnerable. We are going to attack Copenhagen my boy, and teach the damned Danes a lesson in manners!"

"I see sir. Is that not a little close to home? After all the Danes…"

"Yes I know. They are the best candidate. If we bully them into withdrawing from their pact with Russia and Sweden it falls apart. Sir Hyde Parker and Lord Nelson will have all the details and by the time you get back to Yarmouth nearly all the ships will be there. Fifteen sail of the line, with three joining later, and God knows how many smaller craft. A nice Fleet to take on the Danes, not that it is going to be easy.'

"When do I have to return sir?"

"Day after tomorrow. I want you there as soon as possible." Crompton looked at him. "Nelson asked for you, did you know that?"

"No sir, I did not."

"H'mm. Well impressed with you after the other year in the Mediterranean when you had *Amazon.* You will get your final orders at Yarmouth. Now, said I had a surprise for you my boy and I have." He stood up, and Courtenay did likewise. "It is waiting for you at your father in law's house."

"Sir?"

"Took the liberty of informing Lady Courtenay that you would be coming home for a short while. Suggested she might like to come to London for a while about now. Least I could do!"

"Jessica in London?"

"Yes, and your handsome son as well. Suggest you get off now, and make the most of it!"

"I do not know quite what to say sir, except thank you."

"Oh, get along with you. I have work to do. Give your lady wife my kind regards."

"The least I can do is to offer you dinner tonight sir, if you will permit?"

"Rubbish! You will want to be alone with your wife." He looked out of the window at the snow still falling, and then back. "Are you still here Captain?"

Courtenay smiled and left.

When his carriage stopped outside his father in law's house, Jessica was through the double doors and down the steps to the road before he had even opened the door. Oblivious to the surprised stares of onlookers she gave her husband her usual welcome, and hugged him to her. Trafford, getting out of the carriage, smiled and turned to lift down their bags. One the maids came out of the house as Courtenay and his wife entered and smiled at Trafford as he carried the bags up the steps. Trafford smiled even more widely and followed the maid into the house.

Courtenay only had a day or so but he and Jessica made the most of it, spending all the time they had together. There was only one incident which partly spoiled their short time together. The weather improved the day after Courtenay had seen Lord Crompton and they took advantage of a bracing day to stroll in the park in the middle of the square where Sir Geoffrey's house was situate. His house was on the fashionable side of a fashionable square and there were many people of obvious substance taking the air or sitting on benches reading a broadsheet. As Courtenay and his wife, with Courtenay holding his son in his arms, turned round one side of the square he saw a small group of youngish men coming the other way, laughing together and not really watching where they were going. It seemed quite obvious that some of them at least were more than a little the worse for wear for drink.

Courtenay steered a course which would take them well clear, then some of the young men moved to one side and in the middle was a figure in blue and white. A naval officer. Courtenay's eyes narrowed as he saw this. A naval officer and therefore supposedly a gentleman, acting in such a way in public was bad enough but the person in question was none other than Marmaduke Spencer-White. The other man saw him at the same time and nudged one of his companions.

Although Courtenay had tried to avoid them it became obvious that he and Jessica would not be able to. Instead they walked calmly along the footpath until they were face to face with the young men.

"Excuse me," said Courtenay, as the men were blocking the path, "would you mind making way, please?" There was a snigger from one of the men but Courtenay turned the type of glacial stare on him that had left many a seaman or subordinate officer shaking and the man went very quiet.

"Well Captain Courtenay," started Spencer-White, "fancy seeing you here. Are you slumming sir?"

Jessica stepped forward before her husband could stop her. "It seems to me *sir,* that your presence in this Square is lowering the tone to a level which I am sure everyone here will deem totally unacceptable. I would suggest that you leave."

Spencer-White looked at her calmly. Two of his friends were looking daggers and the last one, the one who had withered under Courtenay's stare, started to move away. Without turning Spencer-White rapped, "Stand Whitely, you cowardly scum!" Then he turned back to Jessica and opened his mouth to speak but did not get the chance.

"I would suggest *Mr* Spencer-White, that you do as my wife suggests before you regret your incursion here."

One of Spencer-White's friends stepped forward. "I say sir, just who the devil d'ye thing you are? Do you not know who you are addressing? This is the nephew of…."

"Lord Cairns, yes I know. I am well acquainted with his Lordship. The fact Spencer-White here is his nephew impresses me not one jot." He turned to Spencer-

222

White and smiled but the smile was far from pleasant and just for a moment Spencer-White's friends saw it through their alcoholic haze. "Tell me, how is your wound? How did you come by it may I ask?"

"I was accosted by half a dozen n'er do wells who were after my purse. I made them pay for it, I'll have you know, before one of the cowardly bastards shot me!"

"The last I heard it was one or two footpads and the pistol shot was at some distance. Was the damage to your shoulder at the back or the front?"

Spencer-White reddened. "What the devil do you mean by that sir?"

"Take your choice. One thing is certain. The wound is hardly an honourable one gained in battle. The only time you were supposed to be in combat with me I seem to recall you hurt your leg and had to stay to the rear."

"By God I will call you out for that slur sir, Baronet or not!"

One of his friend's heads jerked up. "Baronet? I thought you said he was just a Captain!"

Jessica smiled grimly. "My husband is not *just* a Captain. He is Captain Sir Giles Courtenay, Baronet. He has some important friends in Whitehall." She turned to her husband. "Did you not tell me the press were operating in London these days dearest?"

"Why yes I believe that I did, but mostly along the River. Still I suppose if I summoned some men." He turned and saw Trafford not far behind them, one hand resting casually on the cutlass he had thrust through his belt. "Perhaps Trafford could assist. I am sure that a spell aboard a man o'war would put some colour in these young mens' cheeks?" He turned back and the men had gone, save Spencer-White, who was standing there still, his face now deathly pale.

"By God sir, you drive me too far!"

"No Mr Spencer-White *you* drive *me* too far and I will therefore give you a warning which if you wish, you can repeat to your Uncle, not that he will care a fig I am thinking. Twice you have attacked either my family or those close to me. Please do not try to dignify yourself by denying either charge. We both know you were behind the attempt to kidnap my wife and we both know it was you behind the attack on Mrs Fenwick and my First-Lieutenant. This is your first and last warning. Keep away or rest assured, I will call *you* out and settle it one way or the other!"

Spencer-White was still pale but he sneered his answer. "Do you think you can better me in a duel Sir Giles?"

Courtenay smiled. It was not a pleasant smile and Spencer-White suddenly felt a chill pass through his body.

"Remember what happened to Matthias Harding Mr Spencer-White. Now I suggest you catch up with your friends before I have you brought before a Court-martial for conduct unbefitting an officer!"

Spencer-White glowered but turned and left. Jessica slipped her arm back through her husband's, kissed Edward on the cheek, and they strolled on as if nothing had happened. Trafford relaxed, looked around for the maid who had been with him and beckoned to her.

"Is everything all right then Alex?"

"Everything is fine my lovely. Thought we were in for a storm but looks like the wind has veered!"

Three days later Courtenay was back aboard his ship and looking through the Orders which had been delivered in his absence. Since he had left to go to London Yarmouth Roads had become crowded. There were now fifteen sail of the line there with countless smaller vessels from lithe frigates downwards, including some bomb vessels. Hyde-Parker was there, his flag raised in *London,* 98. Vice-admiral Lord Nelson had also joined, his Flag being in the *St George,* 98.

Courtenay knew that very shortly they would all be leaving. It was a question of when. Fenwick had made sure they were as ready as they could be for anything. The holds were full of food and other provisions. The Purser had been left in no doubt at all as to what was expected of him and he had purchased fresh vegetables and as much fresh meat as he could lay his hands on with all the other ships at anchor. Water casks were full and Fenwick had even managed to obtain some more sailcloth from the Port admiral's office.

Eventually the signal was made from *London* for all Captains to repair on board, and everyone knew what that meant. Courtenay was away for three hours and when he returned, even as the boatswain's mates were blowing on their calls and the Marines were stamping to attention and presenting arms, he was opening his mouth to speak to Fenwick.

"I would like all officers not on duty to join me in the cabin in fifteen minutes James, together with senior Warrant officers and the Midshipmen."

Fenwick touched his hat and simply nodded.

"Well gentlemen, I expect you are wondering what exactly is happening." Courtenay was saying later to the gathering. "The answer is very simple. Most of you know that this 'Armed Neutrality of the North' has been formed with the specific object of preventing the Royal Navy from searching neutral ships for cargoes bound for France and her allies. You all heard about the *Freja,* of course. Somewhat embarrassingly of course the Navy had to pay to have her re-fitted after she refused to allow the ships she was guarding to be searched. It has been decided that something has to be done to break this 'Armed Neutrality' and the Navy has been given the somewhat unenviable task of being bully boys. It has therefore been decreed that we will attack Copenhagen. Denmark, it is felt, is probably the weakest of the three and the most vulnerable. If we can defeat her then we break this treaty. Three more ships of the line will be joining us in the North Sea. Tomorrow we up-anchor and set a course for the Skagerrak. Their Lordships are however hopeful there can be a negotiated settlement to all this, and even now a deputation is headed for Denmark. We will not know the answer until we arrive in the Skagerrak, but we have to be ready for whatever Admiral Sir Hyde Parker requires us to do. Are there any questions?"

Martin Stevens stood up. "What sort of Navy does Denmark have sir? Forgive my ignorance, but I have only ever fought the French and the Spanish!"

Courtenay smiled. "I have never fought the Danes either Mr Stevens. Denmark is believed to have about 23 sail of the line but only 10 at Copenhagen. They do however, have many unserviceable craft. Do not underestimate them any of you. The Danes are tenacious people. They will fight hard to protect their country and their main City and they fight in the same way as we do. Unlike the Frogs the Danes aim for carnage 'twixt decks!" Stevens sat down, brow furrowed in thought. "We do not know yet exactly what we will face gentlemen but whatever we do, our ship bless her, will be ready for it!"

There was a ready cheer for his words and then Kingston and two seamen helping him, passed round with trays loaded with full glasses.

Courtenay raised his glass. "To the ship lads!" More cheers, and glasses emptied quickly, to be replaced just as quickly.

Two days later on the 12th March the fleet quit Yarmouth Roads. One by one the heavy ships of the line set their sails and moved slowly away from their anchorage, settling into line ahead as they did so. Courtenay looked abeam as his ship tacked astern of the *Ganges,* a 74 similar to the *Pegasus,* and three ships ahead of them was the *St George,* carrying Nelson's flag at the foremast truck. They had with them a number of bomb vessels but Courtenay was looking at a lithe frigate which was tacking clear of its bigger brothers and setting all its sail. It was soon surging ahead of the heavier ships but Courtenay found he was not envious. He had accepted his role as a Captain of a ship of the line and was content with the same. That was not the case with some of his officers and more than one could be seen wistfully looking at the smaller ships. He smiled, and when Trafford saw where he was looking he realised what his Captain was thinking.

He was drawn from his thoughts by harsh words from the same person.

"Mr Stevens, are you or are you not the officer of the watch?"

"Yes sir, I am."

'Well then, take note of the leebrace on the foretopsail. Would you not say it needed attention? See to it Mr Stevens and less of the daydreaming!"

"At once sir!"

Courtenay turned away, and as he did so he winked broadly at Trafford.

Smythe, the Midshipman of the watch, turned and called out, "Sir, the Flagship is signalling! *General, repeated St George. Make all sail conformable with weather."*

"Acknowledge if you please Mr Smythe."

Courtenay looked out abeam again. The frigate had already disappeared to the head of the phalanx of ships.

Adverse and very strong winds hampered the progress of the Fleet across the North Sea, into the Skagerrak, and down into the Kettegat, which led them towards the Sound, a narrow strip of water separating Denmark from Sweden. Between the batteries of Helsingborg and Elsinor was just three miles of water.

At length Hyde Parker ordered all his ships to anchor at the entrance to the Sound and many of the ships which had been separated during the storms eventually joined them.

Courtenay paced the quarterdeck of his ship, fretting at the delay. Fenwick, looking at him carefully first of all to judge his mood joined step with him as he paced the decking.

"Do you know what we are waiting for sir, apart from our missing ships?"

"I am not entirely in the confidence of Lord Nelson and Sir Hyde Parker James, but as I see it there are two matters holding up any action. First of all we are waiting to hear from the delegation which went to Copenhagen to try and avoid any action at all and secondly it would seem the pilot aboard *London* is dithering over proceeding any further. I have to confess, there is a delicate matter ahead. We will have to sail between two batteries and the Sound is only three miles across at that point. It would be disaster if we sailed through and were pounded to matchwood on the way!"

"I see sir. I am glad I am not the Admiral!"

Courtenay laughed. "Yes, I think I am as well!"

Courtenay was glad that the bomb vessels were in company. He had the feeling they would be very useful.

Eventually the delegation returned and it was obvious that it had not been successful almost immediately. Nelson, after a conference with Hyde Parker struck his flag aboard *St George,* and went aboard *Elephant.* She was a slightly smaller ship of the line of 74 guns, as opposed to the 98 which the *St George* carried. However, she was also of smaller draught and that would enable her to get closer inshore. There was then a signal for Captains of certain ships to repair on board *Elephant.* Courtenay was one of the Captains so summoned.

When he returned Fenwick saw he was smiling. "Conference with all officers James in ten minutes."

Gathered again in the cabin, the officers of the *Pegasus* were not kept waiting for very long as to what was about to happen.

"Whilst Sir Hyde Parker was waiting for the delegation to return I understand he sent a message to the Governore of Elsinor enquiring as to whether we would be fired upon if we force the Sound. I think I could have told him the answer to that one and not surprisingly gentlemen the answer was, 'of course I will!'" Courtenay shook his head. "I really do not know what else he expected! Very well. In the morning Lord Nelson will lead a selected number of ships through the Sound. He will of course fly his flag in *Elephant,* and we are to be part of his division. Sir Hyde Parker will lead the centre division, and Rear-admiral Graves the rear division. We are directed to take our place third in line gentlemen. Once through the Sound we will again anchor and there await further instructions from Parker. We can expect to be fired upon and you know very well that to fire back will be a waste of powder and shot although the bombs might have better luck. Make sure that chain slings and nets are rigged. Ensure a good supply of water and sand on all decks in case of heated shot. Hopefully we will not need either, but if we do we will be prepared!. Very well gentlemen, good luck to all of you."

The following morning Nelson hoisted the signal on *Elephant* for his division to up-anchor, and slowly they moved into the Sound. Courtenay noted that Nelson was edging towards the Swedish side of the Sound and Davies did not need urging to alter course a couple of points to follow. They were part way through when the batteries at Elsinor started to fire. They were actually aiming at the ship ahead of *Pegasus,* but Courtenay was relieved to see that in fact none of the shot struck home and he did not detect any heated shot. He did not even order that the gun-ports be opened, and instead the ships all carried as much sail as they safely could to get through as soon as possible. One or two of the ships were less patient, and two of the bomb vessels carried out a bombardment. The Swedish batteries did not open fire and by noon the ships were through and anchoring again, this time at a point some fifteen miles from Copenhagen. The stage was set.

TWELVE

Once again, there was a conference in Courtenay's cabin. It seemed to him there had been one long round of meetings between the Commander in Chief, Hyde Parker, Lord Nelson and the other Captains.

Courtenay leaned tiredly against his desk as the officers filed in, and looked down at the chart once they were seated. Davies came to stand next to his Captain, and Trafford was on the other side. There was tension in the air as they all realised they were almost at the gates of Copenhagen and none of them really knew just what to expect.

Courtenay looked down at the chart and then at Davies before turning back to his expectant officers. All the Midshipman, excluding the junior one on watch, and all the warrant Officers were present.

"Sir Hyde Parker has agreed to allow Lord Nelson to make the attack on Copenhagen," he began. "and he will have ten sail of the line. *Pegasus* is one of the ten although Sir Hyde Parker did hint that he may well allow some more ships to join Nelson's division. The channel down to Copenhagen is difficult. It has been made more so by the fact that the Danes have removed all the marker buoys. Therefore, Lord Nelson tonight will make use of a small lugger, and with some friends mark the channel, or at least try to." He looked up. He had their rapt attention. If Nelson failed, the trip through an unmarked channel probably under fire was a daunting prospect. "Once we are through the channel there is another problem. Opposite Copenhagen there is a shallow area known as the Middle Ground. Between that and the City is a channel called the King's Channel. At least, that is what we call it. The main entrance to this channel is from the northwest. That is not the way in which his Lordship intends to force it. We will sail around the other side of the Middle Ground and attack from the south." There were a few gasps from the gathered officers. Most of the Midshipmen had little idea of what was really happening, but the warrant Officers knew the problems and the dangers.

Courtenay allowed the murmurs to subside. "Now, Nelson has been very busy because he has also surveyed the defences of the City. They are impressive, but not because we face a large number of active ships since we do not. However the Danes have gathered an impressive array of out of service ships and smaller craft, and they are little more than floating gun batteries. On addition, there are batteries. The Trekroner battery is at the northern end of the defences. Then there is Amag Island, which is little more than a floating battery of guns and mortars. That is at the southern end of the Defences. In all there are 18 ships moored between those batteries and the entire defence line is a little over one mile in length. The entrance to the City itself is more or less in the centre but there is a heavy chain across it.'

"What is the plan of battle sir?" enquired Fenwick, standing looking down at the chart and rubbing his chin.

"Each ship will anchor abreast of the one it is to engage and open fire. We will continue to fire until we are out of ammunition or we have sunk the enemy or been sunk ourselves. I think that is clear enough would you not agree?" He looked at Fenwick and smiled.

"Very clear sir! What about the Trekroner batteries sir?"

"Some of the ships, including some of the frigates, are to engage the Trekroner batteries and in addition there are soldiers on board those ships who will storm the batteries. The bomb vessels will anchor outside the line and throw their missiles over onto the City. At least gentlemen that is the idea!" There was laughter as he knew there would be.

"Very well. We make sail at first light. Down the eastern side of the Middle Ground and then we anchor off Draco point. Carry on gentlemen if you please."

They all filed out silently, and with very thoughtful expressions on their faces.

Trafford looked down at the chart. "Them Danes will not be easy to crack Cap'n, if they are anything like us! Don't like the sound of those batteries. Heated shot?"

"Certainly on the Trekroner but we will be at the other end, closer to but not at, Amag Island."

"I know that look on your face sir. What have you got up your sleeve now?"

Courtenay smiled. "I think that if Amag island gives us too much trouble we will give our bullocks some work to do. We will have to see but I am worried that the Admiral plans that we shall anchor by the stern. We may anchor with a bower as well, and run out a spring. We will have to see what happens."

"Shall I get you some coffee sir?"

"That would be most acceptable Alex. Thank you." Trafford left.

The following morning Nelson signalled his division to up-anchor and the ships moved slowly down the eastern side of the Middle Ground. As soon as the division moved away from the upper channel Hyde Parker ordered his ships to take up the places

233

vacated by Nelson, thus placing himself in a position where he would be able to oversee the forthcoming battle.

That night, with the ships at anchor off Draco point, Courtenay went right around his ship with Fenwick and McBride following him. As he climbed down a ladder to the lower gundeck, which also served as home for the ship's company, he removed his hat as did Fenwick and McBride so that the men would know it was not an official visit. They therefore remained at their scrubbed tables enjoying their evening meal. Each man had been given a full measure of beer and Courtenay had already ordered the Purser to break out a double tot for all hands in the morning. Many of the men knew what was about to happen. The more experienced ones had chatted with the Warrant officers and some had even asked intelligent questions of their division officers. Courtenay had told his officers to try and let their men know what the following day would bring. He would have none of the attitude of many officers, 'Do as you are told and never mind why'.

As he passed through the gundeck the men stood although they did not have to, and many knuckled their foreheads. Some smiled and one or two, old shipmates, grinned and even reached out to shake his hand. Those that did found a firm grip and a ready smile. As he reached the ladder to go back to the upper deck Courtenay turned and faced his men.

"What we have to do in the morning may not be pleasant. It is necessary. We do not have to like it but we do what we have to in order to ensure that we can continue to keep the Frogs bottled up in their harbours. If we be seen to be bully boys, then so be it!" He looked at them. "Good luck to you all, my lads. Aim true, waste no shots!"

As he climbed up the ladder there was a roar of cheering from the men. He stopped on deck, breathing in the night air. He listened for a moment to the cheering, smiled at Fenwick and McBride, and left them.

McBride looked at Fenwick. Soon, if he lived through what was to happen the following day he would sit his exam for a commission. He wondered if he was ready for it.

"Mr McBride, would you care to join the officers for a glass? I am sure your days in the gunroom are numbered and it might not therefore be a bad idea to gain some idea of what life is like in the wardroom?"

McBride grinned. "That would be *most* acceptable sir!"

The following morning found most of the ship's company up and about even if they were not on watch. Trafford and Kingston knew Courtenay had been up before dawn, prowling around the quarterdeck. Lieutenant Burton, who had the hated middle watch, had mentioned it to Fenwick in the wardroom when they were having breakfast.

"I have not known our Captain to be quite so nervous before, James." He had said.

"He knows just how important this is Roger. This is not going to be the same as a fight in line of battle. The Danes have got everything possible to throw at us including shore batteries. On the other side we have that damned middle ground to avoid, and mark my words someone is going to go too close to that and go aground!"

"Not this ship James, not with old Owen Davies keeping a beady eye on things!" They laughed together for a moment, then became a little introspective.

At first light the signal came from *Elephant* for all Captains to repair on board for a final conference or as Courtenay put it, a last 'council of war'. He felt the importance of the occasion and as Kingston was making sure his best uniform was perfect, he slipped the ribbon of the Nile Medal over his head.

"Looks right fine sir!" said Trafford, but Courtenay could see that his mind was back in August 1798 at Aboukir Bay. Courtenay smiled, and walked out his cabin.

In Nelson's cabin on board the *Elephant* the mood was almost light-hearted. Courtenay knew that only two of the Captains commanding line of battle ships under Nelson were at the Nile. Foley, at the moment Nelson's Flag-Captain as the Commanding Officer of the *Elephant,* and Thompson of the *Bellona.* The two Captains saw the medal Courtenay wore with pride and smiled and nodded, also reliving that terrible night.

Courtenay had a surprise when there was a movement at his side and the slight form of Vice-admiral Lord Horatio Nelson appeared next to him.

"Sir Giles, I am most pleased to meet with you again and I see that like Foley and Thompson, you saw fit to wear the medal commemorating one of our finest victories over the French!"

"It is an honour to meet you again my Lord."

"Kind of you to say so Sir Giles. You have an enviable record. I am pleased to have you here with us. I need all the experienced and fighting Captains I can lay my hands on!"

"Another two or three two-deckers may have assisted sir?"

Nelson smiled. "Yes, but Sir Hyde Parker wanted to keep enough for his own purposes. We will make do with what we have. It has been good to speak with you Sir Giles. May God keep you safe."

"And you, My Lord."

Nelson moved away and the conference began.

Courtenay was back aboard *Pegasus* an hour later. As soon as he was on the quarterdeck he beckoned to McBride.

"The Flagship will give just one signal Mr McBride. *Up anchor.* There will be no other signal. Each ship will weigh in succession."

"Aye aye sir."

Courtenay turned to Fenwick and Davies. "We will follow the *Defiance.* We will anchor by the stern as we reach the point we are allotted. I fear with the current we will have to also anchor by bower, but as I said last evening we will run a spring in case we have trouble bringing the full weight of our broadside to bear. Hyde Parker will bring his ships to bear on the north wing of the defences although I fear the wind will be against him and he will not be able to do much more than sit and watch!"

He turned and walked slowly to the windward side of the deck. Many pairs of eyes followed him as he strolled leisurely up and down. Davies put another man on the wheel just in case, and many of the seamen were loading muskets. The Marine detachment stood in a slightly wavering line as the ship wallowed slightly in the offshore swell, their red uniforms and black leather shakos standing our starkly. Their officer strode along the line picking out a fault here and there.

Trafford sidled up alongside Courtenay and muttered. "Bloody bullocks. They would be smart at the jaws of hell!"

Courtenay smiled, and then there was a cheer as the rum ration appeared. "I'll wager that did not please the Purser!"

Courtenay had just opened the cover of his watch when McBride turned formally and said "Flagship is signalling sir, *General. Prepare to up anchor.*"

"Thank you Mr McBride." He looked at his watch. It was precisely 9.30am.

"Execute, sir!"

"Up anchor Mr Fenwick, if you please!" Courtenay said calmly.

The men on the capstan pushed and dragged the ship up to its big anchor. It rose from the sea-bed, the men aloft set the topsails, and with men on the foc's'sle setting the jibs and staysails, *Pegasus* slowly gathered way as the rest of the ships moved towards their date with destiny.

They were slowly approaching the southern end of the Middle Ground when the mainmast look-out reported that some of the ships were in difficulties. Then *Bellona* went too close to the Middle Ground.

"*Bellona* 'as grounded sir!" called Davies, who had been peering over the starboard side at the ships which had been trying hard to get as close to the Middle Ground as they could. "Went too damn close!"

Courtenay jumped into the starboard nettings, trying to see what the other ships were doing. Ahead of him were *Elephant* with Nelson's flag at the fore, *Ganges* and *Defiance*. He called to Davies from his vantage point. "Nelson is changing course a couple of points to larboard Mr Davies. We will do likewise as we close on the *Bellona,* but not before!"

"Aye aye sir!" Davies turned and gestured another man to the big double wheel. "Current is quite strong hereabouts sir!"

It was two hours before the remaining four ships got into their positions. The firing had started an hour and a half earlier but with three of the British ships out of action by grounding, it did seem clear that the remaining liners were going to face more than Nelson had bargained for.

"In position sir!" called Davies, the noise all around deafening.

"Anchor Mr Davies, and be ready to lay out the best bower just in case we start swinging! Mr Fenwick, open ports and run out and let us teach the Danes how the Royal Navy executes gunnery!"

He watched for a moment as the gun ports opened and the larboard battery trundled out into the daylight. He also saw Oates getting the anchor party to be ready with the starboard anchor, the 'best bower'. He knew in his heart they would need it. Davies had already commented on the strong current. There was a loud splash alongside as a ball slammed down and spray burst over the side and scattered across the decking.

"You may open fire when ready Mr Fenwick. I think that Danish ship yonder is our target!" From what he could make out she appeared to be an old two-decker which had been cut down, something like a razee, but when he looked at her through his telescope he saw age and neglect. As he looked there was a ripple of flashes, smoke wafted over the ship and there was the roar of cannonballs passing overhead. There was also the sound of a hit as wood could be heard splintering. Then his ship fired, the whole larboard broadside as if one hand was pulling the lanyards. Smoke funnelled in and made everyone cough then the guns were reloaded and being run out again just as another ripple of flashes ran down the side of the old Danish ship. There was another crash and then the larboard broadside roared again. What masts were standing on the Danish ship came down at the rush after the second broadside and when she fired again, Courtenay realised there were not so many guns firing.

Another crash, on the maindeck this time, and a section of bulwark went flying high into the air as dangerous splinters. Two men reeled away from their gun one laying still on the deck with a pattern of blood forming around him, whilst the other man stared stupidly at the end of his right arm where he used to have a hand. One of his friends pushed him against the side and hurriedly formed a tourniquet. The man fainted away but two of the Surgeon's mates appeared, picked him up and carried him down to the orlop deck. Sand was spread over the blood. The firing had continued without a break.

"Current is swinging us sir!" called Davies.

"Starboard anchor will be down soon Mr Davies!" There was a loud splash and the anchor went down. Courtenay walked to the rail, ignoring the sound of splintering wood as another shot hit home, and cupped his hands for the Boatswain.

"Mr Oates! Run a spring from the starboard anchor to the stern!"

Oates waved his hand by way of reply and beckoned to his men.

Fenwick, hatless and his hair blowing in the breeze, turned to Courtenay after waving his gun crews on. "Warm work sir! Those Danes…" He broke off as a ball came through a port on the quarterdeck, overturning an 9 pounder and killing three of the crew. "Hell's teeth!" Blood was spreading over the decking. Courtenay took hold of a fire bucket full with sand and tipped it over the decking, then turned over one of the men lying face down.

"Too late for the Surgeon. Get some more men up here James and get this gun back into action immediately! We need all the guns we can get!"

"Aye sir!"

Courtenay looked again at the other ship and saw hardly any of the guns were firing. His broadsides were telling. He also thought the ship was listing and when he looked through the telescope he saw it was. She was down by the bows.

He caught Fenwick by the arm. "That ship is sinking. Get Oates to take a turn or two on the spring and let's concentrate on the next ship in line. Get the forrard guns to traverse and carry on firing at that one until she strikes!"

"Aye aye sir! With all this damned smoke I am not sure which our target should be! I think there are two ships of some kind out there!"

Courtenay hurried to the side of the ship and levelled his telescope at the moored line of ships. He ducked as a large ball slammed down close to the ship and spray burst over the nettings. Elsewhere he could hear balls hitting home and he hoped that not many of them would be below the waterline.

He turned away and yelled at Fenwick. "There is a prame and a cut-down frigate over there! Lower battery to the prame. That should dispose of any further bombardment from them and then look after the frigate. Damn that battery!" Another ball had hit the ship and a section of timber flew skywards, with splinters fanning through the air. Three men were down and another was being carried below.

Fenwick was yelling to the gun crews and he spoke briefly to Hughes, the junior Midshipman, who hurried down to the lower gun-deck. As he turned back, a ball ploughed past and slammed into the other side of the ship but he was unharmed. When Courtenay looked down at the main gun-deck he saw the Second Lieutenant, Martin Stevens, tying a handkerchief round his arm, the sleeve of his uniform being saturated in blood. Fenwick received a report from Hughes and turned to Courtenay.

"Mr Kingman is dead." Kingman was the Fourth Lieutenant. Courtenay looked around for McBride.

"Mr McBride! You are now Acting Lieutenant. Go below and take over Mr Kingman's division. Ask Mr Smythe to take over your duties."

McBride touched his hat and hurried away.

Courtenay turned again to Fenwick. "James, we need to do something about that battery. I think it is about time our Bullocks earned their pay. Pass the word for Captain Connell."

The immaculate Marine appeared on the quarterdeck in a matter of moments, one elegant eyebrow arched.

"Sir? Have you need of my services for some reason?"

Courtenay winced as another ball crashed down alongside and more water burst over the side. "Yes. You know there is a battery on Amag Island. We have enough to contend with at present let alone put up with that damned battery taking pieces out of us every so often. I wish you to take your men Captain and take that battery. Can you do it?"

"Of course sir but won't the boats be right in the line of your fire?"

"No. You will take your men along our disengaged side and row round the stern keeping clear of the guns. In the meantime we will blow that prame out of the water and I intend a boat action against what is left of that frigate we are about to exchange shots with. As soon as you please, Captain?"

"Consider it done sir." He turned and left, yelling for his Sergeant.

"Trafford? Clear away the barge, the jolly boat, the gig, and anything the Marines will not be using. James? Volunteers. Gunners from the starboard side. I want a full boarding party. Let the men arm themselves with whatever they want. Ten minutes, yes?"

There was smoke, thick acrid smoke everywhere, with little wind. The guns were still blazing away but with the boatswain's men on the capstan the ship was turning away from the cut-down two-decker, which was now so far down by the bows that water was beginning to reach up for the figurehead.

"One more turn Mr Oates!" yelled Courtenay. The men put their weight on the capstan bars, the spring on the two anchors was adjusted, and now the main armament was aimed at the small prame, which would not have more than about 20 guns, and the small cut-down frigate. Flashes rippled along the side of the latter and were followed by flashes from the prame. They were answered immediately by a salvo from the lower deck 24 pounders. Even from *Pegasus* the men could hear screams from the crew of the small ship as the massive balls thundered all around, then all firing ceased. The prame was a vessel more used to carrying horses than standing in the line of battle and stood no chance at all. Thus silenced, guns were traversed and a whole broadside flashed out against the frigate.

Trafford was back. "Barge cleared away sir. The men are getting aboard now."

Courtenay thrust two pistols into his belt, made sure his sword was in place and threw his hat into a corner of the quarterdeck. He looked down onto the larboard side and saw the other boats filling with men, whilst on the other side the Marines were shoving off. He turned to Fenwick. "Keep firing on that frigate for now. Upper deck guns only. I will try to keep the boats out of the line of fire. Take care James!" Courtenay smiled briefly at Davies, but looked back in surprise as Davies grabbed a cutlass and a pistol and said firmly. "This is one fight I'll not sit out sir! You don't need the Master to be aboard at the moment!"

There was no time for arguing and Davies followed Courtenay down to the side. He went down into the barge and Courtenay followed. Trafford was already bellowing orders.

"Out oars! Give way together lads and put your backs into it!"

The barge turned away from the side, and followed by other boats, full to the gunwales with men and arms started to head quickly for the frigate in the line of ships opposing them.

In the meantime the upper battery on *Pegasus* continued to fire, the balls passing well over the heads of the men in the boats. With all the smoke it was impossible to tell what was happening but as Courtenay peered through the murk and saw the frigate approaching, he heard loud cheering and yelling from over to their left and guessed the Marines had reached the battery and were storming ashore.

Smoke had partly hidden their fast approach but now they could be seen from the Danish ship and small arms fire was all around. One of the oarsmen cried out as a musket ball took him in the back and he slumped forward but another man took his place and with barely a break in the stroke, the barge curved towards the enemy ship's side. Courtenay felt balls hitting the barge and looked astern to see the boats following him in. Burton was in one them and Oates in another. Even as he watched he saw the Boatswain stand, take hasty aim with a musket and fire. There was no scream from above but a musket landed in the water with a splash and told its own story.

The barge was alongside and Courtenay was jumping for a handhold. He saw out of the corner of his eye a swivel gun being depressed, but before the gunner could pull the lanyard one of the oarsmen had grabbed a musket, aimed quickly and fired, and the man fell back with a ball between his eyes. Courtenay's men from the barge were following swiftly as he climbed the side. Trafford was right next to him, cutlass in his belt and a knife between his teeth. Even as he climbed over the rail, he took the knife in his right hand and threw it then pulled out his cutlass.

Courtenay was up and over the side. He pulled out a pistol, transferred it to his left hand and drew his sword. Danish seamen were running towards them. He dropped the first one with a pistol ball then as another closed in, threw the empty weapon at him. It struck him a glancing blow on the head but it was enough to slow him and before he had time to recover, Courtenay's sword had taken him in the chest. The blade was forced in and he slumped away not even uttering a sound.

An officer charged down the quarterdeck ladder raising his sword, and fell away as a pike came out of somewhere and took him in the side. Courtenay jumped down onto the maindeck and crossed swords with someone who looked as if he could have been Oates' opposite number. The man slashed and cut but Courtenay stood his ground and then started to force the man back with a series of lunges. The man was clearly no duellist but he fought with determination and Courtenay had just a moment of compassion for a brave foe as he slashed away the man's guard and plunged his already red blade deep into the man's stomach. There was a shrill scream and the man slumped to his knees, hands to his wound. Courtenay drew back the sword for a final plunge but a seaman raced past, a boarding axe flashed in some watery sunlight trying to pierce the smoke, and the man's head rolled away between two upturned guns.

There were plenty of Danish seamen but they did not have the training and experience of their British counterparts.

Back on the *Pegasus,* Smythe reported the flagship had been signalling. It appeared Hyde Parker had signalled that the action should be discontinued.

"What does Nelson say Mr Smythe? He is in command of the attack!" asked Fenwick.

"Flag 16 still flies sir!"

"Then Mr Smythe, close action it is! Can you see what the Marines are doing?"

"No sir, there is too much smoke!"

"Keep me informed, lad!"

Courtenay in the meantime was fighting two seamen, and driving both of them back. They were doing their best to take him with their cutlasses but he got under one man's guard and ran him through and the other man decided discretion was the better part of valour and decided to head for the shore. He got as far as the side of the ship. An axe took him neatly between the shoulder blades.

Courtenay was gasping for breath. His sword was red to the hilt. Trafford was next to him and struck out at another man who came too close. Then it was over and the Danes were throwing down their weapons.

"Mr Burton! Release the prisoners provided they swim for home. Then fire the ship!"

The Danish survivors took Courtenay up on his offer and were clambering over the side quickly in case he changed his mind. Everyone having gone except the dead enemy sailors, Courtenay, Trafford and Burton fired the ship, climbed down into the waiting boats and headed back to the *Pegasus*.

Back on his own quarterdeck again, Fenwick smiled grimly.

"It appears the Marines silenced the battery sir, but they lost quite a few men including Captain Connell. Are you missing many men?"

"I think we lost several dead James. The wounded are with us. Best to have a word with Mr O'Keefe. Now then, any instructions?"

"The Flagship did order the action be discontinued sir but no such confirmation appeared on the *Elephant,* and Flag 16 continued to be flown."

Courtenay laughed. "I daresay Nelson looked at the signal through his blind eye!"

Eventually the superior weight of British gunnery told and by about 2pm, the Danes had ceased to fire from most of their ships. Even though rumour had it Nelson had sent a letter of truce ashore some of the Danish ships continued to fire until silenced by British ships and the Trekroner batteries also continued to fire.

Then, the Trekroner batteries ceased firing and it soon became apparent why. A boat carrying the Crown Prince of Denmark himself was going to the *London,* with a flag of truce. All firing ceased.

Courtenay came back on deck clad in some clean clothes and immediately noticed a hoist on the Flagship.

"What does he want now?" he asked of Smythe.

"*All ships are to up-anchor by succession* sir."

"Acknowledge if you please, Mr Smythe." He turned to Fenwick. "It would seem we are to quit this place. I would imagine that Sir Hyde Parker will have us anchoring near the Upper Channel again so I suggest you keep the anchor party at their stations! When we are settled you will instruct the Purser to issue a double ration of rum to all hands." He smiled but only briefly. "Then, we will have to count the cost of this exercise!"

And so, His Britannic Majesty's ship *Pegasus* 74, survived the Battle of Coenhagen, although when the losses were counted she had suffered a great deal of casualties. Twenty men lost their lives on the ship including Lieutenant Kingman, with a further 50 wounded. Ten more died in the fight aboard the Danish frigate with twenty wounded, and with Captain Connell, ten Marines lost their lives in silencing the battery on Amag Island.

Courtenay felt the loss badly. In all he had over 100 of his men killed or wounded, some very seriously. McBride, in taking over Kingman's division on the lower gundeck, had been wounded by a splinter in his leg but he had remained at his station. Henson, the junior Lieutenant, not long out of the Gunroom, had been badly hurt but O'Keefe expected him to survive.

He, Courtenay, had come out of it without even a scratch. Fenwick also was unscathed and Owen Davies only had a slight cut on the arm from a Danish seaman who rashly attacked him with a knife he did not how to handle properly. The man had had a cutlass thrust through his throat and was left pinioned to the bloody planking of the cut down Danish frigate. The frigate had been consumed by fire which had spread to the prame moored next to it. They had sunk in shallow water.

The ship of the line approached Plymouth Sound slowly, almost as if it was a strange harbour which the ship's Master had never seen before and he was feeling his way. Courtenay watched some seabirds circling overhead and then looked at the Sound opening up in front of them as they slipped past Rame Head.

After the battle Sir Hyde Parker had decided to take some of his ships through into the Baltic Sea and teach the Russians a lesson. From what Courtenay had read the Russians had been taken very much by surprise and fortunately, Parker had had to do nothing further. The Danes had been forced to agree that the Royal Navy could stop whoever it wanted to and whenever they thought appropriate, a very necessary requirement if the blockade of France and her allies was to continue. However Parker had not taken all the ships and because *Pegasus* had sustained quite a lot of damage which really needed the attention of a Dockyard, she was sent home. Courtenay had been called upon the Flagship before they left and praise had been heaped upon his shoulders for what his ship had done. Three ships destroyed and a battery silenced.

As was the tradition he knew James Fenwick would be promoted to Commander. He would be very sorry to lose his friend. He knew however that Fenwick deserved it.

At length *Pegasus* was at anchor, sails neatly furled and all hands making sure that everything was as neat and tidy as the damage they had suffered would allow. Some repairs had been made on the way home. The carpenter and his mates had been very busy. Others would need more specialised attention. Courtenay knew that within a few days his ship would be warped closer to the Dockyard, but for now she was still.

Courtenay looked back at his ship, Union Jack streaming from her mainmast, as his barge crew bent to their oars and made the barge surge across the calm water. He looked at the quayside but could see nothing. Perhaps she had not received word that he would be back today.

Then, as Trafford brought the barge round in a sweep to come alongside he saw her, and his parents and her father. Oars were tossed as smartly as Courtenay had ever seen and he was out of the barge without even realising it.

Oblivious to the fact the crew of the barge were doing their best to look at them whilst keeping their eyes in the boat, Jessica Courtenay threw her arms around her husband and kissed him. Then Courtenay turned and held out his arms for his son and with arm around his wife's waist walked up the steps.

T H E   E N D

But…..watch out for the next Giles Courtenay adventure, *The Greek Warrior.*

Printed in Great Britain
by Amazon

58430799R00142